"Well, Miss Carollan?"

"Well, what?" Her voice was soft as the fabric of her gown, yet with a husky undertone that grated deliciously.

"Well, may I kiss you?"

Oh yes. Please. "Why . . . why would you want to do that? Your family . . . ?"

Now Jason's face was inches from hers, so close that his breath ruffled the fine curls at her temples. "They are probably watching. Not that it matters. I am sotted, Aurelie— remember?"

She had no intention of denying him, nor of being sorry for her own desires. In the end, what brief and contrived warmth he had given her would be a haven on cold Somerset nights.

His grip on her gown kept her from swaying toward him, but she raised her face, her lips parting of their own volition. As his head descended those last inches, she saw the gold lights in his eyes deepen into molten bronze. . . .

CHOICE DECEPTIONS

Emma Jensen

FAWCETT CREST • NEW YORK

To my mother, Jeanne Newman, for teaching me, with boundless love, to believe in love. With all my heart.

A Fawcett Crest Book
Published by Ballantine Books
Copyright © 1996 by Melissa Jensen

Library of Congress Catalog Card Number: 95-90700

ISBN 0-449-22401-5

Manufactured in the United States of America

First Edition: February 1996

10 9 8 7 6 5 4 3 2 1

1

L ORD TARRANT NEEDED a woman.
He needed a woman badly, and soon, before the situation got any worse. At this point it did not matter what she looked like, nor did it particularly matter who she was. As long as she was young, willing, and intelligent enough to follow his instructions, she would do.

No, that was not precisely true. Had his needs been of the carnal nature, those specifications would have sufficed. But as his dilemma was far from physical, there were other criteria to be met.

The disciplined strategist in him took over and he reached across the mahogany desk for pen and paper. *Young,* he wrote. *Intelligent, well bred, unattached.* He crossed the *t*s with neat, precise strokes, thought for a moment, then added *Not from London.* Yes, that about covered it. Satisfied, he wiped the point of his quill and returned it to its stand.

Now the question was where he would find his young lady. Most of the women of his acquaintance were members of the ton. The others were courtesans. None of them would be of any help whatsoever. He would have to try other channels and he knew the quickest place to begin.

Reaching for the day's *Times,* he opened it to the advertisements. He scanned the columns methodically, stopping whenever something caught his eye. After a short time he had found a few possibilities. The first two he discarded after a second reading—the women were clearly too old to serve his purposes. The next three were too close to London and he discarded the sixth simply because he did not like the phrasing. That left only two, Somerset and Yorkshire.

Yorkshire was preferable, if for no reason but its distance. Still, Somerset might do as well. It was far enough from Town to suffice and had the added advantage of precluding the possibility of a heavy Yorkshire accent. Then again, an educated woman would most likely have lost whatever accent she might once have had. He would simply respond to both advertisements. Better to have the option of choosing.

Again Tarrant reached for his pen. He wanted to waste no time in embarking on his scheme. But before he could begin writing, a knock sounded at the door and his butler entered. "Begging your pardon, my lord, but a message has arrived from the earl." He held out a sterling salver on which a letter rested. "His lordship's footman insisted that I give it to you immediately."

"Thank you, Kenyon." Lord Tarrant reached for the missive. "A summons no doubt." He broke the seal, one black brow quirking as he perused the contents. "It appears I have forgotten Lady Heathfield's garden party." He smiled faintly as he read the thinly veiled command to appear forthwith. Then, setting the letter aside, he turned back to the waiting butler. "Tell Phillips I wish to see him here immediately. And inform Cook that I will be having supper at my club."

"Your club, my lord? But what about the earl's missive? And Lady Heathfield . . . ?"

"My parents," Tarrant replied tersely, "will have to continue their little fete without me. Now summon Phillips."

"Yes, my lord."

Minutes later, the viscount's secretary appeared. He was a pale, nervous young man who tended to swallow convulsively in his employer's presence. Had he not been admirably organized once set to a task, Tarrant would have dismissed him. It was devilishly hard to be patient and unthreatening with every order. At the moment, the man's Adam's apple was bobbing with rather impressive rapidity.

"Phillips," Tarrant greeted him with deliberate smoothness, "there is a section of the *Times* on the desk. I wish you to respond to the two advertisements circled. Enclose directions to the Sussex house with the request to report there on the twelfth." He walked past the silent secretary toward the door. Behind him he could hear Phillips shuffling through the papers and winced at the sound of a stack of correspondence sliding to the floor.

He was in the hall collecting his coat and hat when Phillips came scurrying after him. "My lord, please." The young man's natural pallor was now mottled a nervous pink. "I have found the circled advertisements . . ."

"I am so glad, Phillips." Tarrant settled his curly-brimmed beaver hat on his head and turned toward the door. "That accomplishment will make the rest of the task all the more simple."

This ironic announcement momentarily stymied the young man, and Tarrant heard several audible gulps. "But my lord . . . you cannot possibly wish to . . ." Phillips made a concerted effort at recovery. "I mean, these advertisements are for . . ."

"Phillips." The viscount snapped the single word and, with a last swallow, the other man fell silent. "Perhaps there is something in the air. This is the second time today someone has questioned my orders." Now the secretary's face was dead white. "Have you ever known me to give a command I did not mean?"

"N-no, my lord."

"Or to make a decision without thinking it through first?"

"No, my lord."

"Then take yourself back to the library and write the damned letters!"

"Yes, my lord." The poor man spun about so fast that Tarrant expected him to get tangled in his own legs and go sprawling onto the marble tiles. After a rather alarming flailing of limbs, Phillips regained his equilibrium and rushed off.

Lord Tarrant found himself muttering vague invectives as he headed into the sunlight. The green boys who had served under him on the Peninsula had never caused nearly as much trouble. It was certainly not too much to ask to have his simplest orders obeyed.

Unbidden, his thoughts turned to his father. The earl was undoubtedly being driven to a fit of apoplexy by his son's refusal to come to heel. "That is just bloody well too bad," Tarrant grumbled as he mounted his waiting horse. The old coot was meddling where he had no right.

Spinning the horse about, he headed along St. James Square toward his club. A group of young dandies crossed in front of him, chattering loudly and looking rather like a flock of peacocks in their brightly hued coats. Younger sons, no doubt, with their carefree laughter and unlined faces. Pulling his confused mount to a halt, Tarrant watched wistfully as they cantered away.

For a moment he thought how pleasant it would be to live simply as Jason Granville, young enough at thirty to approach life with laughter, and wealthy enough to buy what cheer did not come on its own. Then his mouth thinned. Such simplicity was impossible. He was Jason Roderick Maitland Granville, Viscount Tarrant, and heir to the Heathfield earldom, old enough at thirty to have seen the harsh responsibilities of life, and wealthy enough to understand that money, in itself, did not guarantee happiness.

There was no doubt the earl also understood, and was doing no more than trying to see to the family's future. But Jason was tired of the interference, of the scheming and manipulation, and was determined to put a stop, even temporarily, to it. Face set in grim lines, he resumed his trek toward his club. It was a safe haven for the moment, but it was clear that he needed to get out of Town. It would take no great intelligence to track him to Sussex, but he would have a head start. And, if all went as planned, he would have his woman by the time his family caught up.

* * *

"Must've taken one look at her and run for his life." Lionel Oglesby belched heartily and stabbed his fork into another piece of beef. "Didn't stay long enough to get more than a brief look." With his mouth full, he dropped his fork long enough to reach for the platter of creamed potatoes. He jumped and nearly dropped the platter when his wife reached out and rapped his knuckles with her own soup spoon.

"Honestly, Lionel, how can you eat as if we had not just suffered a terrible blow?"

Lionel regarded his injured digits for a moment before shrugging and reaching again for the potatoes. "Can't pretend it's a surprise, m'dear. Why should I let it spoil my dinner? There'll be another lad along soon enough."

"Another lad? Our scope of acquaintances is not without limit and she has already frightened off *eight* suitors!" Edwina Oglesby sniffed eloquently and pursed her thin lips. "If only we could open the London house. There are so many young men in Town. . . ."

"Can't afford it. Dash it all, madam, must we go through this rot again? Till we get a settlement for the girl, you'll have to cease your squawking."

His wife's eyes narrowed, but she refrained from striking back. Instead, she ran her fingertip along the edge of her knife and muttered, "If only her father had not been so stupid in his arrangement of the girl's affairs, we would not be in this fix now. Of course, her appearance has done nothing to help matters. What man wants to face *that* each morn?" She reached up her free hand to pat at dubiously yellow curls.

"Don't forget her tongue." This time it was their son, Fenwick, who spoke, "Good deal sharper than the knife you are holding, Mother. And I daresay more lethal than her appearance."

"I will have none of that, young man! If you would take her, we would have no need to continue this way."

"Once again, Mother dearest, the devil will be knee-deep in snow before I do any such thing. And my dear cousin's

5

lamentable lack of beauty has little to do with it. A man who needs the blunt badly enough might marry an ugly chit—he can always close his eyes, you know. But 'tis near impossible to do one's duty with hands clasped over one's ears." He ignored both his mother's reproving sniff and his father's amused chuckle. Twirling his wineglass between his fingers, he gave an unpleasant smile. "I would say it was rather brilliant of Uncle Warren to set the rules he did. The girl needed a guardian, but he wanted to make damn sure the money was safe. Other than the piddling allowance, she cannot touch the fortune. And neither can we."

"Really, Fenwick," Edwina began, but he cut her off.

"How many months now, Mother? Three till she is one-and-twenty and gets control of the blunt? I would say you'd better dig deep among your friends and find a man who is willing to pay you your ten thousand and ignore the drawbacks. Otherwise the entire fifty will be gone with the girl."

This piece of advice, certainly no more than plain truth, was greeted by a pinched frown from Edwina and a rather frightening sputtering from Lionel, whose creamed potatoes had gone down the wrong way. Leaving his mother to the task of thumping her red-faced husband on his ample back, Fenwick pushed himself away from the table and took his leave.

Aurelie barely had time to pull her ear from the door and hurry to the far end of the hall before her cousin emerged. He paused to flick an imaginary speck of dust from his primrose coat before looking up. She thought she saw him wince at the sight of her, but it was hard to see much through the thick lenses of her spectacles and he was quite far away.

"Good afternoon, Cousin," he greeted her with mock politeness, striding forward. "You are looking radiant as ever." By this time he was close enough and Aurelie could see the ill-veiled disgust in his eyes as he surveyed her shapeless muslin gown.

"Thank you, Fen," she replied with equal coolness. "You are too kind." It was clear that he thought he *was* being too

6

kind, and Aurelie stifled a grin. So he could not stand to look at her—all the better. Pretending great interest, she studied his cravat, which looked rather like a small child had fashioned the knot. "I do not believe I have ever seen that particular style before. Is it one of Brummell's?"

Fenwick swelled visibly. "My own design," he announced with pride. "I call it the Fenwick Fall."

"Fenwick Folly? Oh, yes, most appropriate." Aurelie tried her best innocent smile, but her cousin was not fooled. He flushed a dull red and his fingers clenched and unclenched at his sides.

"Impudent shrew," he muttered and, spinning on his heel, strutted from the hall.

"Fatuous coxcomb," Aurelie shot back, laughing as the slick heels of his boots skidded on the smooth floor, nearly causing him to land on his tightly encased rump. Fenwick did not turn back, but continued on his slippery way, impotent fury trailing in his wake.

Aurelie's amusement did not last long. Fen was a paltry creature, but harmless. He was far more concerned with slicking pomade onto his blond hair than with her. His parents, however, were a different matter, especially Edwina. The conversation Aurelie had just overheard made the situation all too clear.

She was in a fix, to be sure. Perhaps, she mused, she ought to be truly worried. She was instead more than a little peeved with herself for letting the situation get as bad as it had. After six months, she should have been prepared.

She had been surprised when the Oglesbys' letter had arrived half a year earlier. Since the death of her parents in a carriage accident three years before, Aurelie and her grandmother had lived modestly yet happily. For two and a half years there had not been a word from her mother's brother. Then, suddenly, she was being summoned to Oglesby Grange and the bosom of a family so loving they had not bothered to so much as acknowledge her existence in the past.

Lionel Oglesby, the letter said, had been appointed her

guardian some years before her father's death and, as Warren Carollan had never altered his papers, was desirous of fulfilling his responsibility. Shocked as she was, Aurelie realized that her father had chosen Oglesby purely out of necessity as there were no other close male relations to be found on either side. Warren certainly had not expected to die before his daughter reached her majority, and was undoubtedly distressed, even in his grave, to know the present circumstances. He had never had much good to say of his brother-in-law, even less of the man's wife, and had often teased Aurelie's mother, whose generous nature ever prompted her to offer half-hearted demurrals on her stepsibling's behalf, about her less-than-ideal relations.

As much as Aurelie would have liked to refuse, she could not. Until she reached her twenty-first birthday, Lionel Oglesby had every right to demand her presence. And he was doing so, vehemently. It took very little thought on her part to realize the summons must have something to do with her inheritance. Most likely, she decided quickly, the idea was to marry her off to her cousin. She had met Fenwick only once, when she was ten and he twelve. He had been an arrogant, preening creature even then, and she had no reason to think he'd changed.

Whatever he had become, good or ill, she had no desire to marry him—or anyone else for that matter. So, as Granny Carollan thumped her cane and loosened a string of Gaelic maledictions that made Aurelie smile and would undoubtedly have blistered Oglesby's ears, her granddaughter made her plans. Into her portmanteaus went none of her own clothing. Instead, she summoned a seamstress and commissioned the astonished woman to create a new wardrobe of drab colors and no shape.

Aurelie knew she was an ordinary-enough-looking girl, but she decided with pleasure that the new ensembles, complete with unadorned mobcaps covering her hair, made her positively hideous. The stunned expressions on the faces of the Oglesbys on her arrival were infinitely gratifying. Fenwick took one look, shuddered, and disappeared for the next two days.

In truth, Aurelie expected her uncle and aunt to put her right back into the coach and send her home. Instead, they politely, if not warmly, welcomed her into the Grange. The first several weeks went pleasantly enough, if being virtually ignored could be termed pleasant. In the case of the crass Lionel and viper-tongued Edwina, Aurelie found their lack of attention a blessing. All she had to do was weather a few months until her birthday arrived and she would be free to return to her grandmother.

The cool quiet was merely the calm before the storm. Within a month of her arrival, the men began showing up. Thinking it had merely been her aunt's careless tongue in informing her neighbors of Aurelie's fortune, she turned the first few away with pleasant firmness. Soon enough, however, it became evident that Edwina had, in fact, all but summoned the hapless swains. As her annoyance rose and the men became more frequent and less charming, Aurelie took to playing the termagant. She even went so far as to throw a vase at one particularly persistent suitor. The man left at a quick trot, water and rose petals dripping down the front of his coat.

Soon, she became the target of the collective Oglesby temper. Lionel grunted and belched, Edwina screeched, and Fenwick took to baiting her cruelly at every opportunity. Too proud to show her misery, Aurelie merely lifted her chin and snapped back. But at night, she cried herself to sleep, praying fervently for the coming months to pass quickly.

When she overheard Edwina insisting that one young man be more "forceful" in his attentions, she knew it was time to act. Her aunt was actually condoning *rape*, and Aurelie's anger quite matched her horror. While she managed to dispatch that suitor with a volume of Shakespeare's complete plays aimed at his skull, she knew she might not be so lucky in the future.

In desperation, not knowing what was possessing her relatives to treat her so, she sent the letter to London. A mere three weeks later, she was nearly frantic. The visits from the gentlemen, if they could be called that, had become less frequent but doubly unpleasant. The most recent was a middle-aged neighbor whose cruel mouth and cold eyes made her more than believe the rumors she had heard that he'd beaten his last wife to death. She had greeted him that very morning with a pistol purloined from Uncle Lionel's desk. He had not stayed long enough to take off his hat.

Now, standing in the hallway in the wake of her encounter with Fenwick, she found herself shaking. The conversation she had overheard held nothing specific, but it had been enough. She was reluctantly forced to admit that her aunt's plan was cunning at best and closer to verging on brilliant. The Oglesbys, who would never benefit directly from her inheritance, had seized upon the perfect solution. The gentleman would pay them ten thousand pounds to orchestrate the marriage and, in doing so, would gain control of the fifty thousand that made up her inheritance.

Aurelie knew a little of the 'Change and investments. She also knew of London's gaming tables where men won and lost fortunes at the turn of a card. Neither came close to the assurance of winning fifty thousand pounds with an investment of ten. Quite brilliant really. And utterly despicable.

As she stood, trembling with anger, the Oglesby butler shuffled by, bearing the day's post on a tarnished tray. "Jonas," she called, just loudly enough to catch the nearly deaf retainer's attention, yet not loud enough to reach the dining room. "May I look through the letters?"

Mrs. Oglesby would undoubtedly have a fit if she learned of it, but the elderly butler, along with most of the staff, had been unable to resist young Miss Carollan's genuine warmth and kind words. With only the briefest of glances toward the dining-room door, Jonas handed over the tray.

Aurelie shoved her spectacles into her pocket and scanned the meager stack quickly. Bills, mostly, from local merchants and Fenwick's tailors. Then, at the very bottom, she saw her name. With a vibrant smile, she stuffed the letter into her pocket, placed a kiss on the astonished butler's wrinkled cheek, and hurried out the door. It did not matter that she would miss luncheon. Cook would slip her something later. Right now she needed to read the missive.

Hurrying to her favorite spot beneath an ancient, twisted oak, she tore at the seal. Her delighted smile at reading the opening lines faded somewhat at the sender's identity. A viscount. She had been hoping for something far simpler, a rural squire's family at most. But she could not afford to cavil. She had to leave the Grange as soon as possible, and she had nowhere else to go. Before striking on the idea of advertising, she'd considered going home, but the Oglesbys would have found her instantly.

She read the direction. Havensgate Hall—Newhaven, East Sussex. Viscount Tarrant. Tarrant. There was something a bit unsettling about the name, something stormy. Perhaps it was the similarity to the word *torrent*, like unrelenting rain. Then again, there was something equally appealing about the name Havensgate, as if once she passed through the doorway she would find sanctuary and solace.

Aurelie shrugged at the romantic thoughts. It did not matter if Lord Tarrant was stormy as the sea in winter, or if Havensgate was Hades incarnate. It was a way out of Somerset and the Grange, and she was going.

She had forty pounds hidden in the toe of a slipper, more than enough to get to Sussex. Should the position not work, she would still have enough money to reach London and live fairly comfortably while she looked for something else. One way or another, she was leaving. The Oglesbys could have the allowance that would arrive for her. There was no way she would alert them to her location, not until her birthday and she was free of their hold.

Greatly heartened, she planned her escape. The Brighton coach came through town early each morning. She would be on the next one. From Brighton, it could not be more than thirty miles to Newhaven. She could make that leg of the trip in less than a day . . .

"Aurelie!" Edwina's shrill tones cut through her reverie. *"Aurelie Kathleen Carollan, you answer me!"*

Aurelie sighed, wondering if she could ignore the summons. No, she decided. If she failed to respond, Edwina would undoubtedly send Jonas out looking for her, and the butler was too old to be walking over the uneven ground. She folded the precious letter and tucked it deep into her pocket. Then, pulling out her spectacles, she perched them on her nose and started back toward the house, careful to watch where she put her feet. It would be a disaster if she were to twist an ankle the day before her escape.

She saw her aunt, fists planted firmly on bony hips, standing on the steps as she approached the house. On spying her, Edwina dropped her hands and, as if to obliterate the fact that she had recently been howling like a scalded cat, cried daintily, "La, there you are, dear. I was wondering where you had disappeared to."

When her niece did not bother to respond, Edwina's eyes narrowed. She maintained her composure, though, and continued, "I really ought to scold you for being so ungrateful as to spurn Sir Higginbottom's attentions, but as it turns out, you are to have a much more important visitor tomorrow. Lord Cavander. You will receive him, miss, and you will be gracious."

It was all Aurelie could do to keep from groaning aloud. So they had got down to Lord Cadaver, had they? Old enough to be her grandfather, the baron had few teeth in his mouth and, should local gossip be true, even less groats in his pockets. Aurelie sincerely doubted that he could manage to come close to the ten thousand pounds her relatives were demanding. Apparently the price had gone down, and very quickly. She had the perverse desire to ask her aunt just how much of a bargain she had become, but she did not really want to know, and certainly did not want to let on that she was aware of their scheme.

Deliberately steeling her features into an impassive mask,

she replied, "As you wish, Aunt." Ignoring Edwina's mildly suspicious gaze, she pushed past her and entered the house.

The older lady's skepticism at her easy acquiescence lasted only as long as Aurelie had expected—until she reached the stairs. Then Edwina was calling after her again with strident instructions on her reception of old Lord Cavander. Aurelie kept climbing, reminding herself silently that in just over twelve hours she would be leaving the woman's odious presence, returning only to rub her independence in the Oglesbys' faces. The image of just how comical they would all look made her smile and she reached her chamber in high spirits.

Crossing the dusty, threadbare carpet, she threw open the wardrobe. She would only by taking one bag with her and had to choose carefully. Not that her selections mattered, really. Each of her gowns was equally drab. But she did not want to appear too dowdy to Lord Tarrant. Peers of the realms tended to be a bit high in the instep regarding attire, even in their employees. So she pulled out the least offensive of her choices.

The gray silk might improve slightly with the addition of some lace, as would the dark blue muslin. There was not much to be done for the style of the moss green walking dress, but it was not entirely awful when paired with the darker green spencer. Adding two more gowns to the pile, she gathered the necessary undergarments and shoes and packed the collection into a valise. If she hurried, she would have time to walk into town for the lace and be back in time for supper. If she were lucky, she would not run into any of the Oglesbys in the process.

In the end, she purchased not only the lace, but also an impractical but irresistible dove gray cashmere shawl. Chances were that she would not have the opportunity to wear it for many months, and there was no question but that her money would have been better spent elsewhere. Still, it felt so lovely against her skin and she knew it matched the silver lights in her eyes, so she put down the money with only the slightest twinge of guilt.

It was close to suppertime when she returned to the Grange. Adding her purchases to the valise, she shoved it deep under the bed and descended for what she hoped would be the last meal ever with the Odious Oglesbys.

"Hear you're to have another visitor," Lionel commented after the first course, punctuating the words with his familiar belch. Well trained by that point, Aurelie managed not to flinch with disgust. "Damme, girl, he'd better be the last. Can't abide all these young bucks tracking through my home."

Young? Hah. The last four or five had been older than Lionel himself. Still, Aurelie held her tongue. When he saw that he was not going to get a response from her, Oglesby turned his attention back to his mutton. Thankfully Fenwick was not present, but Edwina seemed happy to take up where her husband left off.

"I certainly hope you appreciate all the trouble we have gone to, young lady, to see you happily wedded. Another year or two and you will be quite on the shelf."

"A year, Aunt?" Aurelie knew she should keep her mouth shut, but the temptation was too strong. "Would not three months be a more appropriate time period—at least as far as you are concerned?"

For a moment, she was afraid she had gone too far. Edwina's lips thinned dangerously. Then, to her niece's surprise, she gave a faint smile. "We hardly need to discuss time, my dear. I'm sure we shall find a husband for you."

Something about that smile sent chills down Aurelie's spine and she hurried through the rest of her meal, happy when she finally was able to excuse herself and leave the table. Her aunt and uncle made no move to adjourn to the drawing room and, instantly wary, she turned back as soon as she'd closed the door behind her and pressed her ear to the keyhole.

Almost immediately, Edwina started speaking. "After tomorrow, we will be free of her."

Terrified that they had somehow discovered her plan, Aurelie was ready to bolt upstairs and quit the house then.

Her uncle's response, however, stilled her flight. "So you've arranged to have the vicar here. How do you plan to force him into performing the ceremony?"

"Money. The old fool will do anything for ten pounds, and Cavander has promised to pay it."

Lionel grunted. "Least he can do after cheating us out of half our fee. I still think we can find someone willing to pay the entire ten thousand."

"Perhaps, but we haven't the time. Cavander will take her, and his five thousand is better than nothing three months from now. At least we can be certain the girl is a virgin. No young man would bother to dally with her and the baron is keen to be the first. The laudanum I will have placed in her morning chocolate should have worn off sufficiently for the wedding night. . . ."

Aurelie did not wait to hear more. Dizzy and nauseated, she staggered away from the door. They were planning on forcing her with whatever means necessary to wed a decrepit old lecher. And they were counting on a supposed man of God to help them.

Unaware of the scalding tears sliding down her cheeks, she raced up the stairs to her chamber. She barely made it across the room before losing her supper into one of her aunt's ornamental and unspeakably ugly porcelain urns.

2

A LL IN ALL, the journey was not too bad. The route
was busy enough that Aurelie did not need to wait
more than an hour at Brighton before the mail coach traveling to Newhaven came along. Knowing it would be an
exhausting ride, but not wanting to stop, she climbed
aboard and settled herself as comfortably as possible on
the poorly padded seat.

They reached Newhaven late afternoon the following
day. Stiff and bleary-eyed from more than a day of travel,
the briefest of stops, and precious little sleep, she climbed
down and weaved her way across the posting-house yard.
Once inside, she secured a room, amazed by how readily
the landlord complied. A young lady of breeding would
have her reputation seriously besmirched by traveling
alone. A young woman of any employed status, it seemed,
need suffer no such worries.

Once settled in the small but neat chamber, Aurelie
caught a glimpse of herself in the looking glass and grimaced. Very respectable, certainly, but decidedly unappealing. Even with the spectacles, she was able to see exactly
how severe and unattractive she looked.

"Well," she sighed, removing the sturdy brown bonnet
and addressing her reflection sternly, "there is nothing to be
done about it now. It is hardly likely that the viscount is
looking for a beauty."

His letter said he would be expecting her the following
day. In her haste to be away from the Grange she had not
thought much about his terse missive. Now she considered

his orders wryly. It appeared Lord Tarrant was not overly concerned with the inconvenience he might cause a potential employee. To expect someone to drop everything and rush to Newhaven was not so very unreasonable—the probability being that anyone placing an advertisement was ready for employment. But to expect that same person to travel more than a hundred and fifty miles in two days was inhuman.

Yes, she had done it, but she was exhausted, stiff, and grouchy. As she wrote a message informing his lordship of her arrival in Newhaven, she forced prudence to overcome pique and tempered her words. High-handed though the man might be, she had no desire to alienate him before they'd even met.

After sending a groom off with the note, she ordered a light supper to be sent to her room and settled in for the night. The innkeeper had offered to provide a hack to take her to Havensgate Hall in the morning. She whispered the name aloud as she donned her muslin nightgown and climbed into bed, testing its sound and feel.

"Havensgate. Havensgate. Haven's Gate."

She needed a haven, if only for the next four months. Her last thought as she fell asleep was that, if the name were to be believed, the manor would not be her sanctuary at all, but merely a portal, leading her to something vast and special just beyond.

"I say, Tare, you're having me on!"

Lord Tarrant took a leisurely sip of coffee, savoring the rich flavor for a moment before setting his cup aside and turning to face his friend. "Not at all. In fact, I have never been more serious."

"But to take an advert from the *Times* . . ."

"Two, Rafe. I replied to two advertisements."

Rafael Marlowe shook his head, wincing as he did so. "Madness. And my poor beleaguered brain is having a dashedly hard time absorbing it all."

"That," Lord Tarrant observed dryly, "is because your

poor abused gut absorbed the better part of a bottle of port last night." While not precisely green, his companion's skin had a distinctly ashen tinge to it, going a shade paler each time Jason took a bite of his breakfast. "It is all very simple, really. I had a position to fill and answering an advertisement seemed the most expedient way to do it."

"Madness," Rafael repeated, reaching for a piece of toast. Jason watched, amused, as he stared at it for a moment—as if not quite sure how it had come to be in his hand, before setting it down on his plate. "Devilish hard to understand, Tare."

"It really shouldn't be. You are an intelligent man and you know the situation. It has become rather dire and hiring a young lady ought to put an end to matters." He speared a bite of braised ham and Rafael winced.

"Actually, I was referring to the fact that you are the only man I know who can drink me under the table. Never have been able to understand it." He pushed his plate to the far side of the table. "But I do have to admit that this whole scheme is a bit beyond the pale. Imagine what Society would say about such an activity."

"Well, then," his friend replied, quirking a black brow, "is it not fortunate that the vipers of the ton will not be able to flick their forked tongues at this one?"

Rafael chuckled, albeit painfully, refusing to be cowed. "No need to go all high in the instep on me, Tare. I am not about to spread news of your folly, especially not as you have seen fit to involve me." He glanced at the bacon this time, taking a moment before abandoning the idea. Instead he poured himself another cup of strong, black coffee. "So you are expecting your angel of salvation to arrive today, are you?"

"My angel? Hmm. Interesting concept. What—or rather whom—I am expecting is"—Jason shuffled among some papers—"Miss Carollan. Aurelie Carollan. She is from Somerset and arrived in Newhaven last night. I expect her here sometime this afternoon." He glanced over the note. "Nice penmanship. Always a good sign."

"What in the devil does penmanship have to do with anything?"

Jason smiled indulgently at his hopelessly ignorant friend. "Everything. Neatness of hand implies organization of mind and person. If Miss Aurelie Carollan thinks and looks as well as she writes, we shall do quite admirably together."

"Bosh. Best handwriting I ever saw was my great aunt Myrtle's. You remember her. Sweet old maid with a mind like a sieve, a mustache, and mussed gowns the color of tree lichen." He ignored the viscount's quelling gaze. "Like the lady's name, though. Aurelie Carollan. Rather pretty."

Jason was inclined to agree. In fact, he had high hopes for Miss Carollan in general, stemming in large part from the fact that he needed her services badly. Never mind that he was merely assuming her to be young and reasonably attractive, all based on an advertisement and brief note. His assumptions were very rarely wrong. The heir to the Heathfield earldom prided himself on being a very good judge of people indeed.

Miss Carollan had certainly made good time arriving from Somerset. This pleased him. Clearly she was a conscientious sort, eager to follow orders quickly and efficiently. Evident, too, that she needed the post as much as she was needed. Her speed said as much.

Yes, he mused complacently, stretching his long legs under the table and leaning back in his chair, Miss Aurelie Carollan would do quite nicely. She would arrive later in the day, giving him plenty of time to prepare his speech, and by the time his parents caught up with him he would be ready.

"I beg your pardon, my lord." Strawbridge, the manor's somewhat fearsome butler, stood in the doorway. Dragging his thoughts from the very tidy and very satisfactory plans, Jason looked up. "I regret disturbing your breakfast, but there is a lady to see you."

Jason's first thought was that one of the neighborhood biddies, delighted to hear of his return to the country and eager to foist her daughter onto a titled gentleman, was deliberately ignoring the fact that morning visits were paid in the afternoon. That speculation lasted approximately five seconds.

"A Miss Carollan, my lord," Strawbridge intoned. Jason's fist hit the table with a hearty thump. The butler did not so much as bat an eyelash. "She claims you are expecting her. Shall I inform her that you are not available?"

"She was not supposed to be here yet—not for hours." Jason did not realize he had spoken his astonishment aloud until the butler gave a satisfied nod and prepared to leave the room. "No, Strawbridge. Tell Miss Carollan I will see her in the library."

Cursing faintly, he rose to his feet and retrieved his jacket from the back of his chair where he had draped it. He was certain Weston himself was bemoaning the creases all the way in London—the early morning ride and Sheraton carved-back chair having left their mark. He had intended to be freshly and impeccably attired for his interview with Miss Carollan, and the fact that their meeting would now be conducted in wrinkled coat and unstarched cravat made him grit his teeth. The only thing more indicative of organization than neat penmanship, he felt, was immaculate dress.

"Shall I come with you? Convince our Miss Carollan that you are not a raving lunatic? Your slovenly appearance would frighten a fishwife."

Jason had momentarily forgotten his friend's presence. His gaze slewed back, taking in Rafe's carelessly loosened cravat and mocking grin. "You," he growled, "may do whatever you damn well please as long as you keep your insolent face away from the library till I call for you."

With that, he strode from the dining room, shoving his arms into the sleeves of his coat with unnecessary force. Had Rafael not been his oldest friend, he would have launched into a serious tirade on the importance of details. Not that a lecture would have done any good. Rafe was a hopeless scapegrace, flying through life by the seat of his pants with no regard for order or logic. And he delighted in making sport of Jason's carefully controlled mien.

"Fishwife," he muttered. "Bloody cheek."

He paused in the hallway long enough to retie his cravat and steel his features into their customary implacable mask. He started again toward the library, only to be halted by Strawbridge. The man was holding a folded missive and, while his countenance was stony as ever, there was a telling pinch to his heavy brows.

"From the countess, my lord."

Jason was sorely tempted to tell the man to cast the thing into the nearest hearth. His parents should not have caught up with him for another week at least. But then, it seemed his treasured peace was to be disrupted repeatedly that day. He accepted the letter and paused at the library door to read it.

After a moment he looked up, feeling his deliberate composure slipping. "It appears," he informed the waiting retainer tersely, "that you shall have to see to preparing the guest rooms."

"Guests, my lord?" Clearly Strawbridge, already bristling with disapproval over Miss Carollan's unannounced appearance, was affronted anew.

"Guests. Eleven of them, fourteen if you count the children."

"Children?" Now Strawbridge was obviously furious—as indicated by the infinitesimal downward quirk of his mouth.

"My nieces and nephew." Jason looked down at the letter again. "The others are my parents, my brother, both sisters, brother-in-law. . . . It is a wonder Mother has not mentioned the family dog. . . ." His mouth tightened. "Mr. and Miss Burnham. And, as the pièce de résistance, the Duke and Duchess of Ramsden and Lady Eleanor DeVane. Fourteen. They arrive a sennight from today."

With remarkable aplomb, Strawbridge squared his already rigid shoulders and nodded. "I shall see to it, my lord." He gave a short bow and spun about on his heel. "Children," Jason thought he heard him mutter as he stalked off, and might have smiled had he not been so angry himself. Catherine's three children were not infrequent visitors and, though they were a lively bunch, were not all that bad. They drove Strawbridge to fits, silent fits to be sure, but Jason rather liked them.

What he did not like was his mother's thoroughly unsubtle maneuvering. Bad enough that she should descend upon Havensgate with the entire family in tow, but including the DeVanes was as unpardonable as it was predictable.

He reached for the library door with a grim sigh, offering a curt prayer that whatever was waiting beyond the portal would be pleasing. He had precious little choice in the matter now. Barring only the worst deficiencies, Miss Aurelie Carollan was about to find herself in his employ.

Shoving open the door, he entered the room, startling the single inhabitant. She jumped visibly and, as he strode forward, spun about to face him.

"Hell and damnation," announced the ever proper, ever controlled Viscount Tarrant, heir to the great Heathfield earldom, and headed directly for the sideboard with its resident port decanter.

Aurelie watched, dumbstruck, as the man poured himself a drink, downing it in a single toss. Then, struggling impossibly broad shoulders, he poured another. She thought he had looked right at her as he entered the room, but she could have been mistaken. Her dark dress did rather blend into the paneling. Perhaps he'd had some unsettling news and, thinking her to be waiting elsewhere, had taken momentary sanctuary in the library. That *would* explain the curse—and the port ... at such an early hour.

"M-my lord?" she queried shakily. "Lord Tarrant?"

He had seemed impressive in profile, but the spacious room seemed to shrink somehow as he turned to face her. Peering through her spectacles, Aurelie got the image of darkness—a great deal of it. Jacket, hair, brows—all dark as midnight. Even his face, the features not much more than indistinguishable angles, seemed dusky against the white of his shirt.

22

She took a reflexive step backward and came up against the wall. She could not see his expression, but the sound he made was somewhere between a growl and a laugh.

"That makes two of us, Miss Carollan." His voice was deep and resonant with a silken edge that registered somewhere under her skin.

"I-I beg your pardon?"

"First impressions, madam."

He made no move to elaborate, but Aurelie was reasonably confident there was no compliment implied. Glancing down, she surveyed her simple brown dress and found nothing to merit much of a response at all. Her garb seemed far more appropriate to her station than his grim black to a viscountcy.

For having spent so much time and effort in making herself unattractive, she was suddenly and oddly irked that he would find her so. "It seems I should apologize," she announced, trying to keep her voice even, "for not anticipating the requirements of the position. I thought myself adequately qualified."

"No matter," Tarrant replied curtly and, when she opened her mouth to speak, cut her off, again with that gruff laugh. "Forgive me. I seem to have forgotten my manners. I am indeed Lord Tarrant." He gave a slight bow. "You are, I assume, Miss Aurelie Carollan."

"I am, my lord." There was, Aurelie decided, something truly bizarre about this experience. But while prudence told her to quit the man's presence posthaste, indomitable curiosity held her in place.

"I trust the journey from Somerset was not too taxing. You did make very good time."

"Yes, my lord, I did. And no, it was not difficult."

"Excellent." The viscount set down his glass and motioned her toward a chair. Far from being reassuring, his sudden politeness was making her wary and she perched rather tenuously on the edge of the seat. "I suppose the appropriate procedure would be to tell you about the position."

As he spoke, he moved forward and took the facing chair. He was close enough now for observation and, despite the fact that he was sitting, Aurelie could not really amend her first impression. He was more than a little terrifying and it was not just his size. She was not a diminutive woman herself, and quickly decided his powerful aura came not so much from his height, which was perhaps an inch or two over six feet, as from the force of his gaze. Even with her flawed vision she could see his eyes were like faceted gold—lion's eyes, sharp and predatorial under slashing black brows.

One of those brows quirked upward and, realizing she had been caught gaping, Aurelie blinked and dragged her eyes down to her lap. "You are looking to hire a governess, my lord."

"I was."

Now she stiffened. "Then why have you offered to explain the position, my lord, if it has already been filled?"

"Please, Miss Carollan." The viscount held up a stilling hand. "I was merely being precise. I believe in precision. I *was* looking to hire someone. You're hired. So I am no longer looking."

"Hired? But—what of an interview? References?"

"Unnecessary. I am satisfied that you will do, and I have not the time to search further. It is now up to you to accept or decline the position." Ignoring her confounded expression, he continued, "The salary is ten pounds a week, plus"—he surveyed her ensemble with obvious distaste—"a new wardrobe."

Aurelie had never heard of a governess receiving a new wardrobe, but then she knew very little about governesses. Ignorance notwithstanding, however, she could not shake the feeling that there was something distinctly havey-cavey going on. She knew nothing of viscounts, either, yet was convinced that this one was not in any way among the ordinary.

"Should not your wife be involved in this decision, my lord? She might have an opinion as to my suitability."

"I am not married."

"A widower?" That could explain a good deal of his behavior. A young man, for Lord Tarrant could not have been much above thirty, left with children, might very well find himself beleaguered to the point of oddness.

"I have never been married."

"But the child, my lord . . . children . . . ?"

A strange smile spread across his face, accentuating rather than softening the sharp angles of his jaw and cheekbones. It was a striking, if not fashionably pretty face and an intriguing, if not calming smile.

"There are no children."

Aurelie took a moment to digest this information. Then, slowly, she rose to her feet. "I have no idea what your game is, Lord Tarrant, but I certainly did not come here to be toyed with. Your behavior, sir, is thoroughly objectionable."

"My day, Miss Carollan, has been beyond objectionable, and it is not yet noon. Sit down." When she made no move to obey, he sighed. "If you please. Hear me out."

Wary but ever curious, Aurelie perched once again on the edge of her chair. "All right, my lord."

"Thank you. Now, I have no children but I did not answer your advertisement in jest."

"No?"

"No. I fully intended to employ someone—if not a governess then a companion—and I am quite serious about employing you."

Now the golden gaze was more compelling than predatory, and Aurelie found herself being drawn into the faceted depths. "So tell me, my lord, whom I would be serving—as governess or companion."

Again that disturbing smile. It was slightly wider this time and she was astonished to see a deep crevice appear in the corner of the viscount's mouth. This saturnine, grim creature had a dimple.

"Me, Miss Carollan. You would be serving me."

3

J ASON WATCHED AS she bounced to her feet for the second time in nearly as many minutes. He debated hauling her back into her seat, but she would certainly spring right back up again and that would make three times, and it would make him rather dizzy. So instead he watched the color rise into her pale cheeks and waited for her to speak.

He did not have to wait long.

"If you are mocking me, my lord, you are a boor. If you are *not* mocking me, you are something far worse!"

Jason decided that when incensed, the girl was not quite as homely. She appeared to have very nice skin, creamy pale under the flush of pique, and he could see silver sparks shooting from her gray eyes. The eyes themselves were a bit overwhelming, seeming to protrude unnaturally behind the bottle-thick lenses of her spectacles. He found himself hoping she would be able to make do with a quizzing glass. The spectacles would have to go, and if he was careful where he positioned her, she would not run into furniture.

The rest of her, from her tightly wound brown hair to shapeless dress, was not tremendously inspiring, either. But at least she was young and spoke well, with an impeccable accent and genteel vocabulary . . .

"Either way, you may take your bloody improper proposition and . . . and *choke on it*!"

This time she actually started across the room, and Jason had to spring from his own seat to stop her. "Miss Carollan, *please*." He positioned himself between her and the door. "I assure you, there is nothing licentious about my . . . er, proposition."

She now began backing away from him and he knew that acquiescence had nothing to do with it. She actually thought he planned to pounce on her. When she glanced about frantically, clearly seeking some weapon with which to ward off his lecherous advances, he could not help but laugh aloud. The very idea was preposterous.

Aurelie had read enough novels to know villains almost invariably preceded their assault on the heroine with a dastardly laugh. The suitor whom she had dispatched with a vase had certainly done so. Even while a small voice in the back of her mind insisted that she was perhaps being just a bit melodramatic, the voice of recent experience was infinitely louder. Finding herself backed against a desk, she groped across the surface, coming up with a letter opener.

She cast the viscount a defiant glance, brandishing the weapon in front of her. "Stay back," she cautioned firmly, noting as she did so that he hadn't advanced so much as an inch. No, he was still standing in the doorway, one broad shoulder propped negligently against the jamb. He hardly looked a man bent on ravishment. In truth, he looked . . . bored.

"Sheath your weapon, Miss Carollan, if you please. It has a fairly sharp edge and I would not want you to do injury to yourself. The rug on which you are standing is a very expensive Aubusson and blood tends to leave a permanent stain."

Aurelie's eyes went from his very calm, very composed face to the rug below her feet. It was obviously just what he claimed, the rich hues and texture testimony to fine workmanship and exorbitant price. She then glanced at the letter opener in her hand. It, too, spoke of wealth and taste, its gold handle adorned with precious stones.

It was evident Lord Tarrant was an extremely wealthy man and, truth be told, a stunningly attractive one. There was no reason she could possibly imagine that he would have any designs on her very ordinary person. She knew

27

little of the society in which he ran, but she did know enough to believe that, with his looks and money, he could have any young woman he wanted.

Slowly, feeling more than a little foolish, she lowered her weapon back to the desktop.

"Thank you, madam. I feel ever so much better now."

Aurelie knew he was mocking her, but she did not particularly care. As far as she was concerned, the bizarre interview was over and it was time for her to be on her way. Deliberately avoiding the golden gaze, she walked back to the chair she had vacated, collected her plain brown reticule from the floor, and headed once again for the door. Lord Tarrant was still blocking her way, but fueled as she was by a combination of anger and mortification, she felt more than capable of walking right through him.

Jason saw the determination written on her face and knew he had to do something, anything, to keep her from leaving. Why, he could not fathom—she certainly was a plain little creature. And nothing in her behavior thus far had indicated the sensibility and pliancy he required. In fact, he was convinced Miss Carollan would be a poor governess indeed, and wondered just how she had fallen into that profession. Necessity most likely. There was little else for a gentlewoman of limited means to do, especially if she had not the beauty to attract a husband.

But that was neither here nor there. He needed a "companion" and Miss Carollan would have to do. If he could keep her from walking out. And it all depended on convincing her as quickly as possible that, while the task he had set for her might not be entirely ethical, it was neither evil nor dangerous.

She would probably want no part of it, regardless of what he said. She was, a bit of loose language aside, a dramatically righteous young woman.

"Virtus est vitium fugere," he muttered to himself and was startled to see her head come up sharply.

He was even more astounded to hear her reply, "Is it not

28

enough that you have mocked me in English, sir? Do you need the further satisfaction of doing it in Latin?"

Then she actually tried to push past him. Jason very nearly let her. Never before had a young lady responded to one of his Latin sallies. It occurred to him quickly that she might not have understood what he'd said and was merely reacting to the sound of the words.

"Auditus an me ludit amabilis—insania?"

She stopped pushing at his arm and gave him an exasperated glare. "Of course I hear you. As for whether you are deluded, I would venture to say yes, on a good many things."

His instant and genuine grin took her utterly by surprise. She had, after all, just insulted him. "You speak Latin," he said delightedly, and she blinked, not at all sure what to make of this abrupt change in demeanor.

"Yes, I do. And I cannot appreciate being ridiculed in that language any more than I would in English."

"I was not ridiculing you, Miss Carollan. On the contrary, really. It is truly a virtue to flee from vice." His expression was earnest as he continued. "Would it be too much to ask for a few minutes to explain that my need for your service is not motivated by such?"

His voice was so sincere and his gaze so compelling that Aurelie could not help but accede. "As you will, my lord. I warn you, however, that I am astute to folly."

"Folly?"

Now it was her turn to smile, albeit unwillingly. *"Et sapienta prima stultitia caruisse,"* she quoted, completing his first Latin statement. "I find Horace an admirable voice—'The beginning of wisdom is to be finished with folly.' Now, you have one minute to tell me why you orchestrated this elaborate deception, and why you wish to employ me."

Jason looked into the face tilted up toward his and tried to decide why he wanted to hire her indeed. A pretty woman would no doubt have been better suited to the task. But there was an undeniable aura of intelligence in her finely-molded features and even a hint of patrician arrogance in the narrow nose and determined little chin.

One minute.

Leaving his position in the doorway, he strode to the fireplace and faced the intricately carved mantel. What could he tell her in one minute?

Only the truth. If she decided to leave then, so be it.

"I am in a rather sticky situation, Miss Carollan, one from which I have been completely and gallingly unable to extricate myself. My parents have made it their crusade to see me wed to a young lady of their choice and, while I know it is my duty to take a wife at some point, I am not ready to do so yet. Added to this is the fact that I know the young lady and I should not suit and would end up making each other utterly miserable.

"I have done and said everything conceivable to make this known, short of being deliberately insulting. Nothing has worked and I find myself resigned to enacting a 'deception,' as you have called it. I settled upon the idea of hiring a young lady to play the object of my affections, my fiancée. Once it is seen that I am committed elsewhere, the other parties involved will be forced to retreat." He sighed then. "So what say you, Miss Carollan. Folly?"

He turned to face her, expecting to see shock, even derision. Instead, she was staring at him thoughtfully, her head tilted to the side.

"Theatric. Is such contrivance really necessary?"

"Yes, it is." He was ready to explain further but the girl nodded, accepting the simple assertion with the same interested yet calm expression as before.

"Then would it not be more efficient to hire an actress?"

A sensible question. Very sensible. Her sudden acquiescence intrigued him but, as acquiescence was the only appropriate response, he was not about to question this gift horse. "I need a gentlewoman, someone who would not be revealed at a later date as anything other."

"Then why not a young lady of the ton?"

This time, Jason gave a short laugh. "I need *intelligence*,

Miss Carollan, and common sense. Most young ladies of the ton possess little of either. Besides, they would expect me to marry them, and that would defeat the entire purpose."

Now it was Aurelie's turn to smile. "Yes, I suppose it would. You have certainly done a good deal of planning. Will you tell me, please, why you chose to answer my advertisement?"

"It was intelligent and precise, with all the information I needed. You said you were young and educated, hinted at good breeding, and expressed a desire for an immediate position where the children were neither too young nor too old to be tractable. Your phrasing was well thought out and to the point. In short, you seemed an entirely possible candidate for the position."

"I see." She chewed thoughtfully on her lip. "For all the care you have taken, you have decided to employ me very quickly. What of other applicants?"

"There was only one other to whom I responded. She had advertised as a companion and seemed the ideal choice. Her response, however, on hearing what sort of companion she would be, was as dramatic as yours—if a bit different."

"She actually attacked you with the letter opener?" Aurelie queried, her natural humor and spirit rising to the situation.

"No," Jason replied, quite seriously. "She fainted."

The girl's responding laugh surprised him. It pleased him, too. Clear and vibrant, it spoke of a spirit quite at odds with her drab appearance. Yes, he decided, Miss Aurelie Carollan just might be able to pull off the charade.

Still, he expected her to decline the position. Hoping certain incentives might change her mind, he said, "The salary I offer should be adequate. I assure you it is more than you would receive as a governess, and I will provide a complete and fashionable wardrobe with all appropriate . . ."

"All right."

". . . accessories . . . I beg your pardon?"

"I said all right. I will accept the position."

Just like that. Momentarily rendered mute, Jason could only stare at her.

"I will do my best to help you—at the salary and accoutrements you've mentioned. I merely have one stipulation of my own."

"And what is that?"

It occurred to Aurelie that he might not agree, her request being a bit limiting. But it must be. "I will stay only three months, my lord. If the time is not adequate to convince your family that their desires will not be fulfilled, it will be up to you to deal with the matter from there."

The viscount did not look overly put out, but he did ask, "Why three months, if I may ask?"

"You may ask, certainly, but I beg you forgive me if I choose not to answer."

Jason searched her face for insolence, but found only calm resolve. "Are there other questions you will not answer, Miss Carollan?" He felt a niggling of concern now that perhaps there was something about the young lady that he should know, something that might interfere with his plans.

His thoughts must have shown on his face, for she raised one small, gloved hand and said, "There is nothing with which you need concern yourself, Lord Tarrant. I will not give you falsehoods. Nor is there anything about me that will serve you wrong." She gave a small smile. "I shall certainly never be seen at a later date treading the boards. I merely wish to inform you that, as this is a bizarre arrangement at best, I reserve the right to a bit of privacy. You may ask what you wish, and I will answer what I can."

It was not precisely to Jason's liking, but for some reason he trusted her. "Agreed. I would like to discuss a few matters now." He motioned her back to her seat and, once she had taken it, began. "It will be simplest if we can stay close to the truth whenever possible. What is your full name?"

"Aurelie Kathleen Carollan."

"Irish?"

"My father was Irish, though he lived in England most

32

of his life. My mother was born and bred in Somerset. Both are dead now."

"I'm sorry," Jason replied sincerely. "Have you other relatives?"

"My parental grandmother still lives in Somerset. I lived with her after my parents' deaths. There might be some distant cousins. My mother spoke little of her family."

"I see. How long have you been a governess?"

Aurelie had anticipated this question and gave as honest an answer as she could. "Not long. When . . . circumstances dictated that I find a situation, I chose the best option. Though my father had no son, he saw to it that I received the quality of education usually reserved for boys."

"Hence the Latin."

"Hence the Latin," she agreed.

"How old are you?"

She did not particularly like the question, but was relieved that he had strayed from the topic of previous employment. "Almost one-and-twenty."

The viscount was quiet for a few moments, then said, "All right. The truth we will use is that you are from Somerset and have lived a quiet country life with your grandmother." He raised one black brow in question and she nodded. "The rest of the story will be as follows: I met you through your distant cousin, Rafael Marlowe, who is an old and dear friend of mine. In the months following our meeting, you were never far from my thoughts and, when you reappeared recently in your cousin's company, the *tendre* developed. So quickly, in fact, that I was driven to offer for you."

"But my lord, surely . . ."

He held up a hand to silence her. "You, of course, have accepted. I am in favor of a short betrothal but you, not having seen much of Society, have persuaded me to wait— shall we say, six months. We will, in due time, repair to London. After three months, you will decide the arrangement is not to your liking and will break the engagement. It would probably be best to say you had fallen in love with

33

someone else. At that point, you may either stay in London or return to Somerset. It will be up to you.

"Meanwhile, I will play the besotted fiancé. Three months should suffice to make my family and Lady Eleanor's realize there will be no match there. I have no doubt the lady will attach herself to someone else fairly quickly. There might be a bit of unpleasantness with the parents, but it does not overly concern me."

Aurelie was very curious about this Lady Eleanor but she refrained from asking about her for the moment. Instead, she inquired, "What if your family does not cease in its demands after the three months? What will you do then?"

"I have long considered a trip to the Continent. Now that the Corsican Upstart has been vanquished and exiled to Elba, I believe I will pay an extended visit to the Mediterranean—southern France and Italy perhaps. A broken heart takes time to heal and I am convinced I can stay away long enough to eliminate any last machinations on the part of my family or the DeVanes.

"And you, Miss Carollan, what will you do? I must ask you to consider the fact that it will look rather odd for the former fiancée of Viscount Tarrant to employ herself as a governess when she could have married into a life of luxury."

The smile she gave him was serene, but somehow wry. "I will manage, my lord. There are certainly places and people who have not heard of the Viscount Tarrant."

Jason could not help but be slightly affronted by her words, even as he admitted their veracity. "I am sure you are right, Miss Carollan," he remarked coolly, "but I think we can find a way to avoid any possible difficulty. I have numerous holdings all over England, many far enough away that my activities are not discussed. I am certain there is a need for a schoolmistress on at least one of them. That position is easier than governessing, and certainly more stable. I will also give you a house and the guarantee of a pension when you retire."

For the character she had assumed in placing her advertisement, it was a generous offer indeed. Aurelie, of course, could not accept, but neither could she demur at present. So, gracing the viscount with her best grateful smile, she replied, "That is very kind of you, my lord. I think, however, we can put off such discussions till a later date. For now it would be better to speak of the immediate future."

"As you wish." If Lord Tarrant found anything amiss with her remarks, he did not show it. "As it happens, all principal players will be arriving here in a sennight's time. That is inconvenient, to be sure, but it should be sufficient time to prepare you for your role."

Miss Carollan's expression had become apprehensive, but before she could speak, the door flew open, admitting a collection of beasts—some four-legged and one two-legged.

"Well, did this one faint? Did she leave in a huff? It's a marvelous day, but I didn't want to go out till I knew . . ." Their uninvited visitor skidded to a halt behind Tarrant's chair. "Oh, I say . . . sorry . . ."

"Miss Carollan," Jason drawled, waiting till she had reappeared from the trio of wolfhounds who had rushed to greet her with lolling tongues and whipping tails to continue. "May I present your beloved and devoted cousin, Lord Rafael Marlowe, Marquess of Holcombe."

Aurelie peered over the shaggy heads. The dogs' effusive welcome had dislodged her spectacles and she automatically straightened them, sending everything back out of focus again. "Lord Holcombe," she said, offering her hand in the direction of the young man.

"Miss Carollan," he replied, actually bending over her hand. "It is a pleasure. I'm always delighted to meet a relative."

It was on the tip of Aurelie's tongue to say that she was delighted to meet a marquess. She had never met one before, and was understandably intrigued. He hardly seemed ducal material, with his blithe words and energetic presence. He was also, she had noted in the moment without her spectacles, very handsome—all rich brown hair and laughing blue eyes.

Odd, she found herself thinking as she tried to push the wolfhounds aside, that she should have fled from the Oglesbys and their string of frightening "guests" into the figurative clutches of two wealthy, important, and undeniably handsome men.

She managed to disengage the dogs long enough to rise to her feet. Immediately, the largest of the trio reared up, placed saucer-sized paws on her shoulders, and commenced to lave her face with its expansive tongue. Again, the spectacles were knocked askew, giving Aurelie a clear view of a wet, black nose and shaggy muzzle. The dog was not nearly as handsome as whichever man owned it, but it was certainly friendly.

"Nolo, down!" Tarrant's sharp command answered the question of ownership. The dog promptly dropped back to the floor. "I apologize, Miss Carollan. They are not usually so effusive in their greeting."

In truth, he had never seen the dogs greet a stranger with such instant approval. They were great, hairy beasts, and tended to send ladies scurrying away with one wag of their tale. But Miss Carollan merely smiled, straightened the odious spectacles, and patted each of the three on its massive head.

"It is quite all right. I like dogs." She looked up at them then. "Nolo?"

"Nolo Contendere." At her raised brows, Jason continued. "Cave Canem and Pace Tua."

Again the lilting laugh. "No Contest, Beware of Dog, and By Your Leave. Very appropriate Latin names for Irish wolfhounds, my lord." She then turned to Rafael. "I fear this is all very odd, Lord Holcombe. I assume you are aware of the, er . . . situation."

"Most assuredly."

"And you approve?"

Rafael looked a bit affronted by the question. "Of course I approve. Rotten business, expecting a man to marry where he's not inclined."

As Jason watched, Aurelie gave a strange smile, shrugged, and announced, "Well then, all I can say is that I hope you will not mind terribly—having me as a cousin."

"Mind? Not a bit of it. I am delighted." Oddly enough, for all his earlier reservations, Rafe actually did look pleased. "I think we shall all manage smashingly." He turned back to Jason then. "Sorry, old man. Almost forgot to tell you. There is some man named Wiggins waiting in the estate room."

That was not good news. Wiggins, the dour steward, never left the northern boundaries of the estate unless there was trouble. Jason scowled as he rose to his feet.

"I am sorry, Miss Carollan. This might take some time." He glanced once more over her serviceable attire. "But the afternoon shall not be wasted." Striding to the door, he called for Strawbridge. When the butler appeared, he commanded, "Summon a maid and two grooms to accompany Miss Carollan to Newhaven."

Then, to Aurelie, "There is a modiste on High Street— Madame LeFevbre. Inform her that you are my fiancée and tell her you need a complete wardrobe to be completed before the end of the week." At Aurelie's soft protestation, he remarked, "She will do it. See what she can give you today and instruct her to send all the bills to me." Already thinking ahead to his interview with Wiggins, he nearly forgot to add, "And buy yourself a quizzing glass."

Moments later, as he headed for the estate room, he was stopped by a grinning Rafe. "She's a decent chit. I think you just might pull this off, Tare."

Remembering his very similar thoughts, Jason smiled. "Yes, we will pull it off." More to himself than to his friend, he muttered, "I just hope the clothes will make the woman."

"What's that?"

"I knew I was pushing my luck, hoping for an attractive governess. Still, it is a shame . . ."

He missed the odd look Rafael shot him as he left the hall.

4

LORD TARRANT HAD not returned by supper time and, in
truth, Aurelie was grateful. She was more than a little
shocked with her own behavior in accepting his proposition. Not that she could have refused—not really. The moment he had spoken of an unwanted marriage, she'd been
hooked. Still, she had managed to commit herself to an outlandish and rather immoral masquerade, on top of the elaborate deception she was already practicing, and she was
feeling decidedly unsettled.

Well, she commented silently as she surveyed her reflection in the cheval glass, one deception would be disposed
of soon enough. The modiste to whom Lord Tarrant had
sent her was unquestionably gifted. No one looking at the
pale green gown would ever suspect it had not been made
especially for her. It had taken only the slightest of altera-
tions to fit it to her slender figure, and the color brought a
hint of green to her gray eyes. She looked very well indeed.
Better, in fact, than even before her trip to Oglesby Grange.

Turning to face the mirror head-on, she gave a slight tug
to the bodice. Plunging necklines were, Madame LeFevbre
had informed her firmly, all the rage. Madame had also announced that the young lady for whom the gown had originally been made had not the bosom to do justice to the
very fashionable bodice. Aurelie had silently speculated that
the young lady had not had the money to pay the very prac-
tical modiste, for Madame had been all too happy to hand
this gown and several others over to her.

Rather, she had been more than pleased to serve Viscount

Tarrant's fiancée. The mere mention of the man's name had sent the entire shop into delighted chaos. Aurelie was forced to admit much of her guilt at her deception had vanished as the modiste and her assistants brought out bolt after bolt of beautiful fabric. She had soon abandoned her notions of fashion, too, as the style plates appeared. Apparently her small corner of Somerset, while lively and sociable, had been sadly out of date as far as apparel was concerned.

With a last tug at her bodice, Aurelie turned and watched as Gilly, her new maid, put away the last of the day's acquisitions. The bulk of her purchases would not be delivered for close to a week. Lord Tarrant had been right, too, in assuming Madame LeFevbre would not balk at the task. Aurelie could only hope that *he* would not balk at the cost. For all that being out of fashion was an embarrassment, it certainly was easier on one's pocket.

The clothing had been his lordship's command. The cost would be his burden. She repeated this assertion to herself a few times, very nearly accepting it. One more glance down at the glorious gown hardened her resolve and, with a defiant swish of silk skirts, she left the chamber.

Lord Tarrant's dour butler was waiting for her in the hall. His face held the same expression as before—stern disapproval. If he noticed that she looked vastly different, he did not show it. Aurelie lifted her chin as he guided her to the parlor where Lord Holcombe waited. The marquess would certainly notice and be gratifyingly surprised.

The young man sprang to his feet when she entered, sweeping into an elegant bow. He looked perfectly pleased to see her, but he did not look in the least bit surprised. "Hello, Cousin," he greeted her cheerfully, then chuckled. "How well that sounds, almost as if I've been saying it for years."

"Good evening, my lord," Aurelie replied, studying his handsome features for anything other than pleasant acceptance. Nothing seemed forthcoming.

"Rafael, please. Or Rafe. We might be distant cousins,

39

but there's no need for the formal rot. Don't you agree?" When Aurelie merely stared at him, he nodded. "Quite. Now, Strawbridge has informed me that supper will be ready soon. We're holding off a bit for Tare. May I offer you something while we wait? Ratafia? Sherry?"

"Ratafia, please." Aurelie watched as he set to the task. He moved with confidence and speed, eliminating the possibility of poor eyesight. "I have had quite a busy day," she offered conversationally.

"Have you?" He nodded again pleasantly as he handed her a glass. "Good day for being out and about."

Now Aurelie was wondering if perhaps he was not a bit thick. It was not so much vanity that made her want to have her alteration noticed as it was simple sense. She did not doubt that the two men had discussed her plain appearance earlier.

She tried another tack. "Lord Tarrant's business has certainly kept him out and about. He hardly got the chance to acquaint himself with his new ... fiancée. Do you expect him to join us, after all, for supper?"

Rafael shrugged. "Can't say, really. Strawbridge will let us know when it's time to eat. Tare will get here eventually."

In the following minutes, Aurelie slipped a few more mentions of her shopping expedition into the conversation. Rafael inevitably replied politely enough, but each time managed to change the topic. Aurelie was happy enough to acknowledge that he was not simple—far from it, and he was without doubt one of the more agreeable men she had ever met. In the end, she decided he was merely too careless in his attitude to have noticed the change in her appearance.

Lord Tarrant did not arrive, and when Strawbridge announced supper, Rafael grinned and offered his arm. "Didn't want to complain," he remarked as they headed for the dining room, "but I was getting awfully hungry. Tare insists on keeping Town hours even here in the country and it is devilish hard on my stomach."

She dragged her attention from the richly appointed hall to answer him. "Do you spend most of your time in the country, then?"

"Not at all." Again the disarming grin. "I am always hungry in London, too."

Aurelie studied her companion carefully as the liveried footmen served the first course. He could not have been much younger than the viscount, perhaps in his late twenties, but had none of the other man's imposing grandeur. Instead, he was youthful and warm, and hardly likely to inspire awe in his acquaintances, despite his lofty station. Lord Tarrant, she had concluded even after their brief encounter, probably frightened half the people who crossed his path.

She wondered, then, why he was having so difficult a time in avoiding an attachment to Lady Eleanor. He did not seem the sort to do anything he did not wish to do, regardless of the parties involved. Intrigued, she abandoned some of her manners and tried to engage Rafael in a bit of good old-fashioned gossip.

"Do you know Lord Tarrant's family well?"

"As well as my own," was the ready reply. "We've been friends since childhood and spent much time in each other's home."

"How nice." Aurelie momentarily debated using discretion, but decided against it. Rafael was not one to indulge in the formalities. "Will you tell me about the arrangement with Lady Eleanor?"

He looked slightly taken aback at that. "Didn't Tare explain?"

"Not really. There was not time."

She half expected him to suggest that perhaps she ought to wait to let Lord Tarrant tell the tale and was pleased when he shrugged and said, "The DeVanes are old friends of the Granvilles. Though Eleanor's quite a few years younger than Tare, the two families decided they would make a match of it. Nothing formal, mind you, just a happy understanding."

"I see." But she didn't, not really. "If no formal betrothal was ever enacted, why is it so difficult for his lordship to decline?"

Now Rafael looked completely surprised. "Why, honor, of course. Tare eats, sleeps, and breathes uprightness. It would be dashed poor ton for him to offend the earl and countess, not to mention the duke and duchess. He won't overtly slight anyone, not even the lowliest servant."

Aurelie, reminded of the viscount's less-than-polite reception of her own person, tactfully refrained from comment. It was obvious Rafael admired his friend immensely. Instead she asked, "And what of Lady Eleanor? Is she so eager for this match?"

"Of course she is. What girl wouldn't be?"

One girl felt slightly guilty in her silent assertion that *she* would not be so eager. True, her meeting with Lord Tarrant had been brief. But it had also been highly disconcerting. Very little of what Rafael said harmonized with her own perceptions of the viscount's character. The man had made no effort to be courteous, nor did the proposition he had offered exactly ring with great integrity.

For a few minutes she turned her attention to her supper, which was, she realized, quite the best meal she'd had in months. She had grown accustomed to the Oglesbys' unimaginative tastes and salt-laden dishes. Her blade-thin aunt barely picked at her food and gluttonous Lionel was content to stuff his gullet with anything not still moving.

The excellent food, however, was not enough to still her rising curiosity. "What is Lady Eleanor like?" She could not be very beautiful or accomplished, or Lord Tarrant would have been far more particular in choosing his faux betrothed.

Rafael set his fork aside and looked thoughtful. "I suppose I would have to say she is the most smashing creature I know. Diamond of the first water, an Incomparable."

The slight was by no means deliberate, but eminently Comparable, topazlike Aurelie sighed nonetheless. So the lady was a Beauty after all. Well then, she must be dull—

insipid perhaps. If the viscount could not fault her appearance, it must be that her company left him disinterested.

"Is she accomplished? I imagine a duke's daughter must be very concerned with the finer activities, yet too busy with social obligations to give much attention to any one thing."

"Eleanor," Rafael replied promptly, "is a dab hand at everything she does. Splendid conversationalist, too. Never prattles on about flounces and fripperies like most chits of the ton."

Again, Aurelie was reminded of her own deficiencies—this time her repeated references to shopping earlier. Rafael was certainly making no such comparison, but the comment struck home. Belatedly, Aurelie scolded herself for indulging in gossip. Her little foray had served two purposes, neither of them good. She was more confused than before as to Lord Tarrant's aversion to Lady Eleanor, and she was thoroughly cowed by the task she had taken on. How could she possibly hope to convince anyone that the viscount had chosen her over a veritable paragon of female perfection?

If Rafael noticed her sudden silence, he did not comment. He chatted pleasantly through the rest of the meal and Aurelie did her best to respond. Her appetite was quite lost, however, and she was happy to leave the table and return to the parlor. She knew the time would be best spent in learning about Rafael and elaborating the story of their connection. Unfortunately, she did not think she was up to the task and seized gladly on his suggestion of a game of piquet.

He played much as he seemed to do everything—with a good deal of enthusiasm and confidence but casual attention. A proficient player herself, Aurelie did not have to concentrate too hard to win more often than she lost. As her hands automatically played her cards, her mind was whirling furiously, trying to figure out just what she had got herself into. When no brilliant conclusions arrived, she was forced to resort to berating herself for an irrationally impulsive decision.

Perhaps it was not too late to decline. There was, of course, the matter of the clothing. And the fact that she could expect a less than accommodating response from his lordship. She thought she just might, if she was exceptionally lucky, come out of the encounter with no more than a few lashes from Tarrant's sharp tongue.

"You know, Aurelie," Rafael said from across the card table, pulling her from her contemplation of the viscount's ire, "I am awfully glad you took the job. The fact that you're helping Tare aside, I am pleased for myself. You are going to make a smashing cousin."

And that was that.

Giving up her idea of leaving, Aurelie smiled warmly at Rafael. "Thank you. I think you will make a smashing cousin, too."

As she climbed into bed a short time later she was still smiling, this time wryly. What a spineless creature she had become. She had been unable to resist the viscount's tale of an unwelcome match—only to discover that the young lady in question seemed to be every man's dream. Then she had all but melted at Rafael's simple admission of his approval—and Rafe undoubtedly liked everything and everybody.

She was stuck. And, as she gazed around her bedchamber with its warmly paneled walls glowing softly in the candlelight, she could not help but feel that her premonitions had been correct somehow. Even owned as it was by a mercurial master, Havensgate held a feeling of safety and solace. Unfortunately, every Eden must have a serpent. The problem, she mused irritably, was that she could not quite decide whether the danger came from Lord Tarrant—or from the fact that she seemed to be losing every last vestige of common sense.

It was too late to go to bed and too early to be up.

Jason stared moodily out the window at the sloping lawns. Green and lush, they spoke of affluence and the best care that money could buy. Beyond the grass was the collection of stone outbuildings, and beyond that the thousand acres that made up Havensgate.

He had traveled that expanse only hours before, returning after a long day and even longer night on the northern edge of his lands. Wiggins had been right to alert him to the problem. The flooding of the estate's best oat field was a critical matter. Jason had not paid much attention to the recent rains, and he should have. Not that he could have cleared the storm clouds from the skies, of course, but he could have foreseen the possibility of flooding and made certain the river bordering much of the estate had been monitored.

He would not have been the only one concerned, regardless. Wiggins had been on top of the situation and, in truth, had not an irresponsible neighbor's dam broken, the problem would never have occurred. As it was, the neighbor's fields had suffered far less than Jason's, and the man could be counted upon to take absolutely no responsibility whatsoever for the matter. Lazy and uncaring, the rotter had not so much as sent any of his men to help fight the water.

Jason grimaced as he flexed aching muscles. He had thought himself to be in top physical condition, but hour after hour of hefting bags full of sand had proven him wrong. In the end, working alongside his men, he had watched as the makeshift dike slowly grew higher than the river. But the damage was done and there was nothing to do but wait until the water receded to see just how bad the loss would be. He was beyond exhausted, sore, and the chill from standing nearly knee-deep in water had not quite left his legs. In short, he was bloody miserable, and his weakness made him furious.

He turned from the window and glanced speculatively at the bed. No, better to stay up and face the day. During his time in the military, he had grown accustomed to staying awake for more than a day at a time. It had been more than a year since he had resigned his commission. It would not hurt to try to regain some of the stamina his time away had weakened.

45

Servants had just been stirring when he had arrived home and breakfast would not be served for at least an hour. He thought about going down to the library to deal with his correspondence, but decided instead to go outside. There was a soothing restfulness to the gardens that appealed to his beleaguered senses.

Little had been done in the way of sculpting in the twenty years since his father had succeeded to the earldom and his mother had left the Havensgate gardens for those at the family seat. Jason vastly preferred the present, deliberate abandon to the neat borders and elaborately shaped hedges of his mother's time. He had never quite understood this preference of his, demanding precision in everything else. But the gardens remained unconstructed at his command and he headed out the door now with a feeling of calm anticipation.

He saw the girl as soon as he entered the second tier of flower beds. She was standing in the midst of blooming rose bushes, her pale pink gown blending so perfectly with the blossoms that Jason instinctively thought of the woodland faeries from childhood tales. But this creature was real enough. No nymph ever had such a mass of sun-touched chestnut hair.

She could not be a maid. Her dress was too fine and her profile, with its smooth, pale skin and sculpted features, had the patrician lines of a classical cameo. No, she was not a member of his household, and Jason realized he had less than no idea who she was. Or why she was in his gardens so early in the morning. Rather than being annoyed at her curious presence as he ordinarily would have been, he was pleasantly intrigued.

"Good morning," he said quietly and she lifted her glossy head from the roses. "May I help you?"

She did not answer immediately, but regarded him with silvery, widely spaced eyes. Then her generous lips spread into a soft, amused smile. "I thought, Lord Tarrant," she replied brightly, "that I was here in order to help *you*."

5

"M*ISS CAROLLAN?*"

"Good morning, Lord Tarrant." Aurelie forced her smile to remain neutrally pleasant. She wanted to grin broadly. His reaction was every bit as gratifying as Rafe's had been disappointing. "You must have come in very late last night. I hope your business has been settled to your satisfaction."

He was blinking rapidly as if to clear his vision. "I . . . yes, quite," he replied finally. It was clear that bafflement was not one of his customary expressions, for his features shifted jerkily as they rearranged themselves into a comfortable scowl. "You have changed."

Aurelie tilted her head to the side and regarded him curiously. "Do you not appreciate the alteration?"

"Of course," he snapped. "But that is hardly the point. I do not appreciate surprises. I do not like . . ." He broke off at her soft laugh. "What in the devil are you laughing about?"

"You must make up your mind, my lord. You are pleasantly surprised, yet annoyed by the means. What would you have me do? Metamorphose slowly? I was under the impression that time was of the essence."

Jason realized his jaw was still a bit slack and closed it with an audible click. He realized, too, that he was being irrational. The caterpillar had metamorphosed into a perfectly acceptable butterfly. Without the spectacles, her gray eyes were actually quite lovely. Large, certainly, but with none of the excessive prominence he had earlier suspected. Nor

47

was their brightness obscured by demurely lowered lids. The young lady was staring at him with a rather disconcerting directness, almost as if it was he who had turned into something odd and unfamiliar. In fact, he decided, she was thoroughly enjoying his discomfiture.

"Come here," he demanded sharply and felt a distinct satisfaction in seeing her blink.

"I beg your pardon?"

"Come here. I would like to see the full extent of this transformation."

Aurelie sighed as she complied. At least he had not asked her to turn in a circle—or to show him her teeth. She advanced until she was only a few feet from him and stopped. Even so, she had to tilt her chin up to see his face clearly. He no longer looked surprised, or even annoyed. He was studying her intently with his lion's eyes, and she resisted the urge to drop her head.

At last he gave a faint nod. "You look very well, Miss Carollan. But you should have told me."

The authoritative tone rankled. "Told you what, my lord? That I was not as unattractive as you so obviously found me? It should not have been necessary of me to beg your indulgence for my appearance. Nor should I have had to answer to your opinion, which you made abundantly clear."

To her surprise, he greeted this outburst with a faint smile. "Touché, Miss Carollan. I owe you an apology. Although," he added, "you seemed no more pleased with me."

There was something in the slight curve to his lips that made Aurelie think he might be teasing her. But no, such a man would never tease. Still, she could not help commenting, "It is just that I have never been greeted so ... emphatically. You must admit it is hard to respond favorably when one's host heads directly for the bottle."

"Touché again. My conduct was reprehensible." Jason suddenly found himself shaking his head at the memory. He had never behaved so before. "I beg you to make allowances for my state of mind, and to offer me another chance." Be-

48

fore she could reply, he took a step back and swept into a courtly bow. "It is a pleasure to meet you, Miss Carollan."

She was staring at him with that forthright gaze again, and he noticed her brows and lashes, though dark, were a deep ginger—as if her Gaelic heritage, hinted at in the chestnut brown of her hair, blazed its existence there.

After a moment, she gave a quick nod and dropped into a graceful curtsy. "My pleasure as well, Lord Tarrant." Then, as if theirs was but a typical Society meeting, she offered, "The weather is uncommonly fine this morning, is it not?"

"Yes, certainly." Jason gave the blue sky the obligatory cursory glance. "Very nice. And very early. What are you doing up and about?"

"I am an early riser, my lord. But I shall have to change that." She was no longer looking at him, but at the wild roses beside the path. "It is not fashionable to rise before noon."

Fashion be damned. In fact, Jason was already contemplating rousting his unwelcome family from their beds at the crack of dawn each morning of their visit, if only so they would see Miss Carollan in the early light. Sally Jersey herself would be able to find no fault with the girl. Nothing whatsoever remained of the dowdy governess.

"Why, Miss Carollan?"

"Why what, my lord?" Aurelie still did not look at him. She knew precisely what he was asking and was not quite ready to answer. He was far too human this morning, with his rumpled ebony hair and relaxed jaw. It was easier to lie to a paragon of stiff reserve.

"Why the elaborate ruse? I cannot believe hiding your, er . . . attributes would serve you well."

"Can you not?" How very like a man, Aurelie thought a bit waspishly. A woman's duty, of course, was to make herself as attractive as possible to show her worth. She swallowed a sarcastic response to that effect and answered instead, "I was merely dressing as I thought a governess ought."

49

"I see." Jason surveyed the faint blush in her cheeks and quickly surmised that Miss Carollan must have had a difficult experience, perhaps with her last employer. Some unfamiliar, chivalric instinct welled up within him and he found himself wishing he could seek the bounder out and plant a fist in his gut.

The urge was as startling as it was strong and he shook his head in astonishment. This woman was nothing more to him than a means to an end, certainly no damsel to be rescued. It must be the fragrant wilderness of the gardens, he decided, and the exhaustion of the night before, playing on his senses. Any man faced with a fey Celtic faery after so little sleep would feel much the same way.

No matter that this sprite stood a good half head taller than most women of his acquaintance and positively radiated fiery spirit. There was something unquestionably fey and elusive about Aurelie Carollan—and it disturbed him.

"We will speak no more on the matter," he announced gruffly, though he had no intention of abandoning his curiosity. He would simply be more subtle in his questions in the future.

"As you wish, my lord," Aurelie replied pleasantly. Her annoyance with his male arrogance had quite vanished. Whatever conclusion he had arrived at would certainly be amusing, but she was willing to let it pass. It seemed she would not have to create a tale for him after all.

When he gestured toward the rest of the gardens with a silent query she accepted, slanting a surreptitious gaze at his profile as they strolled. He, too, had altered somehow during the night, the strong lines of his face seeming less severe. He looked weary, if still eminently handsome, and she wondered if he had returned to the house at all. Something about the set of his jaw implied a sleepless night.

She knew it was presumptuous, but she could not resist asking, "Your estate business—was it very serious?"

He seemed surprised by the question, but not offended. "Yes, it was."

"And quite settled to your satisfaction?"

"Settled for the moment. But come now, Miss Carollan, surely you do not wish me to bore you with dull estate business. Not on such a glorious morning."

"I do not mind."

Jason was not sure why her soft assertion pleased him so. It certainly was not his habit to discuss such things with a lady. But he needed to tell someone of his night in the fields, and something about the girl's aura of intelligence beckoned to him.

So, as they walked, he told the story—quickly and concisely, but with quiet fervor. She listened carefully, her glossy head tilted to one side, waiting until he had finished before commenting, "There must be a way to hold your neighbor at least partially responsible. He should not be allowed to turn a blind eye to what happened. After all, it was his irresponsible behavior that caused the flood."

"Actually," Jason countered, both amused and pleased by this opinion—so much like his own, "it was the heavy rains that caused the flood. His carelessness merely caused it to flow onto my land." He watched as her ginger brows rose. "Whatever the result, I will not suffer."

"Perhaps not," she shot back, "but there is the matter of justness. You should not lose something of yours because another is concerned only with his own welfare."

Hearing the vehemence in her own voice, Aurelie wondered if perhaps she ought to back away from the subject a bit. It was just that she was far too familiar with harmful greed. The viscount, however, seemed no more than mildly curious at her retort and, considering the very specific reason for her being in her present position, she was more than ready to vent a bit.

"I think," she announced firmly, "that it has become altogether too common in our Society to think solely of one's own benefit, with little or no regard for those one might be treading upon."

"Ah, a philanthropist."

Aurelie darted a glance up at her companion. He had spoken blandly enough, but there was a faint smile playing about his mouth and, unfamiliar as such an expression was, she could not determine if it was derisive. Shrugging, she explained as best she could.

"I have done too little in the way of improving the world to be called a philanthropist, my lord, though I like to think I could perhaps help someone someday. No, what I meant is that at worst, too many people use and abuse others to better their own lives. At best, they seem to stomp about, not caring what they crush beneath their heels."

"Like stepping on ants, Miss Carollan?"

"Are you comparing people to ants, my lord?"

Jason had certainly not meant to do so. He had merely been speaking the image that came to mind at her descriptive words. Usually he was very careful to think before speaking. It must have been the late night, he mused, ready to demur. "No, I do not ..."

"Because, if one is to compare lesser people to ants, one must consider the fact that each ant might seem unimportant, but each has a purpose, especially when thousands band together to move a fallen tree."

Now Jason had never heard of ants moving anything larger than a sliver of apple, but he was suddenly struck with an image of a thousand tiny Miss Carollans moving Havensgate right off its foundation. He thrust the absurd vision from his mind and glanced down to see the single, not-so-tiny Miss Carollan glaring up at him. Offending her had not been his plan at all and he wondered momentarily when the conversation had slipped out of his control. They had been speaking of flooded fields, had they not? And she had been supporting his concern for his lands, had she not?

Damn it all, he had spent the better part of the night battling rising water so that his people would not starve, and she was berating him. Or was she? Jason shook his head, trying to regain some degree of linear thinking.

"I like to assume," he said wearily, formulating an apology that would not require apologizing unnecessarily, "that I do not tread upon too many ... ants, Miss Carollan. In fact, I rather think my kitchens supply a good deal of sustenance for those who come within any distance of my feet."

His features appeared drawn again, and Aurelie silently chastised her sharp tongue in the heavy silence. Something told her instinctively that Viscount Tarrant cared for those who depended upon him. If he did not concern himself overly with the welfare of people unknown to him, it was understandable—if not acceptable. He was, after all, a wealthy peer of the realm whose scope of responsibility extended no farther than the prosperity of his title and lands.

In truth, she had spent little time contemplating the well-being of those outside her own home and town, wanting no more, even now, than to be allowed to return to Somerset and her grandmother and live a quiet life. Maintaining a pleasant rapport with this man had a good deal to do with attaining that goal.

"Do you think it is too early for breakfast?" she asked with deliberate lightness. "The mention of your kitchens has made me hungry."

Now Lord Tarrant was looking at her blankly. At least the deep grooves bracketing his mouth had softened somewhat. Aurelie was quite certain that few women of his acquaintance ever mentioned their appetites aloud, even in the country. Well, she *was* hungry, and she imagined he was as well after his hard night.

"Breakfast, my lord?" she prompted. "Is it too early for your staff?"

"It is never too early for my staff," he retorted automatically. "They are well trained to provide . . ."

"Lovely. Then shall we go?"

With that, she spun about, sending the sunlit waves of her hair into motion, and set a lively pace back toward the house. Jason stood for a moment, watching as she again blended into the profusion of blossoms and trying to remember what they had spoken of before food. Then, as she disappeared behind a vine-covered trellis, he remembered that he ought to be following.

He rounded the corner to find her standing in the middle

of the overgrown path, gazing intently at her feet. When he reached her side, she looked up and smiled. There was a single dimple near the right corner of her mouth and he stared at it for several moments before he realized she was pointing at the earth. He followed the elegant line of her arm down to a slender tapered finger.

"Ants," she announced brightly. Then, lifting one pink-slippered foot, she stepped gracefully over the almost invisible queue.

She waited then, a look of amiable expectation on her face. Unsure of what he was supposed to do, Jason glanced down. Contrary to what he had told her, he never paid any attention whatsoever to ants, and saw little point in changing that. He started to look up when one particularly large insect caught his eye. Closer examination showed it not to be an ant at all, or rather, it was a flower petal traveling along, presumably on the back of an ant. Jason glanced up in surprise to find Miss Carollan watching him with a wider smile.

Wordlessly, he stepped over the line and, offering her his arm, which she accepted, walked out of the garden. Aurelie checked his expression as they reached the house. He still looked tired, but he was not scowling. If anything, he looked pensive and she found herself wondering if he, living his life as Viscount Tarrant, ever got a chance to pay attention to the little, inconsequential things. Probably not.

As she stepped through the door ahead of him, she remembered her comment about wanting to help someone someday. *I am going to help you, my lord,* she proclaimed silently. *We are going to help each other.*

As promised, the staff had a commendable breakfast prepared within minutes of the viscount's request. Separated by the vast length of the table, the two spoke little and passed the time in not uncomfortable silence. Tarrant drank coffee rather than tea and Aurelie could smell the strong brew from where she sat. She had never developed a partiality for the bitter taste and watched curiously as he sipped contentedly from the steaming cup.

Funny, she had not noticed before that his upper lip was a perfect, sculpted bow. When taken with the rest of his face, his mouth had seemed as hard and chiseled as everything else. Now, centered above the rim of his cup, that single feature seemed almost feminine. No, she amended, recalling a word she had once overheard. Lord Tarrant's mouth was not feminine. It was quite male and completely, utterly *sensual*.

Feeling suddenly uncomfortable, she glanced up to find the viscount watching her watching him. Not wanting to give her untempered mind a chance to come up with a word for his tawny eyes, she dropped her own gaze and rose awkwardly to her feet. She heard him push his chair back and hurriedly announced, "No, do not get up, my lord." She had no idea whether he obeyed, as she was now staring at the middle of the table. "If you will excuse me, I believe I will . . . um, go upstairs."

Pitiful, but no reasonable excuse came to mind. Not waiting for his response, she headed for the door. His resonant voice stopped her just as she reached for the handle.

"I think perhaps I ought to thank you in advance, Miss Carollan."

"I . . . I beg your pardon?"

She turned back toward him, and Jason caught her gaze from across the room. "You have undertaken what could prove to be a mighty task." She merely stared at him, her gray eyes wide in her face. "My family," he explained after a moment. "I expect a governess must be prepared for many situations, but my family can overwhelm the hardiest soul."

"I understand," she replied with, Jason noticed, admirable conviction.

"You could not possibly. I have full faith in your capabilities, but I thought I would thank you in advance, just in case. You are helping me immensely, Miss Carollan."

She blinked at him then and opened her mouth as if to speak. She promptly closed it again and stared at him silently. After a moment, she dropped her gaze and said, "I will do my best not to disappoint you, Lord Tarrant."

"Jason."

"Who?"

He could not prevent the chuckle that burst forth. "Me. I do have a given name—several actually. Jason Roderick Maitland Granville. I think if we are to be convincingly affianced you might try calling me Jason once in a while." When she did not respond, he smiled and shrugged. "You do not have to do it now. Practice in the hallways. There is a portrait in the gallery that is probably easier to talk to than I am. It was done many years ago when I was far younger and far more pleasant."

He had no idea what imp was controlling his tongue. He had never been one for teasing, and certainly never one to indulge in self-deprecating humor. But here he was, shocking Miss Carollan—no, *Aurelie*—back into prim speechlessness. Deciding it was time to end this particular exchange, he announced, "That is all for now . ... Aurelie."

She left then, quickly, or rather tried to leave. Her path through the door was suddenly blocked by an upright and dressed but clearly not-quite-awake Rafael. Rafe, ever needing some morning sustenance, clearly comprehended that there was some mannerly behavior involved in meeting a woman in a doorway. He just could not quite seem to grasp what it was. He stepped forward and, as Aurelie stepped back to let him pass, remembered and bumped up against the door frame as he tried to get out of the way.

Instead of being offended, she graced him with a brilliant smile. "Good morning, Cousin," she said warmly.

" 'Morning," Rafe replied, returning her smile with a vague one of his own. "Sorry. I'm a proper noddy before noon."

"As am I," she agreed, her bright countenance belying her gracious words. "Have some of the curried eggs. They will perk you right up."

The mention of food brought an instant brightening to Rafael's face. "Is there any rum-currant bread?"

"I believe so."

"Smashing. No one bakes like Tare's cook." With that, he launched himself into the room and Aurelie disappeared into the hall.

Jason waited until his friend had settled himself behind a plate overflowing with bread and sausage before speaking. "I need another woman, Rafe, and I think you can help."

"Another one?" Rafael blinked at him. "Whatever for?"

"Propriety. It is all well and good for Aurelie to be here alone with us now, but once my family arrives, we will need to provide an adequate chaperon."

"Hmm. Hadn't thought of that. How can I help?"

"Your great-aunt is here in East Sussex, is she not?" Jason caught himself smiling. "The one with a mustache and dresses the color of tree lichen."

"Aunt Myrtle. But remember that she is also the one with the mind like a sieve . . ."

"All the better. She seems far more likely to accept Aurelie's sudden presence in your family than anyone else."

Rafe regarded him thoughtfully. "Quite right. All I have to do is tell her she has not seen Aurelie in some time and she will be regaling us with stories of the girl's childhood." He grinned. "Brilliant as always, Tare. Don't know how you do it."

Jason let the compliment pass. Rafael was forever decrying his own intelligence. "Then you will send for her?"

"Gladly. Whenever you like."

Once the matter was decided and a footman dispatched with a request for Aunt Myrtle's presence, Rafe tucked into his meal with relish. The thought that had been niggling at the back of Jason's mind since his friend had entered the room burst forward and he fixed the other man with a sharp gaze.

"You were not surprised."

"Surprised?" Rafe regarded him over a loaded fork. "You always have a flush table."

"Not the food. Miss Carollan."

"Aurelie? What about her?"

57

"What ... ?" China rattled as Jason set down his cup with unnecessary force. "Despite the effort to which you seem to go to make people take you for a careless fool, you are one of the most observant fellows I know. You cannot tell me you did not notice the transformation. She has ... well, she is quite acceptable looking."

Rafe took several bites of his breakfast, chewing appreciatively, before replying, "You are quite right. *I* am observant."

"And what in the devil does that mean?"

"It means," Rafe announced, reaching for the blackberry preserves, "that *I* never found her unacceptable. I knew the minute I saw her she was a looker. I thought about setting you straight on the matter ..."

"Well, why in God's name did you not?"

"I should not have had to."

Jason, finding he had no response whatsoever to that, closed his jaw with a click and watched as his friend tucked into the curried eggs.

6

"IT WAS A very *tall* tree, as I remember. The dear child managed to get all the way to the top, but could not quite seem to get herself down, bless her heart." Aunt Myrtle paused to give Aurelie a cherubic smile. Aurelie grinned back. "I do believe the gardener had to tie two ladders together to get you down. And we very nearly had to fetch a groom to get *him* down. Is that not right, dear?"

The good lady had arrived on Aurelie's third day at Havensgate, descending from her carriage in a cloud of lilac perfume and mossy-looking gauze wraps. True to Rafe's promise, she had taken to her new charge with alacrity, after two days having created a history of visits that could have fooled Aurelie's own family. Far from minding, Aurelie was delighted with the tales and with Myrtle herself, whose affection for the girl rose proportionally with the workings of her quirky mind.

"I do not remember two ladders, Aunt Myrtle," Aurelie began, but was cut off by a growl from across the room.

"I hardly think, madam, that such stories are appropriate for the future wife of a viscount."

Myrtle turned guileless blue eyes in Jason's direction. "Nonsense, dear boy. Even a viscountess has a childhood. Though Aurelie did indulge in such marvelous escapades. I have just remembered the time when she was searching for bullfrogs and had to be pulled from the mud . . ."

Jason ran a weary hand through his hair. He was beginning to question his intelligence in bringing Rafael's aunt to Havensgate. The old hen was an appropriate chaperone, certainly, but her sievelike mind was proving to be surprisingly tight, if faulty. She had embraced the fictional relationship with Aurelie with tenacity and was not about to let go. Added to that was the fact that she fully believed every absurd story that fell from her lips.

The problem, it seemed, was that the stories tended to make Aurelie look the veriest hoyden, albeit an endearing and charming one. His mother would no doubt have a field day with any tale involving bullfrogs. On top of that, Aurelie was doing nothing to dissuade Myrtle from her ramblings. On the contrary, she seemed to be enjoying the situation immensely.

"Really, my dear," he addressed his faux betrothed, "I am quite certain you never waded into a river to catch frogs."

The bell-like quality of her laugh was only slightly less captivating than the dancing silver lights in her eyes. "Actually, my lord, I did. It used to drive my mother to distraction. I would arrive home with a gown full of mud and frogs in my pockets."

"A truly lovely lady, your mother," Myrtle offered, fumbling in her sleeve for a wilted handkerchief. "Though I only had the pleasure of her company on few occasions, I found her utterly delightful. Such a shame, dying so young."

"How kind of you, madam," Aurelie offered, leaning forward to pat the older woman's plump hand. "She was fond of you, too."

Myrtle sniffed into her handkerchief. Rafe, ensconced in the settee, chuckled quietly into his port. Jason groaned and slumped back in his chair.

Myrtle recovered sufficiently to recall an afternoon involving young Aurelie, a pianoforte, and a Mozart sonata played backward. Aurelie took the opportunity to study her host's tight features. It had occurred to her more than once that perhaps she ought to drop hints about a more illustrious childhood. The strain of hearing Myrtle's lively tales was obviously taking its toll on Lord Tarrant. His lips had taken on a pinched look not more than an hour into their first meal with Rafe's aunt, and had not relaxed since.

Yes, she decided, she really ought to do something, but her common sense was tinged with reluctance. In truth, she quite enjoyed the older woman's tales. They were close enough to her own memories to make her wonder just how scatterbrained Myrtle actually was. She was perceptive enough to "remember" that Aurelie had not been a dull child.

There, too, was the fact that Lord Tarrant had given her little support in their ruse. He had been gone a great deal during the past several days, urgent estate business keeping him from home too often for Aurelie's peace of mind. Most of her time had been spent with Rafael, taking lessons in being his cousin. Actually, he told her of his life and she listened. It was a flawed situation, but not unpleasant. Rafe was an engaging storyteller and there was little need for her to speak of herself. He had asked the expected questions, she had answered as best she could and, with the exception of a few speculative looks, he had let the matter drop.

There were more fittings, and more pleasant hours in the garden. She had chosen some books from Lord Tarrant's extensive library and, though Rafe amiably suggested that perhaps Taliesin and Homer were not the most appropriate of choices for Tarrant's betrothed—and even provided her with several popular novels—she filled the empty hours with her beloved mythology.

She toured the Tarrant estates with Rafe as her guide, mingled in the village with some of the viscount's tenants, and even attended church in her new persona, smiling in response to the countless curious looks she received. Most importantly, however, at least as far as she was concerned, she was able to put enough bits and pieces together to form an almost acceptable image of the man himself.

He was respected, if not precisely liked, by everyone with whom she spoke. Apparently there had been Granvilles in the area as far back as anyone could remember, though they had never truly become part of the community.

That in itself was not unusual. The nobility tended to keep its distance from all but its own. What was surprising was the diversity of knowledge the local people seemed to have regarding the viscount.

The vicar congratulated Aurelie on having the good fortune to be betrothed to one of Oxford's finest scholars. Colonel Howell, Tarrant's closest neighbor and the area's official expert on everything, hailed the viscount as a war hero. The baker's wife reminisced fondly on the serious little boy who had so liked her shortbread. And one young lady had been so emboldened as to blush and giggle over the raptures he caused in the local female population, even when his only presence was in week-old editions of the London *Times*.

She learned, too, listening especially carefully to words not spoken, that the former Lord and Lady Tarrant, now Earl and Countess of Heathfield, were not so highly regarded. Apparently their residence, now limited to periodic visits, consisted of a good deal of noise and bullying of the village merchants. It seemed the present viscount spent less time in Havensgate than the community would have liked, but at least he was approachable and enterprising when there. And while the local people seemed more than happy to be of service to him, the impending descent of the Heathfields and company brought a tense and grudging flurry of activity to the village.

Curiosity about the group whom, she feared, might very well make her life miserable for the next three months, itched like a creeping rash. Rafe was as helpful as he could be, but his endearing tendency to paint everything in a rosy light brought forth nothing more telling than the comment that the Heathfields were "all that their station demanded." For all of Aurelie's experience with Polite Society, she could well imagine the assertion implied nothing more than expensive dress and grand demeanor.

Myrtle was no more likely to shed any usable light on the matter. By the end of the lady's first day in residence, Aurelie had grown tremendously fond of the old dear but could not count on her for reliable information. Myrtle would, she was certain, provide an endless array of entertaining anecdotes about whatever subject was mentioned, Heathfields included. The problem, of course, was that none of them were likely to be reliable.

In the end, she was forced to beard the lion himself. The visiting party would be arriving in mere days, and there were myriad loose ends to be tied up. So, when Tarrant politely excused himself from the drawing room, clearly having had enough of Mozart and frogs, Aurelie decided it was time for action. Myrtle's less-than-hushed whisper to Rafe that the lovebirds must have a bit of time to bill and coo made her smile. A quick glance at Tarrant's rigid back told her he was not so amused.

She stayed a few minutes longer, enjoying the easy affection and warmth between Rafael and his dotty aunt. She expected a far chillier environment in Tarrant's presence and needed some reserve of good cheer. It was not, she conceded readily, that the viscount was a harsh man. It was simply that his responsibilities, along with a naturally marshaled disposition, made for a cool austerity that was at odds with her own basically blithe character.

She wondered, as she wandered down the hall toward the library, whether Tarrant's family would be fooled at all. No matter how good her manners, or the elegance of her new wardrobe, she was an inherently poor match for the viscount. Lady Eleanor, she was certain even without ever having met her, was not the sort to let a frog anywhere near her person, let alone in her pockets.

Tarrant responded to her knock with a curt, "Enter." Straightening her shoulders and forming what she hoped was an impassive smile, Aurelie pushed the door open and entered his sanctum.

"We really must talk," she announced immediately, noting as she settled herself across from him that he was looking thoroughly exhausted. The grooves bracketing his lovely mouth were pronounced and his hair was uncustomarily mussed. It was an entirely pleasing picture, but disturbing. Steeling herself against the urge to reach across the desk and smooth the ebony locks into place, she cleared her throat and continued. "We should get our story straight."

Jason glanced up wearily from the document he had been studying and was startled to feel his spirits lighten. Odd, he thought, how a mere fifteen minutes after being in the drawing room, he had become so gloomily immersed in business. It had to be the seriousness of the matter before him: the impending breakdown of the mill's primary gear shaft. Something about Aurelie's presence made the situation seem less serious. In his haven of dark wood and somber fabrics, she struck a discordant note, her yellow dress making him think of a daffodil in the depths of a forest.

"Yes," he agreed, "we should." In truth, he had not been avoiding her presence. They had shared nearly every meal, certainly. And, he told himself, he had been meaning to have a serious discussion about their fictional relationship. It was simply that he had been so infernally busy. Then, too, the directness of her gaze was a constant reminder of his deceit.

He pushed the thought out of his mind. He was well used to that gaze. After all, she had fixed it on him often enough during their brief meetings at meals. Not that he had not been watching her first, still a bit awed by how very different she appeared from their initial meeting. Where he had seen dull rigidity was now glossy hair and soft curves.

Now *that* was hardly important. Yes, she had become rather lovely—all the better to suit his parents. What he needed to concentrate on was not the cover, but the book.

"Yes," he repeated, "we should get everything in order." Reaching for a crisp sheet of foolscap, he methodically wrote out a list. "Meeting," he read from the top. "At Myrtle's house, I think would be best. She has already started embellishing her memory with something to that effect. You were staying there for the month of November last year and Rafe and I dropped in on an impromptu visit."

Aurelie doubted that he had ever paid an impromptu visit to anyone in his life, but held her tongue. "I do not think it necessary," he continued, "for you to ask Myrtle to describe her home. She would take a week to impart what I can in one sentence." He looked up from the paper to stare pensively in the direction of the hearth. "Lots of brick, three stories, an impossible hodgepodge of heavy furniture and delicate porcelain shepherdesses, small grounds with winding paths and a profusion of primroses. That ought to cover it."

He frowned then, as if he had missed some crucial detail. Instead of elaborating, however, he sighed and announced, "But that was not a sentence." Shaking his head, he turned his attention back to his list. "When: six months ago should suffice. I was immediately impressed by your intelligence and we discussed . . ." Aurelie had been waiting for him to actually look at her, but when he did the leonine force of his gaze sent an unexpected frisson of awareness down her spine. "Just what are your interests, Miss Carollan?"

You, burst unbidden to the tip of her tongue. *Why there is something so different in your eyes and in your demeanor.* When he lifted one dark brow, waiting for her response, she swallowed and dragged her eyes from his. Hastily, she tried to answer his question. "I . . . er, mythology . . . and . . ." Nothing else was coming to mind and she wondered a bit dazedly what imp had invaded her brain.

"Greek? Roman?"

"Well . . . um, Celtic."

"Celtic." Tarrant rapped his pen against the desktop. "I know nothing about Celtic mythology. Well, we shall just say we shared a mutual interest in . . ."

The list went on and Aurelie did her best to concentrate. This was not what she had wanted to discuss, not really. But her own questions hovered unasked as he spoke. Truly, he was leaving little out, at least as far as mundane details were concerned. It was a wonder he had not mentioned the climate.

"The weather was rather poor, a good deal of rain, and

we were confined much of the time to the house. All the better to get acquainted ..." A small, choked sound from across the desk brought Jason's head up. "Am I going too fast, Miss Carollan? Perhaps you ought to be writing this down."

"I think I shall manage to remember enough, my lord." Oddly, her voice sounded rather dry and Jason took a good look at her expression. Her features were composed, but above the patrician nose her eyes flashed silver. "After all, a woman in love cannot be expected to remember such things as the weather."

It would have taken far less perceptiveness than Jason possessed to recognize her sarcasm. "Am I boring you?" he asked sardonically. "I apologize if so, but you did introduce the topic of consolidating our story."

"Yes, I did. And it is not that you are boring me."

"No?"

"No. Your attention to detail is admirable, my lord, but ..." A fluttery wave of her hand gave her opinion of his details. She leaned forward and the lamplight caught the chestnut strands in her hair, turning it into a fiery halo. "I would rather know ..." She caught him looking at her then and whatever she read in his gaze stopped her words on a sigh.

"Yes? Come now, Aurelie, do not be shy. What is it you feel you need to know which you do not already?" He leaned back and rested his elbows on the padded arms of his chair. "I am thirty years old, born here at Havensgate, educated at Christ Church, Oxford, heir to the Heathfield earldom. I have numerous holdings, some as part of the entail and some in my own right. My parents reside in Staffordshire, when they are not in London, at the family seat. I have two sisters and a brother, all younger, all of whom you will be meeting in two days' time. The elder sister, Catherine, is married and has three children. Grace, the younger, and my brother, Richard, are unmarried. Rickey is currently at Oxford. Christ Church, of course."

"Of course."

He raised an eyebrow at her tone. "I fear I am not giving you the information you desire. Perhaps you would be so good as to help me."

"I . . . well"—Aurelie shrugged helplessly—"that is all very important, but . . . categorical."

"I beg your pardon?"

She sighed, in exasperation and self-reproof. "I suppose this could seem silly, impertinent even. But I am to meet these people in two days and since it is so important that I not offend anyone, not to mention the fact that I am supposed to make them believe you have fallen so in love with me that you would disregard their wishes, I need to know *about* them. Nuances, not rudimentary details."

If possible, Tarrant's brow went up yet another notch. "Are you always so unconcerned with rudimentary details? That would seem rather self-defeating for a governess, Miss Carollan. I have always been given to believe that precision in detail is the core of knowledge."

There was a faint scar above his lip, like a pale crescent moon early in the evening, visible only to someone looking very hard. Aurelie noticed this tiny detail, and found herself wondering about the precise circumstances under which he had got it. When he spoke again, the scar shifted slightly.

"Would you not agree that a good governess pays attention to detail?"

Her own lips curved as she answered. "I never said I was a good governess, my lord. Nor did you ever ask."

For a moment, she thought he was going to say something harsh. The corner of his mouth twitched into the beginnings of a frown. Then, amazingly, there was a flash of very white teeth and he laughed aloud. It was the first time she had heard him really laugh, and it was a marvelous sound, deep and resonant. And very brief.

"You are quite right," he announced seriously. "I did not ask. So, are you a good governess?"

Aurelie thought hard for a moment, hating the deceit that seemed to have become so much a part of her life. "I believe," she answered finally, "that I have it in me to be a very good governess, indeed. I am intelligent and caring, but . . ." She paused, and Tarrant regarded her intently.

"What? A fault, Miss Carollan? I should be very interested in hearing what indiscretions taint your past."

A pained expression clouded her eyes briefly, yet was gone so quickly that Jason wondered if he had imagined it. Was there something deeper in her past than genteel poverty and a boorish employer? He searched her face carefully for any signs and saw only bland humor.

"I am not very good," she said dryly, "at controlling my tongue sometimes. I speak without thinking."

Jason wanted very much to probe, to find out just what had caused that momentary crack in her composure. Instead, he acknowledged her remark with a nod. "Not the worst of failings, certainly, but potentially dangerous. Have you always been so blithe?"

"Have you always been so controlled?" was her instant retort.

Near speechlessness yet again, he did not answer for a few moments. "Yes," he said at last, "I have. I have found that order and detail serve me well." He shook his head then, bemused. "It appears we are at an impasse, Aurelie. You want nuance and I can only give fact."

Watching him ponder that thought, Aurelie was seized by sudden and startling sympathy. Jason Roderick Maitland Granville, she understood with utter clarity, had had little chance in his life to deal with nuances. Everything was black-and-white in his world. Honor and dishonor, beautiful and ugly. It was no wonder that he did not instinctually talk about himself or his family in emotional terms; he had probably never seen either that way.

"My lord," she said softly, "Jason. I do not want to know that your brother has followed in the family's footsteps by attending Christ Church. I want to know whether he *likes* it. I want to know whether your parents are kind . . . whether they enjoy being with their grandchildren." *Whether they enjoyed being with you as a child. Whether you ever really were a child.*

In the silence that followed, she wondered if she had not perhaps gone too far, crossed over the fine line between inquisitiveness and insolence that such a man must maintain in his ordered life. He had turned away from her to stare into the fire, his face all harsh angles and unyielding planes in the flickering light, and Aurelie was actually on the verge of creeping out of the room and back to the easy company of the Marlowes. She had even braced herself to rise when Jason's voice stopped her.

"I do not know if my brother is happy at Oxford. I have never asked. No one ever asked me." That statement was not made accusingly, nor with self-pity. Rather, he was just stating one of his facts. "He is a fine young man, carefree, more like Rafe than me. He would make a very good husband, I think, but a poor earl. He does not want the responsibility and should never have to shoulder it. It would drag him down, make him miserable." He laughed, but this time it was a humorless sound. "I suppose that is why my parents are so intent on seeing me wed. It does not matter that I shall make a poor husband. I shall be a competent earl."

He leaned toward the fire, arm extended as if to banish a chill. "My parents are not kind. Not that they are necessarily unkind, mind you, but kindness has never been required of them. They are charitable when required, hospitable when entertaining, always very aware of their status and their reputation. As for whether they enjoy Catherine's children, I have no idea. As far as I know, they spend too little time with them to have formed more of an opinion than whether they are pleasing to look at." He turned back to face her. "For what it is worth to your edification, Miss Carollan, *I* like the children. They are unruly at times, certainly hard on one's ears when excited, but smart and inquisitive, and not in the least stingy with their affection."

As if something about that last assertion startled him, he fell silent. Encouraged by what emotion she had seen, Aurelie pressed him, "And your sisters?"

"My sisters." He frowned, either reluctant or unable to

69

7

H AD AURELIE KNOWN what would descend upon the house two days later, she would have asked for full biographies—and a shield. Instead she found herself, armed with precious little ammunition and even less confidence, seated at the supper table with a group who could well have participated in the Spanish Inquisition.

"Somerset, was it, Miss Carollan?" This came from Jason's mother, an imposing woman whose pale hair and ice blue eyes could not have been better suited to her personality.

"Yes, my lady. Near Bridgwater."

"Remember, Maman, we had a governess from Somerset once." This came from Jason's sister Catherine, a self-recognized beauty with Jason's coloring. "She was so very rustic. You finally let her go when Rickey started speaking in that atrocious accent."

"Really, Cat, I did no such thing. Niver haid 'n axint in me laife." Rickey grinned engagingly at his older sister who tittered in approval. In fact, the entire table seemed well amused, the countess herself breaking into a frosty smile. "Folks froom Somersait spaik jest laik ennyone eelse."

Jason, Aurelie noted, was not laughing, but neither had he done anything as yet to aid her. She had not expected raptures at the announcement of their betrothal, but the countess had quite outdone expectation. When Jason presented Aurelie as his fiancée, the lady had clasped a heavily beringed hand to her flat bosom and swayed with all the

71

grace and drama of a grand willow. Only her younger son's quick movement to her back had kept her on her feet.

Nor had things improved from there. Lord Heathfield had barked, though not truly unkindly, "Irish?" upon hearing her surname. Her honest and unrepentant affirmation had drawn an audible sniff from several aristocratic noses.

Now, watching the table amuse itself at her expense—or, rather, Somerset's—she noticed two of the women were not participating in the revelry. The first was Grace, Jason's youngest sister. A pretty thing, with her mother's blond hair and the golden eyes that all four children seemed to have inherited from their father, she had said little since her arrival hours before. What she had offered to Aurelie, though, was a sweet and sincere welcome to the family. Warmed by the regard, Aurelie had accepted the words guiltily, sorry to deceive the one of Jason's siblings who had bothered to be polite.

The second nonparticipant was, to Aurelie's surprise, Lady Eleanor DeVane. Instead of sharing in the jest, she was staring at the assembled diners, among whom were her own parents and close friends, with what appeared to be annoyance and even a small amount of embarrassment. To Aurelie's astonishment, she leaned to the left and spoke several short words to the young man there, a Mr. Burnham. Whatever she said must have been pointed, for he flushed dully and quickly turned a guffaw into an awkward cough.

Confused, Aurelie studied the lovely woman closely. From the moment Lady Eleanor had stepped from her carriage, a truly stunning image of golden hair and huge sapphire eyes, Aurelie had expected the worst. Instead, Lady Eleanor had been gracious, responding to the news of Jason's betrothal with no more than raised eyebrows and a faint smile. While her mother huffed and sputtered behind her, she had offered Aurelie her hand and, in a low, musical voice, had said, "My best wishes, Miss Carollan. It is good to know that Jason has found a woman to truly suit him."

The most amazing part, Aurelie decided later, was that,

when faced with the news that the man she had expected to marry was betrothed to another, Lady Eleanor had managed to sound perfectly sincere.

Whether Eleanor's censure had carried beyond Burnham, or whether the joke had simply run its course, a sudden hush fell over the table. At least twelve pairs of eyes slewed back to Aurelie, who could do no more than smile weakly.

"Oh, I say," Rickey stammered, reaching up to push a blond lock away from his brow, "I didn't mean to imply . . . Miss Carollan . . . dashed poor of me. I can be such a rattle-pate at times. Do forgive me. I meant no disrespect."

His genuine discomfort, while gaining him no points with the Heathfields, Burnhams, or elder DeVanes, dispatched some of the chill from Aurelie's core. She had little hope of winning over Catherine or her mother, but it seemed that the younger Granvilles were not wholly against her.

"It is of no matter, Rickey," she offered warmly. "There are fascinating accents to be found everywhere in Britain."

"Irish," came from somewhere down the table. Lord Heathfield, no doubt. Aurelie had, in the course of the evening, decided that he did not mean to be cruel. He just did not seem to find it necessary to constrain his opinions.

No wonder Jason prides himself so on his control, she commented silently. *His family seems to have so little.*

"You must understand, Miss Carollan, that it came as quite a shock to all this afternoon when Lord Tarrant announced his betrothal to a nobod . . . er, an unknown person from the country."

"Lydia, really," Lady Eleanor gasped at her friend's words.

Aurelie, once again amazed to find such unlikely support, raised her hand. "I am certain it was so, Miss Burnham. Lord Tarrant"—she shot the viscount a tense look, hoping to convey the message that it was high time for him to step in—"and I anticipated that our betrothal might come as a surprise. It was simply that we, er ... we ..."

"We could not let such considerations interfere in our affections. While the announcement might seem sudden, our regard for each other certainly is not."

Jason very nearly winced at the grateful look Aurelie shot him and berated himself for not taking control of the situation sooner. He had simply been enjoying her handling of the matter thus far, applauding the graciousness and calm with which she answered every sally.

"It took me several months to get Miss Carollan to so much as consider my offer," he continued. "I believe it was only my persistence that compelled her to accept, and it is only at my insistence that we have even made the matter public at this time."

"Quite right, dear boy," Aunt Myrtle announced from down the table. "Why, I had to convince darling Aurelie that six months of acquaintance was more than enough to signify." She turned to Lady Heathfield. "Jason knew his heart, mind you, but he does approach everything so systematically. Once he had found his viscountess, he was all ready to get her to the altar. Aurelie, however, is a far more romantic soul. She insisted on a real betrothal. I just knew the moment they met in my parlor that a true match had been made. . . ."

It took all of Jason's considerable control to keep from leaping from his seat to plant a grateful kiss on the old lady's wrinkled cheek as she prattled on. A quick glance at Aurelie informed him that she was torn between just such a reaction and sliding in mortification from her chair. A delicate blush stained her cheeks a charming pink and once again he was reminded of roses.

Get the family into the garden, he started a mental list. *Order a dusky pink ball gown for Aurelie.*

"Well," his mother huffed, interrupting Myrtle mid-rapture, "it was a shock to us, nonetheless. Really, Jason, you might at least have hinted at the matter when you invited us here."

Jason was spared the necessity of answering by a spirited laugh from his younger sister. "Honestly, Mother," Grace said cheerfully, "you cannot blame Jason for neglecting to mention his engagement—in his invitation, at least." Her eyes sparkled as she turned to her brother. "Jason *never* invites us. We simply descend upon him."

For a moment, Jason stared blankly at his youngest sibling as if trying to decide whether he had just been insulted. Then, slowly, his lips cracked into a reluctant smile. Grace nearly glowed under the attention and Aurelie's heart melted for the girl. It was clear she adored her brother, and that he had never paid enough attention to her to see her affectionate spirit.

When, at last he replied, "You are always welcome, Grace," Aurelie wanted to clap her hands in approval. His next words, however, made her want to clap one hand soundly over his mouth. "You were impertinent with Mother, however. I suggest you apologize."

The warm color faded from Grace's face in an instant, leaving only two bright patches on her cheeks, as if she had been slapped. As she murmured an apology in her mother's direction, Aurelie turned angrily in Jason's direction. He had managed to deflate his sister's charming vitality with a few sharp words and she wanted nothing more than to take him to task for it.

Her resolve deepened when Catherine announced to the table, "Grace does seem to find it difficult to live up to her name at times." And their mother added, "We have no great hopes for her first Season. She will have to learn to curb her tongue before she will find a husband." Aurelie was ready to remark on the fact that, so far, only one member of the family seemed to have any control over his tongue. She had even opened her mouth to say just that when Lady Heathfield continued. "I trust you have no brothers, Miss Carollan."

Now Aurelie prided herself on her quickness, but it took several moments for the meaning of those words to sink in. *I trust you have no brothers, Miss Carollan. . . . I trust you have no brothers ... who would try to follow your lead in marrying into this family, Miss Carollan.*

Jason watched as Aurelie's cheeks pinkened again, now in a fierce rush. This time, his list skipped over a rose ball gown to a muzzle for his mother. He had expected resistance to his "betrothal." He'd even, he finally admitted to himself, wanted to shock his family out of their tenacious and unrepentant interference in his life. He had not, however, meant to do it at Aurelie's expense.

One retort after another rose to his lips only to freeze there. Damn it all, his mother had just insulted the woman he was going to marry, and he could not seem to call her on it.

The woman I am going to marry ...

Now rendered speechless by the absurdity of that thought, Jason could only gape at his guests, wondering what devil had taken hold of his brain. It was his family, he decided quickly. And company. The assembled group was enough to make anyone go stark raving mad. So mad as to actually forget the very necessary deception upon which he had embarked.

"Well ... bloody hell," he snapped.

In the ensuing silence, he gazed helplessly around the table. Aurelie, to his utter confusion, was smiling anew. So was Rafe. As for the rest of the party, expressions ranged from Lady Ramsden's indignation to Miss Burnham's wide-eyed shock. And, to further Jason's disconcerted state, he suddenly found he had absolutely nothing else to say.

The entrance of a footman bearing the main course sounded every bit as loud as an advancing army regiment. The poor man, on walking into the heavy silence, stopped dead in his tracks. For countless seconds, the scene took on all the characteristics of a very concise, very odd oil painting. Then, "How marvelous—pheasant with almonds!" Aunt Myrtle's voice shattered the stillness. "I always say that a splendid meal is taken to a different plane altogether by a few good nuts!"

76

Jason thought it quite the most appropriate statement he had heard all night.

Some semblance of normalcy had returned by the time the ladies retired to the drawing room. Aurelie had followed the countess's lead reluctantly, not wanting to speculate what horrors of interrogation awaited her in Jason's absence. To her immense relief, at Lady Heathfield's urging, Eleanor settled herself at the pianoforte and began to play. She was, as Rafe had remarked, a dab hand at it and Aurelie stifled a flare of envy. Her own performance was decent enough, but not nearly on a par with this.

She shot a sidelong glance at Aunt Myrtle, who was ensconced comfortably on the settee, eyes closed and a contented smile creasing her plump face. It was difficult to tell whether the old lady was sleeping or merely enjoying the performance. Aurelie rather hoped for the former. Now, with the situation as tense as it was, was not a good time for extended fictional reminiscences on Aurelie's wondrous musical proficiency.

"Do you like Havensgate, Miss Carollan?" Grace asked after a few minutes.

"Please, it's Aurelie. And, yes, I find Havensgate to be . . ."

"Shush." Lady Heathfield admonished sharply. "I desire to hear dearest Eleanor's splendid playing."

". . . welcoming," Aurelie finished dryly under her breath.

Grace, who had been leaning forward to hear, gave a saucy smile and patted her hand in empathy. "Do not concern yourself overmuch with the Dragon Lady," she said quietly, jerking her chin toward her mother. "She spits more smoke than fire."

Aurelie, feeling more than a little scorched by that point, merely smiled. Looking at Grace's pretty face, she decided, but for the eyes, there was nothing to indicate the girl was related to Jason at all. With her fair hair and heart-shaped face, Grace appeared every bit the angel. Her spirit, however, implied something far more devilish and, Aurelie decided, beauty notwithstanding, that irreverence was the girl's greatest appeal.

"You have changed him, I think."

"I beg your pardon?" Aurelie whispered back, catching Lady Heathfield's disapproving glance from the corner of her eye.

"Jason," Grace replied, shooting her mother a defiant look of her own. "He seems scattered, somehow. More disturbed than I have ever seen him."

"I see."

"No, you don't. Please, it was not an insult. Quite the contrary. It is just that all his life, my brother has been so distant . . . so cool. I like the transformation. How have you managed this miracle?"

Smoke and mirrors, Aurelie thought guiltily. *Pure fiction.* "I am not certain I can answer that," she said neutrally. "Your brother is much the same as he was when we met. I really have not known him long enough to compare to . . . before."

"That's all right," Grace said genially, just as her mother spat a bit more smoke in their direction. "I have known him all my life and I do not really know him at all."

Eleanor lifted her hands from the keys then and polite applause from the doorway announced the presence of the gentlemen. Jason was standing at the door, port glass in hand, and Aurelie wondered how long he had been there. Long enough to hear all of Eleanor's talented performance? Or merely long enough to see her whispering rudely with Grace? Neither put her in the best of lights.

"Jason, dear," his mother called, "do come and play that marvelous duet with Eleanor. We all so enjoyed it at Heathfield last month."

"Oh, yes, do." This came from Eleanor's mother and, considering her rigid silence through most of the evening, struck Jason with the unexpectedness of hearing words from a statue's mouth.

Both Ramsdens had sat through the bulk of the meal like

marble effigies, the effect heightened by the fact that the couple shared a gray roundness reminiscent of daVinci's work. The impeccable host in Jason had wanted to draw them out on more than one occasion, but prudence had held his tongue. There was no way of knowing what they might have said. Lady Ramsden's sputterings upon her arrival had boded ill for the matter.

Not that I should give a bloody damn, the now familiar imp announced from the back of his mind. *I never showed any interest in your daughter. Any understanding was in your mind.*

His gaze slewed to Eleanor, resplendent as always in ice blue silk. She had turned on the piano bench and was sitting quietly, hands clasped in her lap. Studying her pleasant if vague smile, Jason wondered if the understanding had existed for her, too. Nothing about her appearance or demeanor hinted at a bruised heart, or even broken expectations. No, she simply looked as beautiful and composed as always.

"I believe I have already had my turn at entertaining," she said softly. "Perhaps his lordship would prefer to do a duet with Miss Carollan."

Miss Carollan, Jason noted when he turned to ask if she would, in fact, be amenable to a duet, was looking decidedly discomposed. Her hair had begun to free itself from its careful coils, errant chestnut curls falling forward to frame her face. She tried to smooth one back, at the same time shaking her head in an emphatic plea that sent one loose hairpin flying.

"I hardly think I can offer so lovely an interlude as Lady Eleanor," she began, only to be cut off as Myrtle sprang into action.

"Poppycock! Your modesty, dearest, is commendable, but heaven knows how very talented you are. Why, you were no more than ten when you announced Haydn's sonatas were too simple . . ."

Aurelie stifled a groan. Haydn's sonatas, to be perfectly honest, tied her fingers into knots. Even thinking about it brought a distinct twitching to her hands. "I am certain I never said such a thing, Aunt," she murmured. "Your memory is far too . . ." *Dangerous.* ". . . flattering."

"I have a better idea." Jason had crossed the room to stand behind the settee, and he rested one hand on her shoulder. "Miss Carollan will partner me at whist. We have enough people for several tables."

The idea met with general approval. Myrtle, Lady Ramsden, and Lord Heathfield declined, leaving the perfect number for three tables. Aurelie found herself seated across from Jason with Rafe and Lydia Burnham partnered against them. With her mind not as sharp as could be desired, she began the game in her usual half-attentive way. Rafe, as before, played with gusto but little attention. Miss Burnham, however, made up for what she lacked in skill with competitive determination. Jason made no complaint the first several times Aurelie lost a trick, but the fourth sent one black brow up a notch. After that point, she turned her attention to the cards.

In the end, they won by a considerable margin, prompting a sullen pout from Miss Burnham and a rueful grin from Rafe. "I suppose I shall have to get used to it, Cousin. Perhaps by the time we're old and gray you won't be able to trump me at every turn." The other games had ended by then, and the group gathered to compare scores.

Aurelie, exhilarated by the win, and by the very basic pleasure of having had such a capable partner as Jason, replied without thinking. "Of course I will not. By the time we are old and gray, you shall be a lofty duke and I an old m . . ." *An old maid somewhere in Somerset. We will not even know each other.* The words very nearly slipped from her tongue and she blanched, searching frantically for something—anything to salvage the moment.

"An old married lady," Jason said smoothly, once again curving his hand around her shoulder. "It is quite all right to say it, darling. The secret is out, after all."

The secret had, indeed, almost come out. And, had Aurelie not been oddly distracted by the fact that the warmth of Jason's palm was radiating right through the filmy fabric of her sleeve and down the length of her arm, she might have worried about it. Instead, she found herself wondering how, in the wake of the heat, she was breaking out in gooseflesh.

Jason, too, was more than a little distracted. Aurelie's skin, pale moments before, was yet again turning a delicate pink. It was the effect of her near gaffe, he decided, and tried to give her a reassuring smile. It might have worked, had he been able to lift his eyes from where the blush disappeared into the bodice of her gown. *A rose-colored, low-cut gown*, amended itself on his list.

". . . bed . . ."

Jason's head snapped up. *"What?"*

"I said, I'm all for bed," he brother repeated cheerfully. "If I am not mistaken, you will have planned some hearty escapade for us tomorrow. So, bed seems like a very good idea."

Yes, it certainly does.

"Richard," the countess snapped, "it is most improper to mention such things in the presence of ladies."

Yes, it probably is, but . . .

"Sorry, Maman. Ladies." Rickey grinned, undaunted. "As I said, it seems an appropriate time to retire. Tare is certainly planning some exhausting activity. . . ."

"Yes, I certainly am." The words, not meant to be spoken aloud, resounded in his ears. "I, er . . ." *Oh, hell.* "I thought perhaps a visit to . . . the abbey ruins."

He thought he heard Rickey groan at the prospect, but Grace clapped her hands in approval. "Marvelous! I do so love the abbey. All the soft grass and shadowed alcoves."

She was staring in the vicinity of his hand on Aurelie's shoulder as she spoke. Had Jason not been perfectly assured to the contrary, he might have thought the gleam in his sister's eyes was decidedly canny.

"It is settled then," he announced gruffly. "We shall have a picnic at the abbey."

Then, taking a step backward and pulling Aurelie with

him, he allowed the rest of the party to precede them into the hall. Good-nights were exchanged by all as they climbed the stairs.

Knowing curious eyes were upon them, he kept Aurelie at the back of the group. When everyone separated for their rooms he stopped and, bending down, brushed his lips quickly over hers. He straightened up then to stare into wide, startled silver eyes. "For our audience," he whispered so she alone could hear.

She did not respond for a moment. Then, with a single, jerky nod, she pulled away and hurried down the hall toward her chamber.

It was not until he was alone in his own bed that Jason allowed himself to admit the kiss had not been for his guests' eyes at all. Nor had it been planned. No, it had been a heady impulse, pure and simple, and it had been for himself.

8

AURELIE STOOD ON a grassy knoll above the abbey ruins with the wind on her face and the feel of Jason's lips on hers. It had been much like the breeze, light and fleeting, but carrying with it the promise of far greater force. Remembering, she shivered slightly, her skin tingling again in a way that before had only been associated with cold.

She knew it was unspeakably silly of her to have been—to *be*—so moved by such a small event. Jason's kiss had been impersonal, restrained, done solely for the benefit of everyone ... everyone but herself, really. Still, it had startled her, in its unexpectedness, and in its impact. Kisses in the past, limited to what her recent "suitors" had been able to steal, had been unwelcome and unpleasant. Jason's had been neither.

What a shame, she thought, that something so lovely could be so false.

He had been nothing but polite that day, giving every appearance of a devoted fiancé. Aurelie was confident she had been the only one to detect the detachment behind the solicitous facade. While his lips smiled, sending more warm tremors down her spine, his eyes remained distant.

With a sigh, she turned to survey the scene at the base of the hill. Jason's staff was busy spreading a lavish picnic over the grass. Rafe waited nearby, his impatience apparent in the yearning looks he kept sending in the direction of the food baskets. Beside him, Miss Burnham was chattering animatedly. Judging from Rafe's forced smile, Aurelie rather suspected the young lady was discussing fashion. With her elaborately styled brown hair and sprigged muslin gown, she was quite the thing. Unfortunately, the petulant mouth and grasping hands spoiled the effect. Aurelie could almost feel Rafe fighting the desire to pry those hands from the sleeve of his customarily mussed coat.

Grace, a reluctant Rickey in tow, was still exploring the ruins, the high crown of her bonnet visible as it bobbed among the rock piles. Aurelie smiled as Rickey's groan carried up the hill. It seemed the young man preferred to take his exercise on horseback and had an inherent distaste for using his own limbs. He appeared briefly at the top of a mound, snatching wildly at a clump of wildflowers. Grace's pale arm rose into view, pointing to a higher spray. Gamely, Rickey acquiesced, stretching to reach the flowers. Seconds later, with a flailing of arms, he disappeared over the edge. Aurelie's breath caught in her throat and she gathered up her skirts, ready to hurry down. Then Grace's trilling laugh drifted upward, indicating her brother had suffered no more than bruised pride, and she relaxed.

Lady Eleanor was holding court near the luncheon preparations, Mr. Burnham and the other members of the party all clearly entranced by her witty conversation. Simon Burnham and his sister, Aurelie decided, could easily pose for a portrait of the consummate ton family. Simon positively exuded dandified ennui, his upper lip drawn into a permanent sneer. Nor was his mode of dress any less contrived. The tightness of his breeches was rivaled only by the stiffness of his highly starched cravat. Upon seeing him at breakfast that morning, repeatedly trying to swallow behind the constricting linen, Aurelie had wanted to suggest that he try the Fenwick Folly. It certainly must be easier on the throat.

Eleanor, for her part, could not have possibly looked more beautiful, or more at ease. From the top of her golden head to the tips of her dainty shoes, she was the epitome of polish and poise. Surveying her own servicable half boots, Aurelie could not help but feel a good deal less than perfect. True, her pale yellow gown and satin-piped, forest green spencer were all the rage, but somehow they seemed gauche, provincial even, when compared to Eleanor's blue-and-white elegance.

"Wonderful," she muttered, kicking at a pebble. She had been hired to displace a goddess, and there was not a stitch of ethereal blue in her entire wardrobe.

She had studied the other woman carefully over breakfast, trying to detect any fault. It was no surprise, really, to find only perfection. Lady Eleanor DeVane was lovely, witty, and—as she had been the night before—thoroughly cordial. She had asked about Aurelie's home in Somerset with sincere interest, listening carefully and asking a series of intelligent, though by no means prying questions.

Now, watching her turn that same, gracious expression on Aunt Myrtle, Aurelie bit her lip. The older woman would tell some outlandish tale, the rest of the group would laugh derisively, and Eleanor would smile and nod as if receiving a veritable pearl of wisdom. Aurelie wanted to dislike her. Desperately. Instead, she found herself sighing in admiration, wishing for even a modicum of that grace and style. And wondering with all her heart what Jason could possibly be thinking to decline such exquisiteness.

He had been part of the group surrounding the goddess earlier, and that was what had sent Aurelie up the hill on her own. Now, she noticed, he was no longer present. Turning full circle, she looked for him. Below her, Catherine's children were tangled in a laughing heap. She was about to look away when a flash of dark green appeared in their midst.

A moment later, a snowy cuff appeared above the younger girl's head, followed by the rest of a sleeve. Aurelie watched, not quite believing her eyes, as Jason rose gracefully from the tangle, his nephew clinging to his shoulder like a plump monkey. Instead of peeling the imp from around his neck, Jason reached up and hoisted him securely onto his shoulder. The child laughed delightedly and thumbed his little nose at his sisters far below.

The girls, not to be outdone, promptly latched themselves onto Jason's knees. Aurelie was already entranced by the scene, but found herself laughing aloud as, ignoring the damage that dusty little shoes were undoubtedly doing to his immaculate Hessians, Jason took a few steps forward with his nieces riding atop his feet.

Her laughter must have drifted down to him because suddenly he was looking straight at her. For a moment he stood with his free hand shading his eyes, then he smiled and waved, gesturing for her to join them. His nephew mimicked both gestures with the cheerful expertise of a small child. The girls were too busy clinging to Jason's knees to wave, but they sent welcoming smiles in her direction. Aurelie could not possibly refuse such a delightful invitation. With a smile of her own, she headed down the hill.

Jason was very much enjoying watching her descent, her slim hips swaying gracefully under her sunny skirts, when two chubby hands slipped downward to cover his eyes. "Freddy," he asked patiently, "is this a game?"

"No, Uncle Jason," the boy chirped. "I'm just holding on. It's an awfully long way down."

"So it is. I will not let you fall. However, I shall be the one to go down if I cannot see where I am going."

"Ooh. Sorry." Freddy moved his hands immediately from his uncle's eyes to his ears, getting a firm grip there. "You don't have to hear to walk."

Jason grimaced in discomfort but held his tongue. At least he was able to watch Aurelie's approach. Once again, she reminded him of some woodland nymph, all leafy green and sunny yellow. She had confined her hair in its customary tight knot, but the ever errant curls were working their way to shiny freedom. Brightest of all, however, was the smile she had fixed on the four of them. As she got close, he could see the appealing dimple that curved to the right of her mouth.

And that mouth. He could still remember how it felt, soft and pliant beneath his. In the split second of the kiss, chaste though it had been, he had sensed the vibrant warmth that

86

glowed beneath her skin. No ice princess was Miss Carollan. No, she was bright and vital, and eminently touchable.

She was also, however, rife with mystery, no matter how simple she claimed her life to have been. Taking in her easy grace and elegant bearing, Jason could not stave off a sudden burst of protective ire. Aurelie Carollan had been meant for something far greater than being a governess. Someone had hurt her, of that he was convinced, enough to send her on a flight that ended in East Sussex. Whether it had been before she had been forced into employment or after, he had no idea.

Three months. She had agreed to stay only three months. He had not spent much time considering the oddity of this stipulation, but now it bothered him. What was waiting for her at the end of that time, and why did he feel so strongly that there was so much more to her than her explained situation? *And when,* he asked himself with some awe and no small amount of annoyance, *did you begin to think her your responsibility? She is a partner in crime, so to speak, nothing more. You will pay her wages, make sure she leaves with some security, and be done with the matter.*

Look into teaching positions on the other holdings, he recorded mentally, *just in case she wants one. . . .*

She reached them then, greeting all four with a lively, "Hello there."

Jason was about to reply in kind when Freddy piped, "Uncle Jason can't hear you, so I'll say hello for him. Hello."

He then released his grip on one ear to offer her his hand. She took it, expression perfectly serious. "We have not been formally introduced. I am Aurelie and you, I believe, are Freddy." She gave his hand a hearty shake. "I am very pleased to meet you." Then, to the girls, "And you are . . ."

"Phoebe," the younger announced brightly, still unwilling to relinquish her grip on Jason's leg. "I'm six."

"You are not," her sister said, rolling her eyes and sighing with all the drama of an experienced thespian. "I am Michaela. I am eight. Phoebe is five, but she has a habit of advancing her years." Aurelie managed to keep a straight face at this very adult pronouncement. "And you are going to marry Uncle Jason. Mother said so."

At this, Phoebe tilted her head, fixing familiar tawny eyes on Aurelie's face. All three children were quite beautiful, Michaela and Freddy sharing their father's fair hair and traditional Saxon features. Phoebe, however, unlike her blue-eyed siblings, was pure Granville—all dark curls and golden eyes.

"I thought you said your name was Early," she announced firmly.

"Aurelie. Yes, it is."

"That's funny." Phoebe wrinkled her button nose. "Mama called the person Uncle Jason is marrying 'Country Nobody.' "

"Phoebe!" Michaela gasped, releasing Jason's knee to raise a weary hand to her brow. "I am sorry, ma'am. She also has a habit of repeating the most distressing things."

"You must not hold it against the child," Jason offered lamely, seeing Aurelie's stunned expression. "Catherine says things . . ."

He broke off as Aurelie leaned forward, bracing her hands on her knees. What started as a suspicious giggle quickly turned to silvery laughter. Jason stood, amazed, as she reached out to tousle Phoebe's mahogany curls. "I am certain your mother would not want you repeating such things," she said at last, straightening up with a broad smile. "And I think it would be best if you were to trust me. My name is Aurelie." Then, to Jason, "Children are the true barometers of life. If a six-year-old tells you you are ugly, you are."

"I didn't say you're ugly," Phoebe corrected. "You're pretty. And I'm six."

"You are not." Michaela sighed.

"I'm six," Freddy shouted, making certain his presence was not forgotten, "and I'm hungry."

"You are four, puppy," Jason said gruffly, "and I would say that you have already eaten enough for five. You weigh as much as a horse."

Not in the least offended by the teasing, Freddy whooped in amusement and recaptured his uncle's ear. "Hungry," he repeated. "Horse, horse, horse."

"I have no idea what their governess feeds them," Jason told Aurelie, poker-faced.

It took her a good ten seconds to realize that he had actually made two jokes in a row. This time, when she laughed, he laughed with her. Joining in the spirit of the moment, the three children giggled and tugged at whichever part of Jason to which they were attached.

"Horse, horse, horse," Freddy chanted happily, and Aurelie grinned up at him.

"Have you met Lord Holcombe, Freddy? I think you will get along smashingly. He is always hungry, too."

Their luncheon was sure to be ready by then so, with Michaela and Phoebe riding on their uncle's boots and Freddy on his shoulders, they made their way slowly up the hill. At the top, Aurelie darted a quick glance at Jason. There was a faint sheen of perspiration on his brow and one dark curl arced damply over his eyes. His breathing, however, was not labored in the least and she marveled at his stamina. Few men of her acquaintance could negotiate a hill with three children aboard and not show major signs of strain.

Few men of her acquaintance, she amended, would even be caught dead with three children, let alone carry them with willingness and obvious enjoyment. This was a Jason she had not seen before, and she was thoroughly charmed. There was a dirt smudge across the bridge of his nose where Freddy had clasped his hands and the sorry state of his boots would, she assumed, throw his valet into a fit of pique.

Best of all, however, was the fact that the grooves beside his mouth were now bracketing a genuine smile and his impressive form had taken on a dependable solidity that was a vast improvement on imposing grandeur. He had told her he liked his sister's children and she had not quite believed him. Her incredulity seemed absurd now. Jason Granville never said anything he did not mean.

He paused as they descended to let Phoebe readjust her grip on his leg, and reached up to make sure Freddy was secure on his perch. He might not, as he had asserted, make much of a husband, but Aurelie was convinced that he would be a marvelous father.

By the time they reached their destination, luncheon was ready and most of the group was assembled. Catherine took one look at Jason and let out a gasp of dismay. "Children, look what you have done to your uncle! Why he is . . . disarrayed!"

"It is only a bit of dirt," Jason remarked evenly as he lifted Freddy to the ground. "Nothing irreparable."

Still, when the children filed obediently to their mother, she frowned and scrubbed at Michaela's pinafore with a napkin. "I specifically remember telling you to behave and not pester your uncle."

Michaela flushed miserably, but Phoebe dodged the encroaching napkin to settle herself solidly next to Miss Burnham. "Uncle Jason doesn't mind," she informed the group at large, watching curiously as Miss Burnham edged her skirts as far away as she could. "An' he's not marrying Country Nobody. He's marrying Early. She's pretty."

This time it was Catherine's turn to blush. At least she was able, Aurelie thought rather waspishly. She had been more than ready to believe that Catherine was every bit as thoughtless as she was elegant. To be fair, though, Aurelie decided as Freddy trundled manfully toward Rafe, she had managed to produce delightful children.

"Are you Lord Hol . . . Hal . . . ?" He looked to Aurelie for support.

"Holcombe."

"Yes, Holcombe. Are you him?"

"I certainly am. How did you know?"

Emboldened by Rafe's welcoming smile, Freddy grinned

and pointed at his loaded plate. "Orly said you were always hungry."

Rafe chuckled and patted the place beside him. "And what else did she say?"

"That we would get along smashingly." With that, Freddy turned and, giving Rafe only enough time to whip his plate out of the way, dropped affectionately into his lap.

"Frederick!" Catherine gasped again, to no avail. After a moment of endearing bewilderment, Rafe laughed. He then proceeded to offer Freddy a piece of roasted chicken and the friendship was set.

Rickey and Grace joined them at last. Rickey had dust in his hair and a dramatic tear in the shoulder of his coat. Grace looked perfectly angelic, smudged skirts notwithstanding, a stunning bouquet of wild violets in her hands. Lady Heathfield took one look at her younger offspring and sighed resignedly.

"Whatever possessed you to arrange a picnic, Jason? It is not at all your style."

Jason, by this time, had procured plates for himself and Aurelie and was reclining in regal splendor by her side. "It would seem," he replied pleasantly, "that my style is changing."

"Hmmph. It is all so very sudden."

"What would you have had me do, Mother?" He caught Aurelie's eye and gave her a lazy smile. "Metamorphose slowly?"

Her answering grin told him she well remembered her own words. It occurred to him that her metamorphosis had been less dramatic than the one his mother claimed he had undergone. Aurelie had merely been temporarily masking her natural beauty. He, on the other hand, was behaving entirely out of character. Or so it seemed. In truth, he could not honestly comprehend why a picnic would be a surprise. He had always liked picnics, had he not? And he had organized quite a few. Had he not?

He made a mental note to ask Strawbridge when he had last ordered a picnic.

As it turned out, there was no need. "Heaven." Rickey sighed, reaching for a slice of quail pie. "You always manage to occupy your guests, Tare. It's nice to be entertained as well."

"Do I not usually entertain you?"

"Now don't go all high in the instep," his brother mumbled, shoving the better part of his pie into his mouth. When he reached for a bottle of wine with which to wash it down, Catherine slapped his hand away and provided him with a glass. "I am complimenting you. We always have mighty treks across your lands or through some godforsaken town. . . ." He grimaced. "Remember the day trip to Seaford, Gracie? Tare insisted that we stroll along the cliffs and you nearly fell off."

"That was you, ninny," his sister shot back smartly. "I was the one who saved you by getting a grip of your coattails."

"Was it?" Rickey reached for a chicken wing. "Hmm, you might be right. Anyway . . . I was saying . . . ?"

"That I make you walk through godforsaken towns," Jason offered dryly.

"Oh, yes. Your outings are ever edifying, but I would much prefer to be amused than improved."

"Fancy that." Jason winced as Aurelie's small foot connected warningly with his ribs. "And you find me . . . amusing now?"

"Not you, old man," his brother corrected seriously, his careless mien momentarily abandoned to display unexpected shrewdness. "You are precisely who you have to be. I am merely saying that adding a picnic to your repertoire was a smashing idea."

The talk turned then to the weather, which was uncommonly fine for early spring, and to the Season that would be commencing soon in London. "I understand you will be coming out this year," Aurelie said to Grace.

"Yes, I will. Mother has been planning the fete for months. . . ."

"I have hopes it will be one of the major events of the

Season," Lady Heathfield cut in grandly. "Absolutely everyone who is anyone will be there. You, I assume, will be accompanying Jason."

So much for only having Persons of Consequence. Aurelie silently completed the thought that was undoubtedly on the woman's mind. But yes, she figured, she would be there as the affair was to take place in the next month. Lady Heathfield did not wait for her confirmation, but commenced to regale the group with her plans for her fete-to-end-all-fetes.

Noting Grace's detached expression, Aurelie leaned forward and said quietly, "You do not seem terribly excited about the matter."

"It's not that," the other girl replied ruefully. "I am delighted to be finally making my debut. It is just that Mother can be so . . . controlling. I am afraid she will have a suitor picked out for me by May, and I am not at all certain that I'm ready to be married, especially to someone I hardly know . . ."

"Grace, do tell Lady Eleanor about the gown I have chosen for you," the countess cut in. Before Grace could answer, though, she had turned back to the group. "She wanted something totally inappropriate—leaf green satin, but I was firm on the cream silk. We would not want the other mamas to think her forward. Especially not those with eligible sons. Now, Grace, do describe the gown."

Throwing a telling glance to Aurelie, Grace gave a small sigh and complied. Aurelie felt heartily sorry for her and, when Jason quietly suggested they take a walk, she agreed readily. Perhaps she could convince him to intervene a bit on his sister's behalf.

Ignoring the speculative gazes they attracted, she took his arm and allowed him to lead the way toward the ruins. She had accompanied the group on the initial tour of the site, but was struck anew by the shadowy beauty of the place. Nature had reclaimed the land with passion, covering the tumbled stones with lush grass and mosses and spilling profusions of wildflowers over the mounds.

Jason guided her through the fallen portal. "I have not apologized yet for my family's reception of you. It was unforgivable of them and remiss of me not to see to the matter better."

Aurelie nodded her acceptance of his apology. The less said on the subject, she decided, the better. She did want to talk about Grace, though.

"Your sister is very concerned about her debut, and understandably so."

"Grace? Whatever does she have to be concerned about? She is more than pretty enough to be a success, and Mother is sparing no expense in the preparations. Why, the whole thing is planned to the last minuscule detail."

"That," Aurelie informed him tartly, "is precisely the problem."

"I do not understand."

Yes, you do. "Choice, freedom. Grace is terrified that she is being rushed into the cabal of Society and might find herself married off within the year, to a man of your parents' choosing."

Jason's eyes narrowed speculatively. "Correct me if I am wrong, Miss Carollan, but that seems to be the primary purpose of a Season."

"Is it? I rather thought that the London Season was intended as a means for the Haute Monde to come together to entertain themselves."

"Did you have a Season?"

This question, come quite out of the blue, momentarily stymied her. "I, er . . . of course not, my lord."

"Yet did you not wish for one?"

Jason watched as her ever direct gaze became uncustomarily distant. It took her a moment to respond, and when she did it was with the brisk, governess voice which had become pleasingly absent in recent days. "What I wanted at Grace's age is hardly the point. What *she* wants is of paramount importance."

"What she wants, yes." Jason found himself wondering what Aurelie had dreamed of even four brief years earlier.

He imagined her glowing and starry-eyed at the prospect of ballrooms filled with candlelight and dashing suitors. "You think Grace does not wish to be married."

"I did not say that. What I said was that she does not wish to be married out of hand, her life given unto the control of another simply because it suits your family. I thought you would be able to comprehend that."

By this time they had wandered to the far side of the fallen chapel, out of the view of the rest of the group. When Jason stopped and turned to face her, Aurelie wondered if, yet again, she might not have gone too far.

"I apologize if my interest seems insolent, my lord," she began. "I just feel compelled to remind you of the parallels to your own situation. . . ."

"What do *you* want, Aurelie?"

"I—I beg your pardon?"

"Out of life. Do you not have thoughts of home and hearth? Of a husband? Children?"

Yes. Oh yes, I do. Of course I do. "That is . . . I mean . . . No," she lied awkwardly. "I have no such aspirations. I am merely a governess, my lord."

"Jason."

"I . . . Jason. I must think to my future placements, not to empty dreams."

Suddenly he was standing awfully, wonderfully close. So close she could see the scar above his lip. "Do you really expect me to believe you do not allow yourself to dream?"

"Of what?" she asked breathlessly, losing the gist of the conversation in his proximity.

"Oh, of anything. Whatever you want."

She felt herself swaying slightly toward the broad expanse of his chest. "I—I have forgotten how, I think. I would not even know where to begin."

"What a terrible shame. I suggest you work on it, Aurelie." With that, he leaned forward, his breath fanning her cheeks. "Perhaps I could be of some assistance."

9

I T WAS MORE than passing strange, she thought hazily, that
Jason would talk of dreams. He was not one to live in
reverie, but in utter certainties.

His mouth hovered there, scant inches above hers and
Aurelie braced herself for its descent. He would kiss her
and she would let him. Such was, after all, the sort of thing
on which her dreams actually did center—a dashing suitor
whose affections were based on emotion rather than greed.

"Omne tulit punctum . . ." The quotation spilled unbidden from her lips, almost lost to a gasp as his hand came
up to circle her ribs. If he spread his fingers even a little,
his thumb would be brushing against the underside of her
breast. *". . . qui miscuit utile dulci."*

The second she realized what she had said, she regretted
it immensely. Like water on flame, the warm promise vanished from his eyes and he dropped his hand. Mortification
swept through her and she took a shaky step back, wanting
nothing more than to turn and run—and keep running until
she hit the coast.

"I am sorry, my lord. I do not know why I said that. It
was insupportable."

"No, Aurelie. Not insupportable. My behavior was quite
beyond the pale. You would have been within your rights to
slap me."

And she had, her words far more cutting than physical
attack. Horace: "He wins every hand who mingles profit
with pleasure." Was that how she thought of him, then? As

an unprincipled bounder who would take advantage of her aid to him by toying with her?

Yet again, he wondered what indignities she had been forced to suffer in the past. More romantic words, probably, like those he had given her. Empty promises and grasping hands. Suddenly and thoroughly disgusted with himself, he took his own step away from her, increasing the distance between them.

"I can only ask your forgiveness, Miss Carollan, though I cannot blame you if you should withhold it. My only excuse is that I am, perhaps, becoming too caught up in this deception."

So it was Miss Carollan again, was it? The return to formality sent Aurelie's heart plummeting lower. It was exceedingly gentlemanly of him to be shouldering the blame for the incident when the fault could be laid squarely at her door. No well-bred young lady would have behaved so wantonly as she had, all but begging for his caress.

"And at the risk of making things far worse, I will add that having a lovely young lady so near in this magical place overrode my sensibilities. That is no more an excuse, to be sure, but I hope something in the way of explaining my reprehensible behavior."

It made things worse. Not far worse, but bad enough. Now, as well as being thoroughly contrite, he was being complimentary, and it was not to be borne. Her own guilt was strong enough for both of them.

Realizing he had effectively headed off her own apology, Aurelie responded with a faint shake of her head. "Think no more on the matter, my lord. As you have said, the magic of this place is invasive."

They stood for several minutes in awkward silence before Jason cleared his throat and said, "We should be getting back. There is dessert to be had and with it the distinct danger of Freddy and Rafael eating it all."

His blatant attempt at humor appeared to work, poor as it was. Aurelie nodded and turned back toward the portal. He noticed that she hesitated before taking his arm and, once she did, her fingers rested light as air on his sleeve as if even the simple touch would somehow pain her.

Nor would she look at him, instead staring fixedly ahead. It was better, he supposed, than having her eyes downcast toward the grassy path. He darted a quick glance at her pale profile, and searched for something, anything to say to bring that damnably direct gaze back to his face. Nothing came to mind until they were nearly back to the glade and his sister's nervous laughter reached his ears.

"I will think on what you have said of Grace's concerns. I can make no promises, but I assure you I have every desire to see her happy."

That did the trick. Gray eyes lifted to his, their previous bleakness replaced by approbation. "Thank you, my lord," she offered softly before letting her gaze slide away.

Then, to Jason's great relief, she fixed a serene smile on her face and tightened her grasp on his arm. She might not look the radiant fiancée returning from her lover's embrace, but she no longer resembled a candle whose flame had been snuffed.

"Oh, there you are," Lady Heathfield called stridently. "I was ready to send Richard after you." Rickey's cheerful grimace clearly showed his opinion of this task. "We are discussing the finer points of our guest list for Grace's ball and need your assistance."

Aurelie released Jason's arm and went to sit by a miserable-looking Grace. The other girl's face brightened at her approach and, as Aurelie settled herself at her side, she leaned over to whisper, "Did I not comment last night on the advantage of shadowed alcoves?"

Aurelie forced a smile. "Yes, I do believe you did." *And I might very well have taken advantage of those alcoves had not my tongue taken it upon itself to interfere.*

For, no matter how improper her impulses had been, they had been real and honest. And they were still there, warming her inside. Several feet away, Jason was listening attentively to his mother, his lovely mouth curved in a faint smile. Knowing that smile was more wry than amused, Aurelie gave her attention to their conversation.

"Of course there is the Marquess of Dearbourne. He has that marvelous estate in Derbyshire."

"And rheumatism," Grace whispered miserably.

"Also the Earl of Ware. Of course, he is said to be considering Theresa Montague—and her family only two generations removed from trade." The countess sniffed disdainfully. "The girl is pretty enough, but I still think it vulgar for her mama to be shopping her about for a grand title. I am certain the earl would be ever so much happier with a wife from his own class. Oh, and there is Lord Fremont. He is a member of your clubs, is he not, Jason?"

"Yes, Mother, he is. Though I think he might be a bit, er, worldly for Grace."

"Nonsense. You will see to it that he attends. Why, I never did believe the story about the opera chorus anyway. The dear man has far too much consequence to be involved in such a sordid matter."

"The dear man"—Aurelie heard Mr. Burnham mutter under his breath—"has far too much money to worry about paying off a feminine inconvenience or two."

At her side, Grace gave a quiet gasp and Aurelie covertly reached over to squeeze her hand. Grace's fingers were cold beneath hers and her heart swelled with pity for the girl. So far as she could tell, Lady Heathfield's only criterion for a son-in-law was that he move in the higher circles of Society.

"What of Andrew Scully?" Rickey offered cheerfully and Grace brightened slightly. "He's a good sort—I've known him since Eton."

"Irish," Lord Heathfield barked from his seat in the shade, and his wife nodded her agreement to this veritable pearl of wisdom.

"Not that it is not a fine family with a respected title," she said sagely, "but he *is* Irish, after all, and Andrew is a younger son. He will have money, of course, but his brother will have the estates."

Aurelie's sympathy for Grace rose with each addition to the list. Not that she knew any of the men mentioned, but Grace's expression and Mr. Burnham's asides told her enough. Jason, for his part, did offer numerous suggestions of his own, though his friends seemed no more appealing to his sister. To one who was only seventeen, Aurelie speculated not unkindly, a man of thirty-odd years must seem to have one foot in the grave.

The wind had picked up in the last hour and a series of ominous-looking clouds began to drift across the sun. It was a clear sign that the picnic had come to an end, and the group hurried to the carriages, hoping to beat the storm back to Havensgate. Aurelie found herself riding with Grace, Aunt Myrtle, Miss Burnham, and Lady Eleanor.

Eleanor had said little during luncheon, conversing quietly with Catherine and her husband, and had offered nothing during the discussion of Grace's proposed suitors. Now, however, as they rolled toward Havensgate, she leaned forward and patted the younger girl's hand with a compassionate smile.

"It will not be so bad, Miss Granville. Trust me. My mama planned my debut with much the same . . . energy." She raised one elegant brow then, as if a much stronger word would serve better. "As I entered my first ball, the only men I could see seemed to be of an age with my father. I spent the first five minutes convinced I would be passing the evening unable to converse with my dance partner because of the loud creaking their stays would make!"

Grace's laugh was a wonderful sound after her recent blue-deviled sighs. Unable to help herself, Aurelie laughed as well, losing her envy of Lady Eleanor's beauty in the wake of her witty kindness to the younger girl.

"But then it did not really matter," Grace said after a time. "After all, you were already in an underst . . ." She broke off with an embarrassed gasp, her cheeks flaming "I mean, you were already understood to be an *Incomparable*," she stammered desperately, the weight of what she had almost said causing her slender shoulders to droop noticeably. "There was no question that you would be a smashing success."

As far as recoveries went, it had been a splendid one, but Aurelie knew the damage had been done. Thus far, no mention had been made of the expected match between Eleanor and Jason, and it had been sinfully easy to assume that no mention would be made of the matter. Now, in a way, it had.

Aurelie could sense three pairs of eyes shifting back and forth between Eleanor and herself, and knew her reaction to Grace's gaffe had not gone unnoticed. There was no sense of pretending she was unaware of the understanding, appealing though such an act might be. So, thrusting cowardly impulses aside, she straightened her shoulders and looked for anything she might say to ease the tension.

She did not have to say a thing.

Composed smile never leaving her lips, Eleanor patted Grace's hand again. "What is unknown is not necessarily bad," she commented softly. "And what is expected is not necessarily good. It is uncertainty that makes life exciting, after all. There is always the promise that something marvelous will happen purely by chance."

"Serendipity," Aurelie murmured unconsciously, and Eleanor nodded.

"Exactly, Miss Carollan. Serendipity."

Some time later, having changed into her evening gown, Aurelie climbed the stairs to the third floor. She had completed her toilette early and had an hour before she was expected in the drawing room. Not particularly wanting to face whomever might already be downstairs, she decided to pay a visit to the nursery. The children, as was expected, were usually separated from the adults, and she wanted to see more of them that evening than the requisite but brief good-nights they would perform in the drawing room before being put to bed.

She found Freddy and Phoebe sprawled on the floor of the spacious room, surrounded by a haphazard arrangement of toy soldiers, engrossed in the art of organizing the figures by uniform color. Michaela was sitting in the cushioned window seat, thumbing listlessly through a book.

Phoebe looked up as Aurelie entered the room and, with a squeal of welcome, jumped to her feet and ran forward to wrap her arms around her knees. "It's Early!" she shouted, all but knocking her off her feet with her enthusiasm.

Michaela glanced up from the book, her instant smile stifled quickly under adult restraint. "You must call her Miss Carollan," she told her sister sharply. "Mama said so. And you are mussing her dress."

Not in the least concerned about the effects small fists were having on the smooth silk, Aurelie patted the top of Phoebe's head and replied, "It is very mature of you to say so, Michaela, but I think we can dispense with the formalities here." She cast a dramatically furtive glance around the room. "I expect we can be reasonably assured that we will not be discovered, hmm?" The older girl's shy smile was answer enough. "Besides," she added seriously, gesturing toward the regiments below, "these fellows will let us know should a foe approach."

This brought a gurgle of delight from Phoebe. "They're not real! Uncle Jason says he played with them when he was a little boy. They were General Burgin and Owl fighting the 'Mericans then." She tugged at Aurelie's sleeve, drawing her down, and whispered, "Uncle Jason says they lost before he was born, but he didn't care."

Aurelie suppressed a smile as she surveyed Generals Burgoyne's and Howe's vanquished troops. "And who are they now?"

"Why, Wellington, of course," was the emphatic response. "'Gainst Boney—you know, Napoleen Boneypart." Phoebe prodded one finger with a small foot. "That's Napoleen. And this"—she reached down to pick up a particularly splendid soldier and handed it to Aurelie—"is Uncle Jason. He helped Wellington make Boney sorry."

"Boneypart," Freddy announced, the word muffled by the fact that he was holding his tongue between his teeth in

102

fierce concentration. "Sorry, sorry, sorry," he chanted in an endearing lisp, reaching out to pound the hapless Bonaparte with a chubby fist.

"Would you like to play with us?" Phoebe asked, renewing her grasp on Aurelie's skirt.

"I don't know," Aurelie replied, sinking to the floor beside the child, heedless of the damage she was undoubtedly causing the silk. "You seem to be routing Boney quite well without my help."

She ran the tip of her finger over the figure in her hand. From the scarlet coat to the trappings on the horse, it was a work of exquisite detail and skill. She wondered if Jason had ever held that very piece, dreaming of wearing a dashing uniform and fighting for king and country. Probably not, she decided wryly. He undoubtedly knew his future in the king's army right down to the colors and location of his regiment.

She could not banish the image of a serious little boy from her mind, however, sitting on this very floor with his dark hair falling over his forehead and his tongue caught between his teeth as he refought the War with the Colonies. Without question these troops, under the command of General Jason Granville, had fared far better than they had under Burgoyne and Howe.

Perhaps, she mused, it had been those very days of childhood that had made Jason the military hero he had grown up to become. How it would irk Bonaparte to know, as he languished in his island prison, that one of Wellington's finest officers had begun his days of valor on a nursery floor in East Sussex.

"Did your Uncle Jason help you find these?"

"Yes," Phoebe chirped. "He even played Boneypart for a few minutes. I," she announced proudly, "was Wellington."

Interest piqued anew, Aurelie stared into the beaming face. "Does your uncle play with you often?"

Phoebe shook her head, setting familiar dark curls into motion. "He never really played with us at all before today. He's changed."

103

"Changed?"

"Mmm." Phoebe turned her attention back to the cavalry. "He's nice."

Something warm and hopeful unfurled inside Aurelie. It would be highly arrogant to assume her influence had anything to do with Jason's interest in his family, but it was gratifying. Somehow he had been able to go from liking his sister's children at a distance to playing with them. With any luck, Grace would be next in his attentions. She adored him, and would blossom under the slightest encouragement.

She looked up then to find Michaela studying her with serious blue eyes and pushed her proud reveries aside for the time being. "Are you not as bloodthirsty as these two?" she queried cheerfully, gesturing toward where Phoebe and Freddy were ruthlessly mowing down the French troops. "I imagine you would make quite a good general."

The girl appeared to take this very seriously and pondered the concept for a moment. "I could never be a general," she said at last.

"And why not?"

"It is terribly simple, really." Michaela gave a dismissive shrug of her narrow shoulders. "I am not a man."

Aurelie could not help the laugh that escaped her lips. "Very sensible of you," she said honestly. "I would tend to spend far more time thinking of the numerous reasons you could be a general than the one very basic reason you could not. I am not very sensible sometimes."

"Tell me the reasons."

"That you would be splendid in command?" Aurelie asked, and the girl nodded. "Well, to begin, you are obviously levelheaded and intelligent. You are also concerned with the proper behavior of those below you"—Freddy let out a particularly fierce bellow then, making both Aurelie and Michaela smile—"and you understand the importance of honor and responsibility." The girl was blushing in gratitude now, and Aurelie wished she could express the equal importance of light-heartedness and abandon. "You like to read, don't you?"

"Oh, yes," was the emphatic reply. "Though Mama does not always find my choices seemly. She picks most books for me." She held up the volume in her lap then and Aurelie tried not to grimace. *Improvement of the Mind*—Mrs. Chapone's decidedly dry collection of essays intended to teach deportment to young ladies. She had tried to read it once and had ended up pitching it out the window. "Do you read, Miss Carollan?"

"Yes, I do. I must say, though, that your mama would undoubtedly find my choices most unseemly indeed. I like folktales and mythology, especially stories set in Ireland."

"Ireland!" Freddy shouted, sounding remarkably like his grandfather.

"Will you tell us a story, Early?" Phoebe asked, having apparently tired of making Boney sorry. "Please?" Without waiting for a response, she settled herself solidly in Aurelie's lap.

"Phoebe!" Michaela gasped in dismay, but Aurelie laughed.

"A story, hmm? What sort of story?"

"Ireland," Freddy repeated, giving Boney a last thump.

"A funny story," Phoebe commanded.

"A funny story from Ireland." Aurelie thought for a moment. "I think I have just the one. It is about two brothers, Flynn and Flann."

"Funny names."

"Yes, Phoebe, they certainly are." Ignoring both her dress and her manners, Aurelie crossed her legs in front of her and settled Phoebe comfortably in her lap. "Now, Flynn and Flann went out one day to pick blueberries for their mother to make a pie. Flynn was very industrious and he . . ."

"What's *in-dusty-us*?"

"It means he was very eager to please his mother, Freddy, and he worked hard."

"Oh."

"So, Flynn worked hard to fill his pail with blueberries. Flann, however, ate them out of the pail as fast as Flynn

105

could pick them. After a while, Flynn became very angry and stopped picking berries in order to find a rod with which to whip his brother. He found a birch rod still growing on a tree. 'You may not have me,' the rod said, 'till you find an axe.' So Flynn left in search of an axe.

"When he at last found one, it said, 'You may not use me till you find a stone to sharpen me.' So Flynn went to find a stone. When he found one, it said . . .'"

"That's silly," Freddy cut in. "Rods and axes and stones can't talk."

"Hush, Freddy," Michaela said before Aurelie could respond. "It is just a story and anything can happen in a story."

"Quite right," Aurelie agreed and, giving the girl a grateful smile, continued. "So the stone said, 'You may not have me till you find some water with which to wet me.' Flynn walked a very long time, looking for water. Finally he came to a river, but the water said, 'You may not gather me till you find a bowl.'

"Now Flynn was becoming very tired, but he was determined to whip his brother, so he walked to a farmhouse. The farmer's wife answered the door and he asked for a bowl. 'Why do you need a bowl?' she asked, and he told her, 'I need a bowl to carry the water to wet the stone to sharpen the axe to cut the rod to whip my brother.' When the woman asked, 'Why do you want to whip your brother?', Flynn replied, 'Because he was eating all the blueberries that we were picking for my mother's pie.' The woman looked at him strangely and asked, 'Did your brother enjoy the berries?' Flynn said that he had. Then the woman asked, 'Could you have picked more berries?' Flynn said that, yes, he could have. 'I have no bowl for you,' said the woman at last, 'but you may have this sieve.'

"Flynn took the sieve and went back to the river. But every time he tried to gather water, it slipped through the holes. It was getting very close to dinnertime and Flynn was getting hungry. When a bullfrog hopped by, saying, 'mud'm, mud'm,' Flynn had an idea. Scooping mud from

106

the riverbank, he covered the bottom of the sieve. After it had dried, he filled it with water."

"How long did the mud take to dry?" Phoebe asked.

"Oh, a very long time, and Flynn was exhausted and hungry. He was still determined to punish his brother, however, so he wet the stone, sharpened the axe, cut the rod, and went back to whip Flann. But there was no one there. Do you know why?"

"No." Freddy and Phoebe breathed in unison. "Why?"

"Because"—Aurelie leaned forward and lowered her voice—"while Flynn was gone, Flann ate all the blueberries and he ... burst!" With that, she bounded Phoebe and reached out to tickle Freddy, sending both into hysterical giggles.

"He burst!" Freddy repeated cheerfully.

"What happened then?" Phoebe asked once the mirth had receded.

"Well, that is not the funny part."

"Tell us!"

"All right." Aurelie smoothed back the wild curls from Phoebe's forehead. "The story ends with Flynn going home very sad. Do you know why he was sad?"

"Because he didn't get to whip his brother?" the girl replied seriously.

"No, sweetheart. He was sad partly because there would be no pie after all, but more because he did not have a brother any longer."

"Oh." Phoebe's small nose wrinkled as she considered that.

"He *burst!*" Freddy shouted and Phoebe poked him in the ribs.

"It'll happen to you, too, piggy, if you don't stop eating so much."

This effectively doused her brother's glee, and his eyes went wide.

"No, it will not," Michaela said sharply. "It is only a story, Freddy, remember?" He nodded in satisfaction. "It is a good story, Miss Carollan. Does it have a moral?"

"I don't kn—"

"What's a moral?" Phoebe asked.

Aurelie smiled. "It is something you are supposed to learn to make you a better person. What do you think the moral of this story is, Phoebe?"

"Don't eat blueberries!"

Everyone laughed but Michaela, who sat in thoughtful silence.

"What do you think?" Aurelie asked her after a moment.

"I think the moral is that we have to see the things that are really *important* to us and that sometimes that means not doing what we have been told is *right* because it hurts us in the end. Is that it, Miss Carollan?"

"You are very wise for being so young," Aurelie said with a sigh. "I think that is precisely the moral of the story."

Michaela nodded, more with simple acknowledgement than with pride. Then she asked, "Did you choose this story for a special reason?"

A clock chimed somewhere in the distance. Aurelie gently lifted Phoebe from her lap and rose to her feet. "I had not thought so," she replied, absently shaking the creases from her dress. "I simply thought it a funny Irish story."

10

IT WAS EVIDENT Lady Heathfield expected rain. Either that, or the marmalade with which she had coated her toast was unexpectedly bitter. Whichever, her expression was enough to curdle milk. After nearly a fortnight of facing the woman over meals, Aurelie was well used to the countess's pinched expressions. This one, however, was enough to bring to mind the adage about not making faces lest one's features froze that way.

For once, at least, the reason for the lady's pique was not Aurelie herself. Instead, amazingly, it turned out to be Catherine. As Aurelie entered the dining room, the younger woman was saying pleadingly, "I'm sorry, Mother, really. I know it is not convenient for you, but it was hardly deliberate on our part. . . ."

"Not *convenient*? Catherine, inconvenient is hardly the word I would choose. The Season is commencing. Beyond the fact that we have a mere ten days till Grace's ball, we have social engagements beginning tomorrow night."

"It is hardly as if they will be coming along at night. Nor will you even have to see them."

"But I will *hear* them, and you know how noise gets on my poor nerves. Honestly, Catherine, why now, with all the preparations to be made?"

Aurelie had not seen Jason standing at the sideboard, but he stepped forward then, plate in hand. "Good morning, my dear," he said upon seeing her. "I trust you slept well."

"Perfectly, thank you." She forced a smile as he hastened forward to hold out her chair. Knowing his next move would be to provide her breakfast, she stalled him. "I think a cup of tea for now."

Lady Heathfield sniffed, letting all present know just what she thought of her son doing a servant's task. Silently, Aurelie quite agreed with her. Since the afternoon at the abbey, Jason had been all that was solicitous and courtly, giving every appearance of the besotted fiancé. Even in the short times when they were left alone together he was charming and attentive. But they did not touch unnecessarily, nor did they really talk.

He was kind, patient, and still handsome enough to make Aurelie's breath catch in her throat. And she was ready to shoot him for being a paragon of perfect deportment.

Just once, she would have liked to have seen him head for the port with a muffled curse, or smile wryly behind Lady Heathfield's back. Instead, he was almost unfailingly polite to all, giving the appearance of utter contentment. Even now, he was smiling benignly at his mother as he summoned a footman for Aurelie's tea.

"You cannot blame Catherine for setting a fire fifty-five miles away. That was the fault of a damaged chimney. Nor can you hold her accountable for the fact that their governess has come down with a nasty dose of influenza."

"Silly woman should never have gone out in the rain. The boy would have returned from the stables eventually. As for the matter of the house, I thought Stephen said it was only one room."

"Two, Mother," Catherine offered, "and the drawing-room wall. It was not the fire that did the most damage, but the water used to put it out. We cannot use the house for at least three weeks. And you know we would stay at Jason's house, but it is not set up to accommodate a family."

Aurelie was finally catching on. It appeared the Heathfields were to have a full house for the next several weeks. She was herself to stay with them, it being thoroughly inappropriate for her to reside at Jason's townhouse. The news that Catherine and her family would be staying with them as well was more than welcome. Between Grace,

Rickey, and the children, she would not feel totally unwanted.

"Hmmph," the countess snorted again, but much of the
steam had been taken from her argument. She gave one last
heated effort. "I still cannot countenance having so many
people underfoot while I am in the midst of preparations."

It was time, Aurelie decided, to step in and play the
proper daughter-in-law. "From what I understand, my lady,
you have been astonishingly efficient thus far. Why, Grace
tells me every last detail has already been seen to, including
her entire wardrobe for the Season. I doubt any other host-
ess in Town can claim to be nearly so well prepared."

Amazingly, it worked. Lady Heathfield's tightly com-
pressed lips relaxed and she even managed a cool smile.
Taking a deep breath, Aurelie pressed on. "I would be more
than happy if I could be of any assistance to you. In fact,
I would greatly appreciate anything you could teach me. I
am not accustomed to running households of any great size,
and I will be required to do a good deal of entertaining
as"—the words stuck in her throat—"Jason's wife."

It would have been overly bold to say the words caused
a melting of the icy disapproval the countess had been casting in her direction for the past two weeks, but Aurelie
detected at least a faint thawing.

"Quite so. Though it is a very great amount of knowledge to impart to one unaccustomed to such a position."
The countess took what was perhaps her first good look at
Aurelie. "I suppose with some training you might make an
adequate viscountess."

"Thank you, madam." Aurelie forced herself to swallow
her pride for the umpteenth time in the lady's presence. "If,
as I am convinced, you have already perfected all the preparations for Grace's Season, perhaps I could be of some assistance with the children. I am certain that until such time
as their governess recovers, we can keep them occupied."

Catherine promptly sent her a look so grateful that it
completely made up for any earlier slights. Lady Heathfield
considered the matter carefully. "As long as it does not

keep you from addressing your social responsibilities as Jason's fiancée, I do not see how it would hurt. The children seem to like you."

"And I them."

Aurelie spoke these words with honest affection, and Jason smiled. The children had taken to her like ducks to water, ever pestering her to tell them a story. He had never stayed to listen to the tales but, as she had said, children were the barometers of life, and they were clearly entranced.

He was equally pleased that, slowly but surely, she was winning over the adult members of his family as well. The DeVanes had departed with the Burnhams after several days, their absence lightening the atmosphere considerably. Not that Eleanor had behaved badly. In fact, he admitted with some admiration, she had been all that was gracious and poised. Her mother, on the other hand, had been a black cloud over everyone's head, refusing to acknowledge Aurelie's existence at all and muttering vague invectives at every opportunity.

In the wake of their departure, a fragile peace blossomed. His father had unbent surprisingly quickly, having discovered over supper one evening that he and Aurelie shared an interest in fishing. Lady Heathfield's responsive sniff had left no doubts as to her opinion on that unladylike activity, but the earl was fast on his way to being charmed. The clincher had been a particularly long-winded soliloquy from Myrtle on a good deal of mud and a huge bass.

Aurelie had gently amended the story, asserting that because it had been a stream and not the ocean, the catch had been a small string of trout. She did not, however, disclaim the mud, and Jason had found himself imagining a scene that might very well have happened—young Aurelie chin to toe in mud, proudly waving her catch. By the time she mentioned a willingness to bait her own hook, the earl was smitten, following Grace, Rickey, and the children into Aurelie's camp.

Now, it appeared, the countess and Catherine were on

their way as well. Jason left them in the midst of a pleasant discussion of current fashion and headed for the library. They would all be leaving for London in a matter of hours, and he wanted a few minutes of privacy.

There was a large stack of papers in the middle of his desk and he knew they should be attended to before his departure. He had virtually ignored important business during the past two weeks, electing instead to play host. It would have been unforgivably rude, after all, to abandon his guests while dealing with matters of estate.

He reluctantly drew the first sheet toward him. A contract for cattle he was purchasing for the Lancashire properties. It would wait. The second was a proposed plan for controlling the river. Jason skimmed it and set it aside. Wiggins would handle it. The third was not so clear. It appeared to be a bill, written in a flowing hand. The amount was negligible—at least it would be if he could decipher what, in fact he was supposed to be paying for.

Linear chemists, it appeared to be. Now what in the devil did that mean? No, not *linear*. It was . . . *linen*. A dozen linen somethings. *Linen chemi*—Good Lord, linen chemises!

Had he not been so thrown off by what he was holding, he would have laughed at the confusion. Twenty-five pounds for Aurelie's undergarments. Delicate and unsubstantial, no doubt, festooned with tiny bows and fancy embroidery. And thin enough to be nearly transparent . . .

Bloody, everlasting hell. He tossed the bill aside and abandoned the desk for the sideboard. This called for a swift shot of whiskey. No matter that it was not yet even noon. He chased it down with a second. He had come to the library with the specific intent of finding a little peace and had instead found himself communing, in a manner of speaking, with Aurelie's chemises. Bad enough that the sight of her fully dressed was enough to make his very teeth ache. Now he had to contend with her in an imagined state of undress.

It had become increasingly difficult in the past few days

113

for him to keep his hands to himself. Even the simple act of sitting next to her had taken on epic proportions. Several nights earlier, after endless pleas from the group, they had joined at the pianoforte to play a duet. He had been able to keep his calm at the onset, pleasantly surprised by her more-than-acceptable skill. Then, as he had leaned forward to turn the page, his thigh had accidentally brushed hers and he had very nearly ended up with his posterior meeting the floor, hard.

She was not the most beautiful woman of his acquaintance, not by a long shot. Nor was she the most seductive, in her demure gowns and blithe innocence. No, it was simply that he had been far too long without a woman. Yes, that was it. It had nothing whatsoever to do with her lustrous hair, sweet scent, or warm smile. Nor did it have anything to do with the nearly invisible scattering of freckles across the bridge of her nose.

He cursed aloud this time, emphatically and descriptively. It was a damnably good thing that they would be in London that very evening. And that she would be several blocks away each night, tucked into some bed in his parents' house. He would pay his discreet visits to the home of a particularly skilled demimondaine, and no one would be the wiser.

That decided, he searched the desk for a clean sheet of paper. He changed his mind quickly, deciding a list including *Visit Madame Millau* was not one to be put in writing.

He committed his plan to memory and returned to business matters. Bills from the modiste were pushed aside with a twitch of his fingers, leaving only such concerns as whether to choose blue or green paint for the new phaeton.

He had reached a comfortable level of concentration when a knock sounded at the door. "Dash it all," he muttered, then, "Enter!"

Apparently his annoyed scowl went unnoticed by Rafael, for the bounder merely shot him a cheerful grin and dropped into one of the facing chairs. "Splendid repast, as always," he commented, patting his stomach. "I am rather dejected at the prospect of returning to my own house in Town. My cook is talented enough, but hardly on a par with yours. Perhaps I could persuade him to part with the recipe for haricot beef . . ."

"Rafael"—Jason was in no mood to listen to his friend's gastronomical raptures—"did you come in here to regale me with tales of my chef's prowess?"

"Of course not. Ridiculous concept. I came in to talk to you about Aurelie."

Oh, marvelous. "What about her?"

"In case you have not noticed, your family is very nearly accepting her position as your future wife."

"Correct me if I am wrong, but that was the point of this endeavor, was it not?"

Rafe rubbed absently at a spot of marmalade on his sleeve. "To be sure, it was. The problem, old man, is that they are apt to raise a breeze when she ups and leaves you. Especially if they make a point of introducing her to Society as the future Viscountess Tarrant."

It had begun to occur to Jason of late that Aurelie's departure might, in fact, cause a rather unpleasant stir among his family. It was not a calming thought. If his mother and Catherine should decide to embrace the betrothal after all, he could be in for a full force gale from the entire Granville clan when it ended. And this whole ploy had been intended to keep things controlled and cordial.

"What," he queried tightly, "do you suggest?"

"You could always marry the girl."

"What?"

"She's a prime article, Tare, and she seems to like you. It would be a damned shame to see her end her life as an ape leader."

The term, meant to describe an old maid—Shakespeare's glib pronouncement that women who did not marry were doomed to lead apes in hell—brought to mind an interesting image. He could see Aurelie quite happily climbing trees, pockets full of frogs, with a troop of hairy clowns in tow.

"What utter rot," he muttered. "If the girl wants a husband, we will find her one in London." This image, of Aurelie arm-in-arm with some fawning fop, was far less amusing.

"And how is that to be accomplished if she is there as your betrothed? Once your engagement is broken, she cannot very well stay with your family. With no money and no one to sponsor her, she will be forced to return to the country and another position. It might be under your employ on some far estate, but even that has a pall about it. Doesn't sound like the end of a fairy tale to me."

Jason ground his teeth. Rafe could pick the very worst times to be astute. "Perhaps," he said grimly, "this would be best left between Aurelie and myself."

"Are you telling me, in your utterly polite way, to mind my own business?"

"I am simply saying that our arrangement, and its conclusion, are our concern."

"Wrong." To Jason's amazement, Rafe's ever smiling visage was suddenly set in tense lines "You made it my concern when you brought me into it. Whether you like it or not now, I am involved, and I do not want to see Aurelie hurt."

Jason forced himself to count to ten. "Do you honestly think my shackling myself to Miss Carollan would prevent her from being hurt?"

"No. I do not. I think Aurelie is going to get the short end of the stick whatever happens. If you marry her, however, she will have the protection of your money and title to soften the blows."

"Rafael," Jason carefully enunciated each syllable, "I embarked on this scheme in order to keep from being maneuvered into marriage. If you are so concerned with the girl's future, why don't you marry her? Your fortune is considerable, and your title is far more powerful than mine."

At this, Rafe rose to his feet and planted his fists on the desk. "Don't think the possibility hasn't crossed my mind," he said tersely. "If it were not for a few rather important factors, I might very well be tempted."

"Come now, don't by shy. Do tell me what those factors are."

A distinctly un-Rafael-like smile crossed Rafe's face. "I don't think I'm going to tell you, Tare. I shouldn't have to. I will say, however, that for such an ordered fellow, you are appearing thoroughly addlepated lately."

That did it. Restraint flew nimbly right out the window. Jason's fist hit the blotter, sending papers sliding across the surface. "Out." When Rafe ignored the order, he thundered, *"Out!"*

"Now that is the Tare we all know and love," his friend said at last. "Polite and in full possession of his faculties." He sketched a mocking salute. "See you in Town."

His lively gait as he sauntered into the hall did nothing to improve Jason's temper and he actually hurled an account book at the door. It hit with a dull thud, scattering pages over the rug. He let out his most impressive curse thus far and slumped back in his chair.

Nervy bugger.

He was not overly concerned with Rafe's anger. It was slow to rise and quick to burn, fizzling almost before it had begun. True, his friend's anger had never been directed at him before, but he was not going to concern himself with that, either. This new interference, however, was not to be ignored.

He and Aurelie had a deal, a mutually agreeable deal if his memory served him right. He was paying her to provide a service, she was doing a very good job of it, and their parting would be as planned. It occurred to him then that he had not actually paid her yet. He owed her thirty pounds. Odd, that the amount was only slightly more than that which he was paying for her chemises. Something about the concept did not sit well—that her salary equaled the cost of something as unsubstantial as undergarments. Still they had agreed upon ten pounds per week, and that would be what she was expecting.

He reached again for the paper and again thought better of it. *Pay Aurelie* was hardly more appropriate than *Visit Madame Millau.*

Damn, but he would miss her.

Of course, if he settled her as schoolmistress on one of his far estates, there would always be the opportunity to pay a visit once a year or so . . . and what? Converse on the aptitude of her students? Discuss the rigors of his life among the Haute Monde? Watch, over the years, as her chestnut hair turned to gray and she became the quintessential old maid—quite literally leading the little monkeys who would be her pupils?

The idea was, as Rafe had said, thoroughly appalling. The concept of allowing her vitality to wither in some distant county left a weight like a brick in his gut. One more shot of whiskey did little more than make the brick float momentarily. Then it was back, settled uncomfortably in the pit of his stomach.

What to do, then? Rafe's suggestion was preposterous. He could not possibly marry her, family expectations or no. She *was* a prime article, certainly, well suited to be a man's partner and helpmeet. But he was not well suited to be a husband, at least not for a few years yet, and his bachelorhood was not something he cared to shed until such time as it became imperative.

He would have to find her another husband. Rafe was a possibility, lofty title notwithstanding. He would be good to Aurelie, make her comfortable and happy. Or another young buck, perhaps not with Rafael's expectations and good looks, but with an acceptable living and pleasant mien.

Now Jason was positively miserable.

Well, the matter could be put off for the time being. After Grace's debut—yes, he would think on it then. *Find Aurelie a husband* imprinted itself on his mental list and, with a vicious curse, he wiped it away.

This time, when the knock sounded, he did not bother to answer at all. Not that it mattered. Seconds later, the door

118

flew open and the dogs charged in, tails whipping and tongues lolling. "Down!" Jason commanded before they could reach him, and the trio promptly collapsed into a wriggling heap on the floor.

"I am sorry, Jason. They have been confined to the stables for so long that they think you've abandoned them."

His head came up sharply at the sound of Aurelie's lilting voice. She was standing in the doorway, her jonquil skirts fluttering lightly in the draft from the open front door.

"Someone close the damn door!" Jason bellowed from his seat and a footman hastily scurried to obey. "Your concern for my dogs' emotional well-being warms my heart, Miss Carollan."

She had moved into the room to seat herself on the edge of a chair by then and he was struck by memories of how she had looked when they had first met in that very chamber. It was not the same woman, this poised Celtic faery with her hair rioting in burnished abandon around her face. Jason found himself wondering what she had done with the odious spectacles and rather wished she would take to wearing them again. The silver gaze was far too clear and searching for his peace of mind.

"What can I do for you, Aurelie?"

At least he had come back from Miss Carollan. His use of her surname always served to set her teeth on edge. Not that he was looking welcoming—or even polite, for that matter. Instead, he looked as he had that first day, all dark and sharp. "I-I merely came to tell you that I will be traveling with your sisters, and that we are to leave shortly." *Not true, but he looks so grim . . .*

"Fine. I will see you tomorrow then. We are all to attend the Kingsley bash, I hear."

"You will not be dining with us tonight . . . ? Yes, certainly, Jason—tomorrow."

He clearly was not dining with them that eve, and she quashed the flare of disappointment. He had to settle into his own house and was probably looking forward to an evening at his club, far away from the demands of his family.

There was little else to be said. She had come in hoping to learn something, anything, about his life in London—whose opinion mattered to him, who she should contrive to please, or avoid. She had wanted, too, to come clean, even in a small way, about her situation. It did not seem likely she would run into any of the Oglesbys in London, but there was always the remote chance and she wanted Jason to be prepared should Fen happen to roll across their path.

Silly, she chided herself. *Fenwick and the viscount hardly run in the same circles.*

Still, she would have felt ever so much better had she apprised Jason of the fact that she did, in fact, have relatives. The matter had been weighing heavily on her mind since she had heard that they were to accompany the family to London. Then again, such a revelation would have opened the door for other questions, questions that she was not willing to answer.

Jason's obvious unwillingness to talk suddenly took on a beneficial bent. Had he been more approachable, she might have loosened her tongue, and that could have been disastrous.

"Until tomorrow then, my lord," she said evenly, and rose to go. One of the wolfhounds—Nolo, she thought—scrambled to his feet and trotted to her side.

"Have a good journey," Jason replied, his eyes already back on his papers.

Nolo nudged his enormous head under her hand, begging for a pat, and she complied absently. The dog certainly was not as handsome as his master, but he was a good deal more predictable and, at the moment, a great deal more friendly. She frowned, trying to think of what could have put Jason in such a surly mood. It could not have been anything she had done—or could it?

Nothing illuminating came to mind, nor did Jason seem inclined to help. So, with a last hopeful glance at the formidable figure ensconced behind the desk, she turned and quit the chamber, closing the door quietly behind her.

Jason looked up after she had gone. It had not been his

intention to be rude. But then, he had not been rude, precisely, merely reserved. It had seemed imperative somehow to keep himself distant and to get her out the door as soon as possible.

Why? he asked himself eventually. *Because, you fool,* the imp replied, *you would have said something you would have regretted.*

"Perhaps," Jason murmured, silencing the little voice. "I might very well have been rude." And she had done nothing to deserve bearing the brunt of his foul mood. "Yes, that is it—I might have been impolite."

And Viscount Tarrant, heir to the Heathfield earldom and Society gentleman was, after all, *never* impolite.

11

AURELIE FUMBLED WITH her fan, silently cursing the blasted thing's apparent unwillingness to be useful. It was unbearably hot in the Kingsley ballroom and a bit of air, even manufactured, would have been very welcome. Attempting to conceal her inept struggle behind her skirts, she tried to figure out how an intelligent woman could be foiled by some sticks and a bit of silk.

"Perhaps I could be of some assistance, Miss Carollan."

Aurelie blushed and tried to smile serenely as her companion removed the offending object from her fingers. Several gentlemen had begged an introduction from Lady Heathfield and, despite the announcement of her attachment to Jason, had requested a dance. Even now, some quarter hour after his set, Theo, Lord Something-or-Other, seemed in no hurry to be displaced.

At the moment, he was earnestly trying to pry her fan open and was meeting with no more success than she had. Under his thatch of blond hair, his pleasant features were drawn in concentration. Aurelie decided she could be in worse company. He was perhaps a year or two older than she, quite a pink of the ton and, she mused, a possibility for Grace.

"Where did you say your home was, my lord?"

He looked up from his task to reply, "My estates are near Ashbourne, in Derbyshire."

Another point in his favor. Derby was very near Stafford and the Heathfield lands. "Lovely country. Do you pass much time there?"

"As much as possible. I much prefer the country to London. . . ." He broke off and flushed. "I mean—Town is quite the place to be, but it can be so . . . I do not mean to imply that I prefer to rusticate . . ."

"I quite understand, my lord. I am myself a country girl and find London a bit much on the senses."

He flushed again, this time in gratitude, and turned his attention back to her fan, which was still resisting his best efforts. Aurelie suppressed a smile. She might not have been to London in many years, and was undoubtedly far less accustomed to the bustle of Society than the young lord; still, she was quite comfortable thus far. True, her senses were rather overwhelmed, especially in this crush of vivid colors and flashing jewels, but she was enjoying the experience.

She resisted the urge to fan herself with her hand and decided the experience would be even more enjoyable if Jason were at her side. He had been there earlier, politely accepting congratulations. As soon as was seemly, however, he had excused himself to visit the card rooms. She had gazed after his departing back, broad and impressive in its austere black coat, and tried to keep her wistfulness from showing.

She had dressed carefully for her first London ball, donning the silver tissue gown with reverent pleasure. The quick, almost imperceptible flash of approval in Jason's eyes when he had greeted her at the foot of the stairs had swelled her heart, registering somewhere deep within her. She knew that years later, when the rest of her time with Jason was naught but a faint and distant memory, she would still see that brief flare of appreciation with all the clarity of the moment.

How very sad it could not have lasted, even for a few minutes longer. But by the time they had walked out the Heathfields' door, he had assumed the aura of polite calm that had remained until he'd left her side.

". . . got it . . ."

"I beg your pardon?" She shook her head to clear it of

Jason's image and turned to Lord Whomever, who was still bent over her fan.

"I think I've got it."

As Aurelie opened her mouth to thank him, there was an ominous cracking and the frame splintered in his hands. Numerous heads swiveled in their direction and Lady Heathfield's sniff carried tellingly. The young man turned a rather alarming shade of puce. He raised the ruined fan near his face, appearing to think that if he stared at it long enough it would repair itself.

"Oh, I do say, I am so sorry, Miss Carollan! What a loaf to have got myself into. I do beg you to forgive my ham-fisted . . ."

"Please, sir," she interrupted consolingly, "do not concern yourself with such a trivial matter. It was only a fan." He did not look reassured. "I quite believe it was defective to begin with, and would have come apart so eventually."

"Dismal affair," the lordling muttered. "So embarrassed."

He looked well past consolation, but Aurelie was ready to try again when a deep voice interrupted the poor man's self-recriminations. "Difficulties with the fripperies, my dear?"

Aurelie could not hold back the bright smile that burst forth at Jason's arrival. "Just a minor mishap with a fan, my lord. Theo, I mean, er, Lord . . ."

"Taking it upon yourself to deplete my accounts, Newlyn?" *Yes, that was it—Lord Newlyn.* "It would not do at all for me to let my future wife go without fans. I shall have to see about buying her a dozen. More, I suppose, if you plan on crushing them."

Newlyn flushed miserably. "Ham-fisted," he stammered, "m-my fault entirely. I will see to replacing . . ."

"Relax, Newlyn. It was a joke."

Jason's assertion did not seem to comfort him much at all. Aurelie was not surprised. She was quite certain Jason did not make a habit of joking in public, and his delivery ranked somewhere well below chummy. He towered a good

124

head above the hapless Theo, making her think of a panther looming over a house cat.

He deftly plucked the mangled fan from Newlyn's limp fingers, dropped it into his own pocket, and turned to face her. "I believe this dance is mine."

"Of course, my lord." Casting a warm smile over her shoulder at the now-pale Newlyn, she accepted Jason's arm and allowed him to lead her onto the dance floor.

The strains of a waltz drifted to her ears as his hand circled her waist, and she was suddenly convinced that, as long as he held her so, she was in danger of making an utter cake of herself. Instead, she fell easily into the rhythm of the music and, finding him more than skilled enough to guide her, allowed herself to enjoy the warmth of his touch.

"You quite frightened him," she commented after a time. "I am afraid he will be too terrified to speak to me again."

She looked up at his face then and caught her breath at the force of his tawny gaze. No matter how many times she stared into his eyes, their leonine beauty always startled her.

"He is a weak creature, my dear. Is it so very important that he speak to you again?"

"No, not to me, precisely. It is just that I thought he might do for Grace. . . . Does that amuse you?"

Jason could not very well tell her his smile came from pleasure rather than amusement. He had stayed in the game room as long as he could stand before the desire to dance with her had driven him back. The sight of young Newlyn wrestling with Aurelie's fan, all the while sneaking surreptitious glances at the creamy skin exposed by her fashionable bodice, had set his blood roiling.

The arrogance of the pup—ogling the future wife of Viscount Tarrant.

Even as he had borne down on the pair he had reminded himself that he did not have a future wife. But the ton assumed he did, and that should have damn well been enough to warn off any buck thinking to sniff around Aurelie.

It had flashed into his mind that Newlyn would make a perfectly good husband for her. He was wealthy, titled, and

125

a decent sort of fellow—at least as far as green-headed fops were concerned. That thought was followed by the emphatic assertion that the young man would make a deplorable husband for Aurelie. He was a bumbling, stammering fool and would have her bored to tears within weeks.

She needed someone stronger, more self-confident, sharp enough to appreciate her intelligence yet caring enough to see the simple warmth behind it. The only man who came to mind was Rafe, and Jason did not want to think about Rafe. His relief at hearing Aurelie's admission that she viewed Newlyn as a suitor for Grace and not for herself waned at the concept of better men honing in, and he cast one more speculative glance at the man over Aurelie's shoulder. He appeared to be stammering his embarrassment to a nearby potted plant.

"In the wake of recent events, do you still think Newlyn suitable for my sister?"

Aurelie's familiar, bell-like laugh made his body tighten. "She would scare him off in a second."

But Aurelie had not. She had, apparently, quite charmed the sod.

From the moment they had walked in, eyes had followed her every move. And people seemed to approve of what they were seeing. She looked beautiful, a celestial faery in floating silver. As they had entered, he had heard someone remark, "Not a Beauty, certainly . . ." and had been ready to step forward and plant the toad a facer. The man had saved his nose by finishing, ". . . but there is something fetching about her. An Original, I think . . ."

He had looked down at Aurelie to see if she had heard the pronouncement. She'd appeared completely oblivious to the attention, her eyes wide as she surveyed the scene before her. In the following hour she had been alternately dignified and ingenuous, charming everyone to whom she was introduced. Jason, for his own part, had been equally charmed and had ultimately been forced into the card room to regain some of his slipping composure.

Returning for a dance, he decided now, had not been the

wisest thing to do. God only knew how much he deplored dancing to begin with, and here he was in the midst of a waltz. He did not dislike the waltz quite as much as other dances. To be honest, he rather enjoyed the opportunity to hold a woman in his arms. There were far better circumstances in which to hold a woman, however, and thinking of them now, with Aurelie in his arms, was doing nothing for his state of mind—or body.

Aurelie nearly lost a step when he suddenly pushed her another few inches away. She wondered fleetingly if she had inadvertently pressed improperly close to his chest. No—there was almost enough room there for a third person. A quick glance up at his face revealed an implacable mask. Only someone who knew him well would be able to detect the displeasure evident in the tight set of his mouth. And she knew him well.

Perhaps not so very well, she amended. His recent behavior was odd, even as it was thoroughly consistent with the Viscount Tarrant she had first met. The softening she had seen in the early days of the house party had been welcome and wonderful, and she had grown used to it, despite its relative brevity.

She wanted it back.

"My lord," she said softly, "Jason."

"Hmm?"

"Are you ... I was wondering—I mean ..." Better to spit it out before she lost the nerve. "Have I done something wrong?"

This time, they both came to an abrupt halt as he missed a step. "What is God's name would make you ask something like that?"

She darted a quick look around the floor and, following her gaze, Jason realized they had attracted the attention of a few dozen pairs of eyes. Narrowly avoiding a collision with a sweeping couple, he drew her back into the dance.

She concentrated on the steps for a moment, her lips moving ever so slightly as she counted. Then she said, "It is just that you have been so . . . distant recently. I thought perhaps I had done something to displease you."

Jason stifled a curse. "You have done nothing wrong. I am merely preoccupied . . . with matters of business." *Matters of business. Right. And Prinny doesn't wear corsets.*

"I am very pleased to hear that. It would be extremely distressing to think that I was not behaving as a future viscountess ought."

Not that she was at all convinced. When compared to the grand ladies around her, especially to Lady Eleanor, she felt very gauche indeed. Eleanor, she was certain, would not need to count her steps in a waltz. Nor would she find Jason's presence so unsettling as to make even the simple act of counting difficult. No, she would be cool and poised, her fan opening with a flick of a wrist, each lock of her golden hair staying in its elegant place rather than slowly slipping into wild disarray.

The music ended suddenly, and Aurelie fought back the surge of disappointment with the conviction that she would be far better off out of Jason's arms. In fact, she vowed, it was the perfect opportunity to visit the ladies' retiring room and see to repairing her hair.

Jason's hand dropped from her waist, and he began to lead her back to his mother. "Aurelie," he said softly as they approached, "look at me." She did, more or less, fixing her gaze somewhere around his chin. "You are everything you should be and more. I am proud of you." With that, he deposited her back on the sidelines, nodded politely to his mother and sisters, and disappeared back into the crush.

How paltry was pride when compared to love, Aurelie thought sadly. For with this parting came the realization that somehow, sometime, in the past few weeks, she had managed to fall deeply, irrevocably in love with the one man she knew she could never have.

Strange that she had not felt it happen. She had always expected love to hit her like a thunderbolt, making her dizzy in its unexpected power. She felt dizzy, a bit nauseous even, but it was not the sensation she had anticipated, nor was it for the same reason. Rather than being exhilarated by the wonder of love, she was sickened by its sheer hopelessness.

News of her betrothal to Lord Tarrant was tearing through the ton like wildfire. She saw frank curiosity in nearly every face she encountered and wondered, hating herself for the weakness, whether she was being found wanting. Well, in the end it would not matter. She would simply vanish, leaving behind nothing to remind Society that she had ever existed. She would be leaving something, to be sure, but no one would see her shattered heart.

Already feeling the fissures, she allowed herself one bleak sigh.

"Handsome devil, is he not? Plenty of sighing in his wake."

Aurelie spun about to face the speaker of those light words. She could not remember having been introduced to the stunning, reed-thin lady who stood there, but she had met so many people that evening she could not be sure.

"No need for you to sigh, my dear. You have netted him."

The woman was not English, and Aurelie tried to place the accent—German perhaps. "Netted, madam?" she replied lightly, hoping levity would hide her heartsickness. "That sounds uncomfortable to an extreme."

From the corner of her eye, she could see Lady Heathfield trying to disengage herself from conversation with a formidable-looking matron. The countess's face seemed abnormally pale. Even stranger was the fact that, above her companion's head, she could see Jason hurrying back, bearing down on them with tight-lipped determination.

"Uncomfortable—quite so!" The lady gave an amused chuckle. "Many husbands no doubt would agree. He is quite a catch, Lord Tarrant. What sort of net did you use?"

"I think it was more of a buoy, actually," Aurelie answered, wondering if she was not perhaps getting herself into deep water.

"Ah, you rescued him. From himself?"

"Not at all. From others with nets."

Jason had, against his will, turned back to look at Aurelie, only to have his heart skip a beat at the sight of Countess Lieven reaching her side. The glamorous Russian woman was a patroness of Almack's and was well known for her elegance and hauteur. Many a girl had lost her chance for a successful Season as a result of the merest frown from the countess's lips.

She rarely deigned to initiate a contact, and Jason silently cursed her for breaking the habit now. Aurelie was thoroughly worthy of the lady's attention, but he hardly expected the countess to agree.

Aurelie needed the nod of one of Almack's patronesses, so an introduction would have been necessary at some point. But why, he wondered grimly, did it have to be La Lieven? Sweet, helpful Maria, Lady Sefton would have been ideal. Or the kindhearted Lady Cowper. Even Sally Jersey, the Grande Dame herself, would have been preferable to the blade-thin, razor-tongued countess.

As he fought his way through the crowd he spied his mother on the same course, her face tight as she tried to avert disaster. They reached Aurelie at the same second, just in time to witness the most astonishing occurrence. Countess Lieven laughed aloud and reached out to touch Aurelie's cheek.

"You are most amusing, my dear. I think perhaps Tarrant has chosen well."

"Thank you . . . madam." It was clear that the woman expected to be recognized, but no names came to Aurelie's mind. "You are too kind."

"Very likely, my dear. Ah, Lord Tarrant, you have returned to your fiancée's side. How gallant. And Lady Heathfield. I hear your daughter makes her bow this year."

"Countess." Jason bent over her hand. "An honor and a pleasure as always. Have you been formally introduced . . . ?" He smoothly drew Aurelie forward. "May I present my future wife, Miss Aurelie Carollan. Miss Carollan, Countess Lieven."

Aurelie had the distinct impression that something very important had just happened, but she could not figure out exactly what it was. "Countess Lieven," she murmured, following Jason's ceremonious lead. Silly, she thought, as she had already been conversing with the woman. "I am very pleased to make your acquaintance."

A near-wicked gleam flashed in the lady's eyes. "You should be," she announced with a smile. Then, to Lady Heathfield, "We will look forward to seeing Miss Carollan and your daughter at the Assembly Rooms soon. I will see that you receive vouchers." With a majestic swirl of silk, she swept off into the crowd.

"Oh. Oh, dear." Lady Heathfield had lost some of her customary rigidity and was standing, shoulders slumped, hand over her heart. "What did she say to you, Aurelie? No, more importantly—what did *you* say to *her*?"

"Nothing, really. We merely discussed fishing."

"Oh, *dear!*" the countess gasped and for a moment Aurelie actually thought she might faint. She recovered admirably, however, lifting her hand from her chest to wave it weakly in her son's direction. "Jason, I believe I could use a drink. Champagne."

"Certainly, madam." And, with a strange smile for Aurelie, he went off in search of something with which to revive his mother.

"Nods for both of us, and I did not have to say a word." Grace settled herself more comfortably on the carriage seat. "Thank heavens for that. Mother has been terrified for years that I would say something untoward to one of the patronesses and thus ruin my chances for a good marriage."

Lady Heathfield could not muster so much as a disapproving glance for her daughter. She was still recovering from what she clearly believed to have been a brush with disaster.

Aurelie was not fooled by Grace's levity. She knew the evening had been a trial for the girl. To be honest, Grace was on her way to being a smashing success. Men had all but flocked to the countess, begging introductions, and Grace's dance card had been filled from the first set. The problem, she had confided to Aurelie in a quiet moment, was that not one of the men had been in the least interested in what she had to say.

"Charming, smooth, gallant," she had said with a sigh. "But not a shred of intelligent conversation among the lot. The polite ones complimented my gown; the not-so-polite were obviously calculating. I could see the pound signs adding up in their eyes—even the wealthy ones."

Aurelie ached to tell her that what she felt was not merely sympathy, but total empathy. It was a horrible sensation to know one was being courted for one's money. Grace, at least, had beauty to recommend her as well—but there were scores of beautiful women in Society. There were, however, precious few heiresses. Aurelie knew this because, where she had expected tongues to be flapping over gowns, the most cherished topic of conversation among the revelers had been money.

After only one evening, she knew that the plain Miss Alyce Britten, daughter of Lord Wincaster, could be expected to bring a hundred thousand pounds to her marriage. The glorious Lady Helena Yarrow, daughter of the Earl of Tonbridge, would provide little more than her beautiful self.

Lady Eleanor DeVane, a reigning Beauty even after two Seasons, was worth an amount so great that no one could agree on it.

Glad for the dim interior of the carriage, Aurelie bit her lip. She was feeling thoroughly heartsick again and was grateful her companions could not see her face clearly. She had never been much good at hiding her emotions and wondered how she was going to do it now. Each time she looked at Jason, she would be thinking how very deeply in love she had fallen. And each time she saw Lady Eleanor, she would be looking at just the sort of woman he would choose when he finally decided to marry.

For the first time in her life, she wished for beauty. She had always been pretty enough, certainly. Enough, certainly, to be forced to hide her looks behind heavy spectacles and horrid gowns. But she was still a topaz amongst diamonds—bright and attractive, but only semiprecious.

"You did well for yourself, girl."

Lady Heathfield's only slightly grudging assertion cut into her musings and she managed a faint smile. "Thank you, madam. It was a very pleasant evening."

"With Countess Lieven's nod, you should be well set. No one will dare cut you now."

Aurelie wondered what possible reason anyone would have had to cut her before. Unless, of course, being Nobody in Particular was a reasonable offense. She thought that perhaps it was. The ton, so far as she could tell, was comprised of a good many high sticklers whose toplofty attitudes were often as hypocritical as they were harsh. Along with learning what various Misses were worth, she had learned which Misses had married into their present station.

She was rapidly learning the rules of Society. They were not terribly complicated. A title forgave many faults. Money forgave a good deal more. Together, they appeared invincible. Well, she thought sadly, her money would mean little once she became known as the one who had jilted Viscount Tarrant. His title and fortune put him near the top of the ton apex, and he would suffer no more than a few weeks of pitying stares. Less if, as he had claimed, he decamped immediately for the Continent.

She was beginning to think his plan was reasonable—with one major fault. His parents might respect his broken heart for a time, commiserating over the fickleness of a woman they had known to be inappropriate from the onset. But there was no question that they would be back at him with a vengeance, determined to see him settled with a paragon of womanly excellence.

Jason might very well find himself returned to an "un-

133

12

HELL WOULD BE a vast improvement. There could not possibly be a worse way to pass a Wednesday night, Jason thought grimly, than at Almack's. The scenery was poor, the food worse, and the very thought of trying to dance on the warped wood floor made his bones ache.

To top it off, he was being submitted to the truly appalling view of Lord Milby's flailing limbs as he danced a Scottish reel with Aurelie. Dressed, as were all men present, in the requisite knee breeches, the man resembled nothing so much as a collection of sausages trying to escape their casings.

Jason desperately wanted to turn away from the sight, but he had already caught the bounder gazing longingly down Aurelie's bodice. Milby had looked up eventually and had had the grace to flush at Jason's fierce glare. Should he relax his vigil, however, Milby would undoubtedly turn his eyes back to lower things.

Aurelie, per usual, seemed totally oblivious to the attention. She was dancing with undisguised enjoyment, a graceful vision in floating green muslin. She also seemed oblivious to the oppressive heat. A good thing, too, he decided, as Newlyn was hovering about, undoubtedly waiting to have a go at her fan. Seeing the thing dangling from her wrist, Jason rather wished it was in his hands. Along with the rest of the Assembly Rooms' miserable architecture, the ballroom possessed only six windows, none of which seemed to be open.

He tugged discreetly at his cravat, regulation white, of

course, wondering why the place had never bothered him so before.

"Seems to get worse every year, doesn't it?"

"So it does," Jason replied, turning to face the figure who had reached his side, "though I cannot figure out why. Same people, same music . . ."

"Same god-awful food. A wise man would repair immediately to White's."

Jason smiled faintly at the mention of his club. "A wise man would certainly do so, Brummell, but I was foolish enough to allow my mother to talk me into doing this instead."

The ton's longtime leader chuckled. "Devilish business, having a sister and future wife enjoying the same Season. Could put quite a cramp in a man's style."

Rumor had it Brummell was not long for his lofty position. Whispers of debt and disfavor with the Prince Regent had begun to quietly circulate through Polite Society. The glee with which this news was received by some was far from polite. Anyone looking at the Beau that evening, however, would be hard put to believe what they were hearing.

Resplendent as ever in formal tailed coat and studied ennui, Brummell was every bit the elegant nob. He appeared to have no question of his own consequence and Jason silently gave the man at least a year or two before fate would catch up with him.

He neither liked nor disliked Brummell. He found his arrogance to be annoying at times, downright absurd at others, but Beau was usually pleasant enough. They were both members of White's and Watier's, and had passed enough amicable evenings at the card tables to have forged a distant friendship.

"Surprised to hear of your engagement, Tare. Didn't think you the leg-shackling type."

"Age and family pressures can change a man's type," Jason replied dryly.

"If you say so. She is a rather fetching thing. Milby certainly thinks so."

Milby had, in fact, taken advantage of Jason's temporary distraction to lean over Aurelie again, no mean feat considering the constantly changing positions of the dance.

"Bloody hell," Jason growled.

"Quite. But the music is winding down. Perhaps I shall rescue your betrothed from Milby's clutches."

"The hell you will." Ignoring Brummell's chuckle, Jason stalked onto the dance floor. If anyone was to do any rescuing, it would damn well be he. "Excuse me, Milby," he muttered, all but shoving the man aside to claim Aurelie's arm. "This set is mine."

The musicians drifted into a minuet. Jason detested minuets. And promptly told her so.

"Then why are we participating?" Aurelie asked lightly. "I would be perfectly content to sit this one out."

That much was true. She would have liked very much to dance a waltz with Jason, but it was unlikely she would have the opportunity at Almack's. As they walked, curiosity got the better of her and she asked again, "Why did you come onto the floor?"

"Because," was the terse reply, "I was convinced that if I did not, Milby would have thrown you over his shoulder and carried you off into the night."

The image of the portly lord doing anything so barbaric brought a laugh to Aurelie's lips. She sobered quickly, though, when it became clear that Jason was not jesting. Heavens, but it was hard to keep up with his moods these days.

Thinking he was censuring some unconsciously imprudent behavior on her part, she bit her lip and fell into step beside him. She had not noticed anything untoward in Milby's behavior. In fact, she had been enjoying the lively dance immensely. Clearly such enjoyment was not seemly for Jason's fiancée, and she vowed to develop greater restraint.

Another rule, another lesson learned.

Feeling suddenly unable to bear his displeasure, she stopped moving. When he turned to gaze down impatiently, she murmured, "If you will excuse me, my lord, I believe I will join the other ladies. I wanted to talk to Grace about . . ." Unable to come up with a clever topic of conversation, she merely raised her chin and walked away.

Jason watched her go. His first impulse was to follow, even to beg her to partner him in the infernal minuet. He held back, thinking he could not stomach the cool expression she had taken to wearing around him, not when she smiled so readily for everyone else.

In the past several days, it had gotten so he was ready to do handsprings across the floor or sing, "Rule, Brittania" backward, just to win a smile. She was endlessly cheerful around his family, especially the children. Had he not known of her naturally sunny nature, he might have thought some of her gaiety was forced. Rafe was the only other human being he knew who could seem so effortlessly cheerful.

And he did not want to think about Rafe.

They had crossed paths several times since arriving in Town, and his friend had been almost impossibly amicable. "Almost," Jason decided, because Rafe had taken to smirking, especially when he led Aurelie onto the floor for a dance. Had Jason been feeling rational, he would have admitted there was nothing to suggest attraction on the part of either person. They merely looked the roles they were playing—cousins and friends.

Jason was not, however, feeling rational. He was feeling mean and jealous and he did not like the sensation. It was alien and thoroughly unpleasant.

Spying Eleanor and her parents across the room, he decided to pay his respects. Ordinarily, he would have walked barefoot over broken glass before willingly submitting to a miserable and awkward situation, but at the moment one martyrdom seemed rather like the next.

"Your Grace," he greeted the duchess. And again, to the duke and Eleanor, "Your Grace. My lady."

"Hello, Jason." Eleanor returned his greeting with pleasant familiarity. Her parents, on the other hand, let out a simultaneous grunt. Jason did not think it was in welcome.

Feeling reckless suddenly, he asked, "Would you care for some refreshment?"

Eleanor's blue eyes glittered. "Perhaps a bit of succulent beef? Or one of the scrumptious pastries? I must confess I find chewing on wood to be quite a challenge."

"A challenge to which I am certain you are equal." When she grimaced, he shrugged and offered, "Lemonade, perhaps?"

"Yes, I think lemonade would be nice—provided they remembered to add the sugar." Accepting his arm, Eleanor allowed him to lead the way toward the refreshment tables.

"You are looking lovely as always."

"Thank you, Jason. I meant to pass on a similar compliment to Grace, but she has not had a moment free since we arrived."

"Yes, my little sister is causing quite a stir."

As he collected Eleanor's lemonade, he searched the sea of heads for Grace's bright curls. He found her completely surrounded by a group of fawning men. Lords Dearbourne and Fremont, he noticed with annoyance, were among them. Dearbourne was in the midst of the crush, rheumatism notwithstanding, and Fremont, in customary hauteur, held himself several feet away.

Funny, he had not noticed before just how lovely his sister really was. In her regulation white, she looked positively angelic. Only the snapping of the golden eyes, seemingly unnoticed by her gaggle of beaux, betrayed the fact that her thoughts were far more devilish than her appearance.

Jason found himself remembering the varied and frequent flashes of deviltry in the child who had been his sister. She had been a lively little thing, forever getting under his feet. Once, she had even gone so far as to leap out of a tree when he was riding past. The next thing he had known, he'd been staring up into her angelic face from the unfortunate vantage point of the ground. She had merely fixed him with a perfectly innocent gaze and informed him that she was playing Robin Hood.

Being designated the corrupt Sheriff of Nottingham had not improved his day.

Now, watching her hold nearly a dozen men in the sort of thrall Maid Marian had held her Robin, he wondered when she had grown up. Whenever it had happened, he had not been there.

"Careful, Jason. Your brotherly concern is showing. It would not do at all to frighten off Grace's suitors at this early date. She might not mind, but your mother would be livid."

"Am I looking so very threatening?"

"No more so than in the past, actually. It is just that you have seemed different lately, more approachable. Your betrothal has softened some of the sharp edges."

Jason wanted to howl, but limited himself to a single harsh bark. Howling in the middle of Almack's—and in the presence of a lady—was not especially proper behavior. The damnable thing, he thought rather sullenly, was that he did not particularly care.

He caught his mother's eye from across the room. Livid was not a word that he would use to describe her at that moment. Her gaze shifted back and forth between Eleanor and himself and, for perhaps the first time in recent memory, her expression held none of the satisfied arrogance the sight of them together ordinarily produced. Instead, she looked bewildered.

Aurelie stood at her side, but she turned away before he could gauge her expression. And began talking to Rafael. Jason had not realized Rafe was present that evening, but there he was, blithe and dashing and obviously enjoying himself. Whatever Aurelie said to him made him laugh. For a moment, they conversed cheerfully, Rafe's mahogany hair blending with Aurelie's chestnut as he bent his head to better hear her. Then, offering his arm, he led her away toward the dance floor.

For a minuet.

Jason was convinced that, in the second before the dance commenced, the bounder had seen him. And laughed.

Seething inside, he turned back to Eleanor who was regarding him curiously. "So you think my betrothal has made me a better man, do you?"

"I hardly meant to imply *better*, Jason. Merely *sans-façon*. Oh, don't scowl at me. I imagine you do not regard being without ceremony much of a virtue, but it can be very refreshing at times."

"My lady, you are doing irreparable damage to my ego with each new word."

"Oh, dear. I *have* offended you. I did not mean to." She laid one gloved hand on his sleeve. "At the risk of doing it once more, I feel compelled to tell you that you take life far too seriously. But I suspect you have been coming to that conclusion on your own."

"And how is that?"

"Why, your choice of brides, of course."

Thinking it was now Aurelie who had been insulted, Jason bristled. "I must insist . . ."

Eleanor raised a hand to silence him. "The fact that you chose her speaks well for you, Jason. I have never been able to guess what you want out of life, but you seem able to find what you need. Now, if you would be so kind as to escort me back—I have promised this set to Mr. Symington."

Aurelie watched from the corner of her eye as Jason and Eleanor rejoined her parents. Eleanor was, as always, stunningly lovely. Her aquamarine gown brought to mind the clearest of Sussex skies and Aurelie, in grass green, felt utterly and miserably terrestrial.

Jason handed Eleanor over to a young man, his reluctance to do so evident on his face. A promenading group blocked Aurelie's view for a moment and when they had passed she could see him still in the company of Lord and Lady Ramsden. It appeared the duke had forgiven Jason for declining the honor of his daughter's hand. The older man was speaking earnestly on some subject and Aurelie's imagination furnished the words.

"... *not too late, young man. You really ought to reconsider tying yourself to that country chit. She's a pleasant enough creature, but nowhere near my Eleanor ...*"

Jason appeared to listen carefully to the duke before giving a thoughtful nod. His eyes slid to Eleanor, moving gracefully on the floor, then to Aurelie, who promptly disgraced herself by spilling punch down her skirt. Even worse, some of the liquid splashed onto Rafe.

"Oh, oh—Rafe, I am so sorry!" Blushing furiously, she dabbed ineffectually at his sleeve with her handkerchief.

"Enough," he commanded cheerfully, removing the tiny lace object from her hand. "If anyone should apologize, it ought to be Newlyn here for providing you with the punch."

Newlyn who had, in fact, offered the drink to Aurelie as she and Rafe finished their dance, flushed a dull red and began stammering very effusive apologies indeed. Taking pity on the poor fellow, Aurelie did her best to console him.

"B-but your gown, Miss Carollan. 'Tis ruined, I vow. You must allow me to ..." As offering to purchase a gown for a woman not one's relation or spouse was somewhat less than proper, Newlyn tried valiantly to find an alternative. Apparently nothing came to mind and he took on the appearance of a landed fish, eyes bulging while he soundlessly opened and closed his mouth.

"Really, my lord, it is of no consequence." Aurelie peered across the room as she spoke but Jason was nowhere to be seen. Lord Ramsden was standing in the same place, however, with a distinctly complacent smile on his thin lips. "I ... excuse me, please," she said to her companions and, not waiting for their responses, headed as quickly as she could, considering the crush of people, toward the ladies' retiring room. If she was going to be emotional, she was bloody well going to do it alone.

Jason reached the spot where she had been standing only to find her gone and young Newlyn eager to apologize for some slight. From what Jason could gather, it had involved spilled fans and dancing punch.

It was almost enough to send him back to the duke, but that conversation had been no more appealing. Ramsden was of the very firm and very vocal opinion that the Colonial upstarts had been allowed to run wild far too long and that it was high time to bring them back to heel. He had appealed to Jason, as a peer and military man, to see that something was done.

Jason has listened politely, nodding when appropriate, and managed to refrain from mentioning that not only had the Colonial upstarts managed to rout British forces quite soundly thirty-odd years earlier, but that they were on their way to doing so again even as they spoke. Jason knew of plans to attack the southern city of New Orleans, but was secretly pessimistic about the outcome. A certain American General Andrew Jackson was proving to be an immense thorn in British sides.

Considering the duke's passion, Jason did not offer his opinion. Nor did he mention that the man's own son was vastly increasing the family fortune by dealing with some of those very people Ramsden wanted to see swinging from English halyards.

In the end, he had extricated himself from the conversation with the rather cowardly act of promising to look into the matter. Not that he would do anything of the sort. He was not an empirist at heart and thought the Americans, despite their national youth, were doing a fairly decent job and ought to be left alone. Besides, he had far more weighty matters on his mind. Like getting Aurelie's attention.

Ignoring Newlyn's ramblings, he looked to Rafe. "Where did Aurelie go?"

"I have no idea," the scoundrel replied lightly. "Perhaps out for a bit of air."

"Alone? Good God, man, you should have known better than to let her wander off like that."

Rafe arched a dark brow. "Why? I am in no position to censor her behavior."

"Damn it, you are her cousin!"

The remark came both for the benefit of Newlyn, who had stopped muttering to listen, and to remind Rafe of the precise, definitive role he was supposed to be playing. In hindsight, Jason realized he should have expected the retort.

"*You* are her fiancé."

"Pardon me, my lords," Newlyn broke in. "I would be happy to go in search of Miss Carollan. It is the least I could do, after . . ."

"No!" Jason and Rafe said in unison and, with grim looks at each other, went off in opposite directions to find Aurelie.

In the end, unable to find any member of his family, he was forced to seek out Willis, Almack's invincible proprietor. "Willis, have you seen Lady Heathfield?" He could not very well admit to the man that he'd misplaced his own fiancée.

"I believe the countess departed not five minutes ago, my lord. Lady Grace and Miss . . ."

"Carollan."

"Yes. Miss Carollan left with them."

"Well, damnation," Jason spat and headed for the door, leaving Willis to gape at his departing back.

A liveried footman rushed up to him seconds later. "Pardon me, Lord Tarrant, but I have a message for you."

"What is it?"

"Your mother asked me to tell you she and the young ladies were leaving. She was unable to find you and, as one of the young ladies was indisposed, asked me to inform you."

The footman, unaware that Lord Tarrant was a customarily reserved man, was not in the least taken aback by the curse.

Jason reached the street just in time to see his mother's carriage disappear around the corner. Unable to come up with a word to express his feelings, he merely ground his teeth and turned back to fetch his cape. There was no point in enduring Almack's any longer.

He had not, for some reason, paid a visit to Madame Millau yet and considered doing so now. But there was no appeal in the thought. A bottle of brandy at White's, however, sounded like a damned good idea.

In his impatience, he nearly plowed over the man who was standing in the doorway, arguing with one of Willis's employees. "I'm telling you, you clod-pated clown, that I have a voucher!"

"And I am telling you, sir, that no one is admitted after eleven o'clock. It is the rule."

"He's going in," the fop exclaimed, pointing to Jason.

"His lordship was already in," the doorman said tersely, his patience clearly near its end.

Jason paused to study the man, wincing at the sight of his chartreuse waistcoat and turquoise breeches. "I would not worry about it, sir," he announced, more from exasperation than generosity. "The party is over."

By the following evening, Aurelie's headache had come and gone too many times to count. At the moment it was back with a vengeance. The day had been spent receiving callers, most of whom had come for Grace. A few, however, insisted on paying their respects to Aurelie—due, she thought waspishly, to overwhelming curiosity about the woman who had finally managed to snare Lord Tarrant.

She would have liked a quiet evening at home. But quiet evenings, of course, were not allowed during the Season. So instead she found herself crowded into a supper box in Vauxhall Gardens with most of the Granvilles, waiting for the festivities to begin.

The children had begged and pleaded to be allowed to come along and, in a moment of idiosyncratic benevolence, Lady Heathfield had agreed. Freddy was perched on Aurelie's lap, making faces at his uncle Rickey, who was sitting with another group in the next box. Michaela was as quiet as usual, staring wide-eyed at the spectacle that

145

was Vauxhall, and Phoebe was tugging at her mother's skirts, asking when the acrobats would arrive.

"Hush, dearest," Catherine admonished. "We would not want Grandmama to regret bringing you with us."

"Grandmama," the countess muttered, "already does."

"But I want to see the man walk through fire. . . ."

"Hush."

Phoebe turned to Aurelie for sympathy. For her own part, Aurelie was intrigued by the advertised entertainment. Apparently one act did feature a man walking a tightrope over burning pitch. It seemed a painful way to make a living, but the crowds flocked to see him, and there were certainly worse ways to earn a pound.

"Come here, Phoebe," she coaxed. "There is a lady over there who is wearing a swan on her head."

The woman was actually wearing a rather alarming hat made of feathers in the shape of a bird. The thing looked a good deal more like a mangled pillow than a swan, but Phoebe was entranced. "Will it fly away with her?"

"Of course, not, silly. It is only a hat." Trust Michaela to be the voice of reason.

A lilting laugh carried from the next box, followed by a deeper one, and Aurelie flinched. Jason and Lady Eleanor had been laughing a good deal in the past hour. He had not smiled much of late, and Aurelie, despite having missed his cheer, wished it gone now. She could not muster up so much as a modicum of gracious pleasure that he had found something to smile about.

He was laughing with Eleanor, and Aurelie wanted to cry.

She jumped slightly when a small hand reached up to touch her cheek. "You look sad, Early," Phoebe announced solemnly. "Why?"

"Oh, I am not sad, sweetheart. I am just thinking."

"'Bout what?"

About love, and why it can hurt so much.

"I am thinking about the story my grandmother told me a long time ago."

146

"Oh, good—a story!" Phoebe abandoned her sympathy in favor of loud glee. "Tell us!"

"I do not think this is the place. . . ."

"Please," Michaela added her encouragement.

"Please, please, please," Freddy added, bouncing on her lap.

"All right." Aurelie took a quick glance around the box. Catherine looked eternally grateful, but Lady Heathfield looked ready to chuck the lot of them into the lake. "I will tell you the story, but let us move onto the grass."

They settled themselves a few yards away on a blanket provided by Lady Heathfield's maid. Phoebe and Freddy argued over who would get her lap, but Michaela silenced them with a patient, "We mustn't muss Miss Carollan's gown. We shall all sit beside her."

As usual when the children were around, Aurelie's gown was thoroughly creased. But she smiled at Michaela's thoughtfulness and managed to make both of the younger children happy by tucking one against each side. "Shall we begin?"

"What is this story about?" Phoebe asked.

"Beautiful women. And love."

"Ick," said Freddy.

"Wonderful," Michaela said with a sweet smile.

"And fierce warriors."

"Wonnerful," said Freddy. Michaela sighed.

Aurelie drew a deep breath and gazed off into the distance. "This is a very old and very important Celtic folktale," she announced. "It is called 'Emer's Choice.' "

13

A VERY LONG time ago there lived near Carraig na Siúire a young woman called Emer, daughter of Forgall the Wily. While her kin were barbarians of the cruelest sort, Emer was sweet and gentle. She was a Treasure of Eire, renowned for six graces: fairness of form, sweetness of spirit, wisdom, chastity, softness of voice, and talent with the needle. She had hair the color of polished bronze, and a heart of purest gold. Her family did not appreciate her value, however, except insofar as it could be used to better their circumstance. So Emer lived in fear of the day she would be sold into marriage to a savage chosen by her father.

Far to the north lived the warrior Cuchulainn, mortal son of Lugh the Sun-god. Cuchulainn was a Treasure of Eire for his fearlessness, strength, and male beauty. Wherever he went—and he had roamed afar, from shore to emerald shore—men revered his talent in battle and women adored him for his ebony hair and sun-kissed amber eyes. During his travels, he heard tales of Emer's glory and journeyed to Carraig na Siúire to see if they were true. Struck by her loveliness and grace, he sought to impress her with stories of his wealth and prowess. Emer could not help but fall in love with the handsome young man and promised to marry him if he could but take her from her barbaric kin.

Hearing of Cuchulainn's plans, Forgall feared losing Emer, for she was a valuable possession. So he set about a rumor that any man who could travel to the island of

Scathach the Amazon would gain such skills that no mortal would be able to stand against him. In truth, Forgall knew Scathach would kill anyone who invaded her isle. He also knew Cuchulainn would not be able to resist such a rumor.

And he was right. When the news reached Cuchulainn, he set off at once for Scathach's island. Such strength as he would gain would allow him to vanquish Emer's entire clan. With the knowledge of her love swelling his heart, he kissed her sweetly once and left her side.

It was not an easy journey and he was forced to conquer many challenges along the way. He crossed the Plain of Ill Luck, where the ground grabbed one's feet and would not let go and the blades of grass were sharp as swords. Next, he passed through the Glen of Perils, where fierce beasts unlike any others known to man attacked with razor claws and teeth the size of ax heads.

After some time, he reached the Cliff Bridge, whose span would shoot straight up whenever anyone set a foot on it. After sliding backward thrice, Cuchulainn decided that trickery was the only means by which he could conquer the bridge. Summoning up all of his strength, he made the Great Jump, leaping all the way to a point just past the middle of the span. This time, when it rose, it was in the opposite direction and he was able to slide down the remaining length to the other side.

At last he made his way to Scathach's home. There he bravely faced the mighty Amazon, holding his sword to her throat. In exchange for her life, Scathach would teach him all of the warrior skills she possessed.

He stayed many days with the great Amazon, and when he left he took with him both her knowledge and her blessing. Again, he conquered the Bridge, the Glen, and the Plain, and arrived back at Forgall's land with powers so great that he defeated Emer's kin in mere minutes. The two lovers were reunited, and wed in the presence of great mortals and gods alike, under the warm smile of Cuchulainn's father, the Sun-god.

For a time, they were very happy together. Emer had given her heart completely and forever to her magnificent husband, and her love grew with the halcyon days. As happens too often with peerless warriors, however, Cuchulainn turned fickle. He was often away from his home, amusing himself with feats of prowess and play with the gods.

It was while he was on one such jaunt that Fand, the faery wife of Manannen mac Lêr, a Sea-god, heard of his strength and splendor. Fand had been abandoned by her husband and promptly summoned Cuchulainn to her side. The young warrior resisted at first, but he had heard much of her incomparable beauty, nobility, and grace, and soon decided to heed her summons.

Fand was a faery queen, and her beauty truly was matchless. Her hair was so fine and bright a gold that it was fair blinding to see, her skin like dewy moondrops on a white rose petal. Cuchulainn, smitten by her charms, stayed with her for a month, leaving Emer alone with her pride and her broken heart. When lordly duties required the warrior to return home for a brief period of time, he arranged with Fand to meet again on his own land, under the yew tree at the Head of Baile's Strand.

Emer, learning of this meeting, made plans of her own. Sharpening a jeweled dagger, she vowed to interrupt the reunion and kill Fand. Such a decision was completely unlike Emer, for she was born warm and gentle of heart. But her heart had been shattered by Cuchulainn's faithlessness and no longer served her.

Still, on the day of the assignation, she wept over the path she was taking and when she strapped the dagger to her leg, the point pricked her fair skin and the blood mingled with her tears. Soul-sick, she set off for the yew tree at Baile's Strand. . . .

A loud cheering drowned out the rest of the phrase. The acrobats had arrived and the festivities were about to begin. Freddy, already bored with the tale, sprang to his feet and ran back toward the box. Phoebe and Michaela, however, did not move.

"Oh, please, don't stop," Michaela begged. "It is such a wonderful story."

"But the entertainment is commencing," Aurelie replied with a smile.

"Tell us how it ends." Phoebe was clearly torn between hearing Emer's fate and watching the acrobats.

"I will finish the tale some other time. How would that be?"

It was fine with Phoebe. Michaela, however, was less pleased with the promise. Aurelie had to all but pull the girl to her feet and push her in the direction of the box. A strident call from Catherine set her in motion, and the girls scampered off. Aurelie retrieved the blanket and was folding it when she noticed the figure standing a few feet away.

"Lady Eleanor, I did not realize you were there."

The other woman smiled pleasantly. "I did not want to disturb the rhythm of the story." She stepped forward to help Aurelie with the blanket. "You are a marvelous storyteller. I confess I am most curious. Does Emer use the dagger on Fand?"

Thinking the gracious woman was merely being polite, Aurelie replied, "Surely you do not wish me to bore you with the conclusion."

"On the contrary, Miss Carollan. I shall not be able to sleep tonight unless I know how the tale ends."

So, as they strolled back to the boxes, Aurelie told her. When she finished, Eleanor nodded thoughtfully. "Perhaps not precisely the ending I would have expected, but fitting nonetheless. It is a wonderful folktale. Thank you for sharing it."

She returned to her seat but Aurelie, her own heartache renewed by telling of Emer's, had lost her desire to participate in the festivities. Instead, she wandered a few yards away and leaned against the trunk of a tree. A quick glance upward assured her that it was an elm—not a yew.

The stars were out in force, and she studied them, looking for constellations. She located the faint W of Cassiopeia, the queen on her throne. Of their own volition, her eyes slid downward, seeking out Orion. He was there, his outline clear. She traced the imagined line of his sword as it hung from the three stars that comprised his belt. The most gloried of mythical heroes, Orion blazed brightest of constellations.

"Aurelie?"

She jumped at the sound of Jason's voice. Enthralled as she had been in the stars, she had not heard his approach and was startled to find him mere feet away. Despite the responding thudding of her heart, her voice sounded surprisingly calm as she replied, "Hello, Jason. Are you bored with the acrobats already?"

He gave a wry smile. "I am afraid the sight of the man walking the tightrope through fire did me in. It was altogether too reminiscent of the lectures on the fires of hell that I received as a youth from an overly zealous tutor. Phoebe, however, is entranced. I am afraid Catherine is presently having visions of the child tying a rope between the canopy posts of her bed and setting the mattress on fire so she can replicate the stunt."

Aurelie could not help but smile at the image. "The thought gives one pause, certainly."

It was the first smile Jason had had from her in what seemed aeons, and he felt it all the way to his toes. He silently gave thanks to his niece the imp. "I have not thanked you, have I, for helping out with the children? Your keeping them occupied has kept them from fraying my mother's nerves beyond repair."

"You must not underestimate your mother's nerves. They are remarkably resilient. And I have enjoyed my time with the children. They are wonderful, and I did, after all, advertise for a position as a governess. Now I can really feel as if I am earning my salary."

Jason had conveniently managed to forget the very reason she was in his life. At least, he had managed to temporarily relegate it to the back of his mind. It was always present in some manner, like a persistent itch he longed to scratch. Now, with her words, it was back with a vengeance and he actually lifted his hand to his head.

"I owe you another ten pounds." He had remembered the thirty but had not been able to give it to her personally. Instead, he had taken the easy route and had a footman deliver it in an envelope. "I shall make certain you have it tomorrow."

"Tomorrow, my lord, will be the worst possible time to have anything delivered to the house." Aurelie heard the slight bitterness in her voice and hoped Jason had not noticed. It was just that it had rankled a bit to have his money arrive like the post. "Your messenger would have to fight his way through flower deliveries, champagne crates, and musical instruments."

"Ah, yes. Grace's ball. The debut to top all others past, present, and future. If all goes as planned, there will not be a flower to be found in London by midday."

"Don't be unkind. Your mother has put an enormous amount of effort into seeing her daughter launched properly."

"Launched. I have always found that word distasteful when used about a woman. Grace is not a yacht."

"I quite agree. Though the way the marriage mart works, the men might as well be shopping for a boat—looking for impeccable lines, strong foundation, and adequate polish."

Jason sighed. "So we are back to that, are we? Would it help to tell you that I am keeping an eye on Grace's suitors?"

"Help whom, Jason—me or Grace?"

Now he had to smile. "Touché. I promise to do what I can to see that Grace is happy. Is that better?"

"Much. Thank you."

"Ah, Aurelie"—he took a step forward—"you have taken it upon yourself to play guardian angel to my family. Did I not warn you that Granvilles thrive on discomfort?"

"Fustian," she retorted, though not with much force. As

153

always, his proximity was doing funny things to her breathing. "And I am hardly anyone's guardian angel."

"An angel of salvation, then?"

Salvation—a buoy, saving him from others' nets. It was fast becoming apparent that he was rethinking his need for rescue. And that, Aurelie mused, was something she could reluctantly understand. Lady Eleanor's net could not be so very unappealing.

At the moment, however, he was by her own side. She could not help but wonder why, even as her heart pounded at his nearness. "Was there something you wished of me, Jason? I am certain you will want to get back before you . . . er, we are missed."

"Missed?" Jason's mouth curved. "Our absence might be noticed, of course, but no one will think much of it. They will undoubtedly assume that we are taking advantage of Vauxhall's numerous promenades. The South Walk, perhaps. Or . . . the Dark Walk."

He took another step forward and debated bracing his arm against the tree to really hem her in. She looked unusually delicate, however, against the sturdy tree, and looming over her might not be the best move. He decided it would be difficult for her to get past him as it was, and kept his hands at his sides. She seemed in no great hurry to go anywhere, though it was entirely possible she was simply being polite. Shoving him out of the way would not look particularly good to anyone who might be watching. And she had played her part well under his family's eyes to date.

Well, hell. He had her there and, performance or no, he was going to take advantage of the situation. "Are you familiar with the Dark Walk, Aurelie?"

"I . . . ah, no." The tip of her tongue darted out to moisten her lips, and Jason wondered if he was making her nervous. Whatever the reason, it was a damnably appealing gesture. "It sounds . . . dark."

"That is precisely the point, my dear. It is also known as the Lovers' Walk."

Why are you telling me this? she wanted to ask. Before she could work up the courage to do so, however, her tongue, ever apt to work quicker than her mind, took over. "Are you foxed, Jason?"

His eyes widened in surprise. "Foxed? Good Lord—why would you think that?"

"The champagne was flowing rather freely at supper. And you are not acting at all like yourself."

"Like myself, hmm? I seem to be hearing that quite a lot lately. The consensus seems to be that this marvelous transformation is your doing."

"M-mine? That is hardly an endorsement. I have done nothing but what you have hired me to do."

"Careful. You might tarnish your halo with such words."

Aurelie was suddenly aware of the bark of the tree, rough against her back from shoulder to thigh. "I am no angel," she murmured, thinking of each deception she had embraced in the past month. "You mock me with your insistence."

"I assure you I do no such thing." Strategically placed lanterns kept the Gardens softly illuminated and he was close enough to see that the baby-fine hair at her temples was nearly gold. "Angels always leave."

"I beg your pardon?"

". . . Angels' visits, short and bright; Mortality's too weak to bear them long."

"You are foxed!"

Yes, he probably was, but the wine he had consumed had little to do with it. Nor did he particularly want to be reminded of that fact, especially by the person whose presence was causing the odd inebriation. "Perhaps I am merely waxing poetic. I do remember more from my years of schooling than a few Latin quotations. It was John Norris, I believe, from 'The Parting.' "

Her heart plummeted at the words. The parting. Was he sending her away already? *Please, no.* "I am not going anywhere, my lord."

"Ah, but you will, will you not? Back to your own life,

155

whatever that will be then. What will I do when you are gone, Aurelie? Without you to charm my family, I will have to find a way to placate them on my own."

"I am certain you will manage." *By marrying Eleanor after all?* "I vow you will hardly notice I am gone."

"I doubt that. You have changed me, remember?"

He was mocking her again, and she wondered if anything was worth the torture of staying out her time. If only she had somewhere to go . . .

"Now you look sad," he commented. "Could it be you are not so determined to leave after your three months?"

"I will not be the one to break our agreement, Jason. I will leave . . . as decided."

"As decided. Of course." A good deal could happen in eight weeks, he mused. By the end of that time he could very well have tired of her presence, banished the faint sadness that the thought of her leaving his life invariably brought. She had not seemed to notice his contrived attention to Eleanor, and appeared perfectly content with the thought of leaving him. "But you are here now."

And now would be a very good time to begin tiring of her. He abandoned his earlier scruples and reached out to brace himself against the tree. In the process, his hand caught a loose fold of her dress, pinning it against the trunk. The sensation of touching half silk and half rough wood sent a tremor up his arm.

"Well, Miss Carollan?"

"Well, what?" Her voice was soft as the fabric of her gown, yet with a husky undertone that grated deliciously.

"Well, may I kiss you?"

Oh yes. Please. "Why . . . why would you want to do that? Your family . . . ?"

Now Jason's face was inches from hers, so close that his breath ruffled the fine curls at her temples. "They are probably watching. Not that it matters. I am sotted, Aurelie— remember?"

All she could remember at the moment was the one, brief, heart-stopping kiss he had given her so long ago.

156

Weeks? It seemed more like years, even as it seemed like yesterday. Whatever the time, she had spent it wishing he would touch her again.

So what if he was cup-shot and would regret his behavior later? The regret would be his alone. She had no intention of denying him, nor of being sorry for her own desires. In the end, what brief and contrived warmth he had given her would comprise the dreams she would have on cold Somerset nights.

His grip on her gown kept her from swaying toward him, but she raised her face, her lips parting of their own volition. As his head descended those last inches, she saw the gold lights in his eyes deepen into molten bronze.

Then she saw enough lights to illuminate all of London.

The crash that accompanied them was loud enough to rattle Jason's teeth. As he jerked his chin up, Aurelie jumped and the top of her head connected solidly with his jaw. His curse was both a result of and muffled by the fact that he had just bitten his tongue—hard.

The proprietors of Vauxhall, on a constant quest to outdo the last year's spectacles, had apparently decided to launch all of Britain's fireworks at once. The crowd's cheers mingled with the lively shrieks of ladies trying to avoid the falling ashes. A new burst, which filled the sky with blue, white, and red lights, inspired a patriotic roar that would have completed the deafening of anyone whose hearing had not been savaged by the fireworks. It was certainly a memorable moment as far as the spectators were concerned.

As far as Jason was concerned, the moment had ended the moment and he heartily wished a long and uncomfortable demise to whomever was responsible.

It was one thing to kiss Aurelie when the air was still and soft under the stars. It was altogether different when the skies were filled with vulgar lights, the cheers of half of London, and the crashing of explosives.

He far preferred to create his own fireworks. In a far more private setting.

"I think," he announced grimly, "I need another drink."

Aurelie disagreed. One more drink would probably make him forget he had even had the desire to kiss her, let alone almost done so. But his face was set again in tensely resolute lines and she knew a protest would be of no avail.

"Shall we return?"

"Of course." He offered his arm and they walked slowly back to the boxes.

The scene that greeted them was enough to send the devil himself fleeing for safety. Phoebe, overexcited by the display, was running in circles, crying, "Boom!" again and again at the top of her voice. Usually stalwart Freddy had been frightened by the huge noises and was howling lustily in his mother's lap.

The countess sat rigidly in her seat, scowling at the world in general. A good many of the elegant people in the surrounding boxes were scowling as well and Aurelie was hard put not to voice her opinion of their attitude loudly and clearly. They ignored the revelry of the lowlier visitors to the park, and turned blind eyes to the carousing of drunken Society bucks. When it was a child causing the disturbance, however, even if it was one of their own class, the ton reacted with stern disapproval.

No wonder young men behaved so outrageously, she mused, her gaze shifting between a group of intoxicated dandies and the children. They had learned that negative notice was all they were likely to get from their parents.

When Phoebe plowed, still shouting, into Jason's legs, he reacted with admirable aplomb. He reached down and caught one of her flailing arms, lifted her off the ground, and tucked her firmly under his arm. Then, wiggling bundle in tow, he announced, "I believe it is time to depart," and walked off toward the gates.

Aurelie stayed long enough to help Catherine calm Freddy. In the end, a piece of raspberry tart did the trick quite efficiently. She made no complaint when, once they were settled in the carriage, he insisted on sitting in her lap, leaving a trail of sticky, purple handprints across her skirts.

Catherine had happily left the children to ride in Jason's vehicle, going off herself to join her mother.

Michaela, demure as always, sat quietly in her seat. Phoebe bounced happily in Jason's lap, declaring him to be much better at "horsey" than her father, until he finally held her still. Aurelie was pleased to see he did not remove her from his lap, but allowed her to curl up against his waistcoat. When, after a while, Michaela shyly scooted toward him, he raised his arm and settled her at his side.

Aurelie wanted very much to ask where he had learned such paternal skills. His parents and sister showed no such proclivity. She decided in the end that Jason was simply and basically a good man. Later, as she stared into the canopy above her bed, she tried to convince herself that she was lucky to have known him for even a short time.

What Jason believed about himself was completely true—he would make a very good earl. And whether he believed it or not, someday he would make someone a very good husband.

Jason gazed moodily into the fire. Bed had not been appealing. Nor had White's, Watier's, or any of the other haunts he usually frequented. Instead, he had returned home to the dubious comfort of his library and a bottle of port. He had not been drunk at Vauxhall, but he was fully determined to rectify the matter now.

If nothing else, he needed to drown the persistent voice that was his conscience.

Seeing Aurelie with the children, and Aurelie gazing up at the stars as the breeze fluttered her skirts, he had come to the firm conclusion that she was meant for far more than governessing or teaching. She needed children of her own to hold and cherish. And a husband to give them to her.

More than that, she needed a husband to tap the deep well of heat and passion that would dry up and vanish if she went back to her country life.

Oh yes, she might someday find a farmer or rural squire who would marry her. That thought was utterly unacceptable. She must have someone who could clothe her in soft, rich gowns and provide her with a life where she would have music and soirées and books from floor to ceiling. Someone who would understand what she wanted, and what she could give.

It was time, he decided, for him to start looking for such a man. He would pay for Aurelie to stay for the Season. Yes, that was a marvelous idea. Myrtle, he was sure, would be happy to act as sponsor if she had the house and funds. It should not take long. As soon as it became known that Aurelie had broken her betrothal to him, the bucks would come flocking.

And he would already have one picked out.

He ground his teeth as he considered the task ahead of him. In fact, he was forced to admit, as appropriate and efficient as the plan seemed, it was beyond his capabilities to act upon it. He could not do it, could not watch Aurelie fall into another man's arms. If he was forced to witness such an occurrence, something inside him would break—and bleed.

One thing was certain. He was going to have to come to some conclusion. Quickly. Before he did the inconceivable and married the girl himself.

14

"The Duchess of Thromberton had her skirts quite crushed when she entered," Lady Heathfield announced gleefully, and the crowd of matrons surrounding her all smiled their approval.

Aurelie had been in London long enough now to understand that the ladies present did not dislike the Duchess of Thromberton. On the contrary, they thoroughly admired the lady and looked to her as a Leader of Polite Society. Her presence was much coveted by the ton's hostesses, and her appearance at Grace's ball was a valuable nod.

Even better, however, was the fact that the entryway was so crowded that considerable harm might have come to the duchess's gown. No party was truly a success unless one had to pinch and squeeze to get in.

For her part, Aurelie was feeling both pinched and squeezed. No less than five persons had trod upon her toes in the past fifteen minutes, and she was certain her maid would never be able to get the creases out of her gown. It was a pity, she thought sadly, looking down at her wrinkled skirts, for it was a truly beautiful creation.

It had arrived with the last of Madame LeFevbre's pieces, reaching her in London some days after her arrival. Made of the finest deep rose satin, with a full train, it swirled and rustled elegantly when she moved and brought an equally polished glow to her skin. As seemed to be the norm with Madame's designs, this one boasted a very low, very tight bodice and, with the silver-embroidered sash gathering the fabric tight under her breasts, Aurelie felt something less than fully clothed.

She was at the peak of fashion, no doubt, and spying some of the nearly scandalous costumes other women were wearing, she felt comparatively modest. Enough, at least, so she only gave discreet tugs at the bodice when she was absolutely certain no one was watching.

One of Grace's acquaintances walked up then, an extremely pretty girl with raven hair, bright blue eyes—and very little behind them. Aurelie thought her name was Julianna or Alessandria, or something similarly complicated, but was saved the effort of trying to remember by the girl's lively greeting.

"How well you look this evening, Miss Carolling." Aurelie did not bother to correct her. "Your gown is simply all that is to be!"

Now that was a new one. "Thank you. Though I am afraid it will not survive the crush."

"Oh pooh. I never wear a gown more than once, anyway."

No, I do not suppose you do. She remembered now that Lauretta or Elisabetta was one of the ones "with fortune." That, Grace had informed her, was the only reason she tolerated the vacuous creature—in the hopes that fortune hunters would find her a far easier target for their covetous attentions.

"And I do so admire the way your hair always seems so carefree. One must remind oneself that it is a contrived look. It seems so very natural."

"It is natural," Aurelie admitted wryly, reaching up to push an errant curl back into place.

"Goodness, you mean you actually leave it as it was created? How very quaint. I was going to ask how your dresser managed to do it."

"I am afraid I cannot help you there. Lady Heathfield's maid gave up on me some time past."

"How novel. A future viscountess who sees to her own toilette. Lord Tarrant must be so . . . proud."

Aurelie was actually beginning to wonder if the girl was quite as stupid as she seemed. There was a sharp edge to the breathy voice that hinted at something not particularly pleasant. She scanned the room casually, searching for any known fortune hunter onto whom she could foist the creature.

"They say he is going to cry off, you know."

This brought Aurelie's head around sharply. "I beg your pardon?"

Now there was no doubt about it. The sapphire eyes held a good deal more calculation than vacant space. "Oh, I am so terribly sorry. What a perfectly dismal thing to have said. I just do so hate to see someone spoken of behind her back."

Of course you do. And the Prince Regent adores his wife. "Your concern warms my heart. But I assure you, such rumors are entirely unfounded. Lord Tarrant and I have made a mutually satisfactory agreement."

"Well, of course you would know best. There is often precious little behind rumors anyway. Still, you must realize how avidly people listen when the rumor involves the possible return of one of the ton's most eligible men to the marriage mart." The girl smiled and smoothed her impeccable skirts. "Oh la, there is Lord Cuthbert. I do believe I have promised him the next set."

Aurelie watched her sway off toward the lucky man, aware her own face was very probably the color of her gown. While she knew such intrinsically cruel interchanges were tacitly de rigueur, she had not been prepared. There was little doubt that what the girl had said carried at least a kernel of truth. It was also clear that she considered herself to be among the first in line to take Aurelie's place should the rumor prove true.

There was a small, very small satisfaction in silently predicting Georgienne a severe disappointment if she truly hoped to become Viscountess Tarrant. Jason would die before tying himself to such a creature. But the words had been spoken and their harm done, even if they were close to the truth. He would be returning to eligibility soon. The only real question was whether that state would last until the end of the year.

She had not seen much of him since the receiving line. He had partnered her in the expected dance, a cotillion that offered little chance for conversation, then handed her off to her next partner and disappeared. She had thought she had seen his eyes darken in appreciation at the sight of her in her gown, which he himself had commissioned. But, considering how little he had looked at her since, she might very well have been mistaken.

The steady stream of young men who begged for dances had done much to boost her ego, as had Grace's whispered assertion that she had been labeled an "Original"—a success, to be sure. Her mind, however, insisted on wandering from pleasant thoughts to those far less appealing. Jason was nowhere to be found. Nor was Lady Eleanor, who had arrived in habitual splendor.

As Aurelie's mind wandered, her eyes continually strayed to the row of French windows opening onto the gardens. Though the moon was full, the terrace offered countless shadowed alcoves where a couple might avoid notice. Then, of course, there were the gardens themselves, with their high hedges and Grecian bower . . .

The more melodramatic her thoughts became, the more she scolded herself for being such a fool. A fool for making herself miserable over a faux fiancé's whereabouts, and an even bigger fool for having fallen in love with him.

"Idiot," she chided herself. *"Idiot!"*

"I sincerely hope you are not speaking to me."

She spun about, face flaming. "Rafe. I did not see you arrive."

"Oh, I've been here for a while—just took me a dashed long time to get to you. You have been quite in demand this evening." When she smiled weakly, he offered his arm. "You look as if you could use something cool."

"Yes, I could. Thank you."

They made their way to the refreshment tables and Rafe

procured two glasses of champagne. He then found a quiet corner and commandeered a pair of chairs. "Now," he said companionably, "who were you calling an idiot?"

"Myself, of course."

He graced her with his usual cheerful grin. "Why in the world would you do that?"

"Because I am an idiot. I am a firm believer in calling a duck a duck."

"So call yourself a duck then. I rather like ducks."

Aurelie laughed for a moment, then said solemnly, "I shall miss you, Rafe. You have been a good friend."

"Miss me? Good heavens, that sounds dire. Are you going somewhere? No—wait. Am *I* going somewhere?"

"Please, Rafe. Be serious for a minute. I think I might be leaving London sooner than I had expected." At his concerned urging, she related her unpleasant encounter with Antoinette. "Not that her attitude was a terrible surprise, but it was distinctly disturbing to hear my own thoughts coming from a relative stranger's mouth."

"Rubbish," was the immediate response. "Christabelle is an unmitigated jade." *Christabelle—of course.* "I cannot believe you would take anything she said to heart. Nor let it run you out of Town."

Aurelie sighed and stared into her empty glass for a moment before setting it aside. "It is more than that and you know it. Jason employed me to, shall we say, divert his family's attentions from Lady Eleanor. I have done so. Now, he appears to be entertaining very real thoughts of courting the lady, making it foolish for me to stay." She turned heartsick eyes to her companion. "It is not that I wish to leave. I have had such a marvelous time." *And I stipulated three months for a reason, after all.* "I will stay if possible and hold up my end of the bargain. Jason, however . . ." She spread her hands expressively.

She thought she heard Rafe mutter something about blithering idiots, but his voice was muffled by the glass he raised to his lips. He drained his champagne in a single swallow then turned back to regard her. He suddenly looked very somber—and very unlike himself.

"Aurelie, there is an alternative to all of this waiting and wondering."

"Oh, and what is that?"

"You could marry me."

Had he suggested that she transform herself into a banshee and wail gloom and doom to the Granvilles, she could not have been more astonished. He was, quite obviously, perfectly serious. "You mean that."

"Absolutely." He leaned forward and took her hand. "Think about it. It serves both our purposes. I need to get married eventually, and you are a marvelous woman. On top of that—correct me if I am wrong, part of your reason for seeking a position was to avoid a miserable situation, probably a marriage."

She was truly astounded. "How on earth did you know that?"

Rafe's smile was wry. "I am a good deal more perceptive than most people think. I noticed in our initial meeting that you reacted to what Tare set out as his plight. And I know what you have done for Grace . . ."

"Now you could not possibly have known *that* . . . unless Jason . . ."

"Grace, too, is far more perceptive than her family wants to believe. She knows you have intervened with Jason on her behalf."

"Oh." She could think of nothing further to say on the subject.

"Look, Aurelie, we are very much alike in many ways. We both approach life with good cheer and we both prefer the simplicity of the country to London. There is a mutual affection and admiration, I think, which would allow us to rub along quite pleasantly."

Aurelie did not misunderstand his phrasing. With a soft smile, she covered his hand with her free one. "A mutual affection, yes. There certainly is that. But you do not love me, Rafe. At least not as anything more than a dear friend."

"True, but the vast majority of Society marriages are based on far less."

"Hmm. I imagine they are. But we are not the vast majority of people, are we? You are a marvelous man, Rafael Marlowe, and I doubt I shall ever be so blessed by another. I thank you with all my heart for your offer, but it would be folly for us to marry. I think we both deserve the best we can get in a mate."

He grinned then, clearly not in the least offended by her refusal. "Are we not the respective best?"

Aurelie laughed with him. "To be sure, we are. Just not for each other."

"You're right, of course. But I needed to ask."

"And I can never thank you enough for being willing to do that for me. I think it is perhaps the single most selfless act I have ever witnessed."

Rafe promptly placed a finger over her lips. "Don't spoil your lovely self-esteem by being noble. I did not offer purely for your good. I know I will be fortunate to ever be blessed by a woman like you."

They sat in amicable silence for a time as the ball whirled around them. Then he said, "He is a fine man and deserves to be loved. Just not by you, I believe."

"I beg your pardon?"

"Come now, Cousin, we are being honest here. You are in love with Jason, are you not?"

Aurelie debated denying it but found she could not. "I hoped I was keeping it hidden."

"Oh, you are. But, as I said, I am a perceptive fellow. The question is—what do you intend to do about it?"

"Do?" She pondered the odd query. "Why, nothing. I shall stay till I am no longer . . . wanted. Then I shall leave. I can go home eventually."

Rafe's eyes sharpened, but he did not press her. Instead, he squeezed her hand and said, "You will do as you see fit, of course, but I hope you do not intend to martyr yourself unnecessarily."

"And what is that supposed to mean?"

"It means," he replied as he rose to his feet, pulling her with him, "that you need to spend less time trying to assure others' happiness, and reach out to attain your own."

He refused to say anything more on the subject but, as he returned her to Lady Heathfield's circle, he whispered, "Should you prove a cowardly failure, however, my offer stands. I do not relish the concept of losing you altogether."

Bewildered, she watched him go. A cowardly failure? She had no idea what he had meant by that and was not quite feeling up to figuring it out.

"You look peaked, girl. Sit down."

Aurelie turned toward the voice. It belonged to one of a pair of matrons who were regally ensconced on a settee. "Madam?"

They were very similar in appearance, perhaps a few years older than Lady Heathfield. Both were handsome women with silver hair and sharp brown eyes. They were elegant to a fault, but there was an unmistakable warmth in their gazes.

"Sit down, my dear, and join us."

It was a command, yet a pleasant one. Unable to do otherwise, Aurelie complied.

"Now you," one lady announced, "are Miss Carollan, young Tarrant's betrothed, are you not?"

"I am."

"Thought so," the second said. "We have not been formally introduced. I am Lady Fielding and this is my sister, Mrs. DeLancey. We are widows."

"I see," Aurelie replied carefully, not at all certain she did.

"I have informed you of that fact because you, my dear, do not look like a young woman pleased with her situation."

Now Aurelie could only gape. Mrs. DeLancey smiled and leaned forward to pat her hand. "Constance has always been a bit ... forceful in her assertions. Do not take offense."

"Really, Felicity," her sister admonished sharply, "Miss

Carollan did no such thing. Did you, my dear? No, I thought not." She rapped her fan against the arm of the settee. "We happened to overhear your conversation with that Christabelle Harrowby. Nasty chit."

"Terribly forward," Mrs. DeLancey added.

"We have heard you are an Original, Miss Carollan. I would venture to agree."

"I . . . thank you, my lady."

"Do not." Lady Fielding now swept her fan in Aurelie's direction. "Being labeled an Original usually means you have far more intelligence than the ton can handle, and it does not know quite what to call it. Both Felicity and I were Originals."

Yes, I'm certain you were. Aurelie was not quite sure why, but she was beginning to like these old hens immensely. "What makes you think I am so intelligent?"

"It is in your face, girl. Right along with the misery."

"I assure you, my lady, I am hardly . . ."

"You really need not deny it," Mrs. DeLancey said kindly. "We are seldom wrong."

"Well, I . . ."

"You have been forced into this arrangement, and it is going badly." Lady Fielding did not bother to wait for affirmation. "We were both married off at our parents' discretion. Not that our husbands were bad men . . ."

"Oh, no," her sister agreed. "They were perfectly decent, but . . ."

"It was not what we wanted, nonetheless. We have had to wait until our widowhood to really enjoy life. You, my dear, should not make the same mistake."

Aurelie was far more intrigued than offended by their interest. "Sometimes a woman must marry to even have a life."

"Sometimes," Lady Fielding agreed. "But you do not."

"I am afraid I do not understand, madam."

Mrs. DeLancey leaned forward. "Why, really, my dear— your father must have left you quite well off. Warren Carollan was an intelligent man."

Aurelie felt the color draining from her face. "You know of my father?"

"Of course, dearest. Sir Warren was a friend of the late Lord Fielding. You have the look of him. Splendid man. Though I must say his judgment was a bit lacking when he left you under the guardianship of your uncle."

Now Aurelie was certain she was going to faint. She had been so convinced that no one in London could possibly connect her with her family in Somerset. She glanced around quickly to see if anyone had been listening. To her immense relief, no one had.

"So they do not know who you really are?" Lady Fielding gazed at her speculatively. "Curious."

Her sister, noting Aurelie's pallor, said quietly, "I believe Miss Carollan has her reasons, Constance, and you have given her quite a fright. Worry not, my dear, your secret is safe with us."

"Thank you, madam." Aurelie's heart slowed its frantic pounding.

"Curious," Lady Fielding repeated. "I do hope you will tell us about it. And why you have got yourself into this arrangement with Tarrant. Which," she added tartly, "is clearly not a good one."

"Constance," her sister chided yet again, then reached into her reticule. "Here is our card, dearest. Do visit. In fact"—she smiled angelically as she pressed the card into Aurelie's stiff fingers—"we are departing for Bath at the end of the week. You might want to join us. Yes, what a lovely idea. Though your fiancé might not approve. He is bearing down on us now with a rather frightening expression on his face. . . ."

"Jason? Where?"

"Right behind you, dear . . . Why, hello, Lord Tarrant. We were just having the nicest little chat with Miss Carollan."

"Good evening, Lady Fielding. Mrs. DeLancey." Jason bent over each lady's hand. "I hope you will forgive me for

170

depriving you of Miss Carollan's company. She had promised me this waltz."

Without waiting for a reply, he pulled Aurelie from her seat and swept her toward the dance floor. She glanced back over her shoulder to find the sisters waving, eyes sharp in their wrinkled faces. She gave a small wave in return and stifled a hysterical giggle. Not only had she received a proposal of marriage from a future duke in the past half hour, but she had also had her identity discovered and a second offer of rescue tendered.

"Bloody hell," she murmured.

"What was that?" Jason asked, swinging her into the waltz.

"Oh, nothing . . ."

Jason rather thought he had heard her curse, but he was not sure. Nor was he particularly interested in listening at the moment. He wanted to look. She was almost impossibly lovely in the pink gown. As always, her hair had managed to escape its confines, and a thick, glossy curl had fallen over her shoulder, pointing an enticing trail down her creamy skin.

And the gown's fashionable bodice did bare an appealing expanse. She had been tugging at the edge all evening, thinking no one was watching. She had been wrong. From whatever vantage point he'd attained, Jason had watched. Watched as she had danced, conversed, rested. He had been ready to intervene when Grace's vacuous friend had approached her, seeing the well-veiled distress in her silver eyes, and again when something the old biddy Fielding said made her pale.

He had quite been ready to do violence when he had seen Rafe holding her hand.

Now, as he held her in his arms, he decided it was high time to do *something*. In the early hours of morning, having reached the bottom of a port bottle, he had come to the conclusion that he was not likely to tire of her any time in the near future, if at all. And nothing had alarmed him as much in his life.

"Aurelie," he said softly, willing her to look up. The top of her head was charming, but he preferred to speak to her face. A second later, he was not so sure, finding himself snared by the forthright gaze. "I believe we need to talk."

"All right."

She hardly sounded enthusiastic, and Jason ground his teeth. This was going to be difficult enough as it was without her making him feel like an utter clod. "I think"—he was forced to pause to clear his throat—"that perhaps we need to discuss our arrangement."

"Of course, my lord." She dropped her head again and was staring somewhere past his left shoulder.

"This is perhaps not the best place to do it."

"As you wish."

I wish you would look at me, damn it! "I cannot very well take you out of the room without attracting notice. Will you meet me in the library in ten min—" He broke off when she came to a sudden halt in the middle of a turn. "What is the matter?" Tilting her chin up, he was astonished to see her face was a chalky white. "My God, Aurelie . . ."

"Please," she gasped, breaking free of his grasp, "please . . . I am . . . unwell. Beg your mother's forgiveness and tell her I have gone to my chamber."

She stared fixedly at a spot behind him for an instant. Then, in a swirl of rose satin, she rushed off toward the doorway. Jason stood rooted to the spot until she had vanished. Finally, he turned away and, ignoring the speculative gazes her hasty exit had attracted, scanned the area at which she had been staring.

Nothing seemed unusual. A few plants, a refreshment table, and a man in a tight, appalling yellow green coat. Jason was ready to turn away when something about the man struck him as familiar. Yes, that was it. He had seen that coat before—at Almack's.

Other than that brief encounter, he could not remember ever having encountered the fellow before. He was not a member of the London set, certainly, and most likely had

172

not been invited to the ball. But it was fairly easy to get into any big affair, even without an invitation. All one had to do was accompany someone on the guest list and look as if one belonged. It happened all the time.

This particular guest, however, had upset Aurelie. Images of former employers flashed through Jason's mind, and he stalked off the dance floor, ready to first get some answers and then to chuck the bounder out the nearest window. By the time he reached the refreshment table, however, the man was nowhere to be seen. Well, in that coat, he could not remain invisible indefinitely. Jason went in search of a drink and prepared to wait.

Upstairs, Aurelie sat trembling on the edge of her bed. She was quite certain Fenwick had not seen her. But he had been there, bold as brass in the middle of the Heathfields' home. She could not believe he had been invited, but that had never stopped him in the past. Always on the lookout for an entrée into High Society, he would know how to ride someone else's coattails, so to speak, into the finer ball-rooms.

The odd part, she decided, when her trembling had subsided a bit, was that he had not appeared to be looking for her. Never the best at hiding his thoughts, Fen could not possibly have looked so unconcerned if he had discovered her whereabouts. Could it be that his presence was a coincidence? Before that night, Aurelie had not been much of a believer in coincidence, but her encounter with the elderly sisters had proven her wrong.

Far from reassured, she tried to decide what to do next. If Fen was aware of her situation, he would be back. Even worse, Lionel and Edwina might be with him. He could not very well drag her out of the Heathfields' home without proof of his father's guardianship. He could, however, tell his family where she was—and Jason's family exactly *who* she was. That in itself was not an insurmountable tragedy. Rafe, she was certain, would stand by his claim that she was a cousin, and his word would carry far more weight than Fenwick's.

So she had a few days at least before anything truly terrible could happen.

The real question was whether her family really had the greatest power to hurt her. In the seconds before she had seen Fenwick, she'd come to the chilling conclusion that Jason wanted to talk to her about ending their arrangement early. That was, after all, the only reasonable explanation. So, in a matter of days—no, he would allow her a week— she would be expected to cry off the engagement and disappear.

And she would have to do it.

15

S HE WOKE THE next morning feeling as if she had im-
bibed a full case of champagne despite the fact that she
had had no more than two glasses. Her head hurt and everything seemed just a bit out of focus. There was, too, a
sick, heavy sensation in the pit of her stomach and she debated staying in bed. Such behavior would attract far too
much attention, however, so she forced herself to rise and
get dressed. There was nothing she could do about the
shadows under her eyes and hoped they would be attributed
to the night's revelry and not to emotional chaos.

Fashionable always, the Heathfield residence did not become active until well after noon, giving Aurelie several
hours to herself before luncheon. After assuring Grace that
she felt quite well and that yes, the ball had been a wonderful experience, she sat back in her chair and hoped no one
would take further notice of her presence. She was not to
be so lucky.

"Jason sent over a message for you this morning." Lady
Heathfield waved the missive in Aurelie's direction. "He
shall be joining us for supper and hopes you will have a
few minutes free beforehand."

Aurelie wanted very much to take the older woman to
task for reading her note but thought better of it. As long
as she did not make a fuss, no one would have reason to
suspect the message was anything more than Jason's desire
to have some time alone with his fiancée.

"I believe it is high time to begin planning the wedding,"
the countess announced firmly. "The end of August, I think.

St. Paul's." Aurelie managed to smother her groan in her tea. "If we visit Madame Junot this week, she should have ample time to create a gown. Pale yellow satin would be nice, with seed pearls."

"Mama"—Grace scolded from across the table—"you must ask Aurelie if she has any wishes on the matter. It is, after all, her wedding."

"Fustian. You have no close family, have you, Aurelie?"

"No, only distant cousins . . ."

"Just so. Lord Holcombe will, of course, stand up for Jason, and his aunt will be invited. Now, Jason will undoubtedly want to provide you with your own jewels, but for the wedding you will have Lord Heathfield's grandmother's pearls. . . ."

It seemed far easier to listen quietly than to protest, and Aurelie managed to do so. When the countess began discussing the names of her future grandchildren, however, she felt her stomach begin churning. Thankfully, she was rescued by the arrival of the three named and animate grandchildren.

"Grandmama, Freddy was climbing on the draperies," Phoebe announced loudly, pausing halfway down the table to grab a handful of cherries.

"Was not." Her brother, unable to reach the food, stopped at Aurelie's side and proceeded to climb her skirts. "I'm hungry."

"Children!" Lady Heathfield's hand hit the table with a resounding crack. "You know you are to have your meals in the nursery."

"It was tongue," Phoebe said disdainfully. "We don't like tongue."

By this time, Michaela had made her way to the table, out of breath from running after her siblings. "I am sorry, Grandmama. I told them not to disturb you." She, too, gazed longingly at the spread of food and Aurelie's heart went out yet again to this child who, at eight, had taken on the adult responsibility of caring for the younger two.

Freddy, while reaching for a piece of ham, managed to

176

upset Aurelie's glass. It was a small spill, but Lady Heathfield treated it like a disaster of epic proportions. Shouting for a footman to clean up the negligible mess, she swatted at her grandson with her napkin. The boy promptly scuttled under the table and Aurelie took advantage of the distraction to tuck a few pastries into her napkin.

Holding the parcel out of sight behind her skirts, she rose to her feet and called to the children. "Come along now. We will go upstairs and entertain ourselves."

Lady Heathfield snorted what might have been approval and gave a last flutter of her napkin. Grace, for her own part, was trying not to laugh and, as Aurelie passed, pressed another napkin into her hand. It was faintly greasy and Aurelie suspected chicken. She passed the parcel to Michaela and, giving Grace a conspiratorial smile, ushered the children out of the room.

She followed them upstairs to the nursery to discover that Phoebe had managed to fill her pinafore pockets with cherries and Freddy had escaped with a chocolate tart as well as his fistful of sliced ham. In the end, the four settled themselves on the floor of the nursery and enjoyed a make-shift picnic. From the looks of the luncheon arranged on the table, they had indeed been given unappetizing fare. Aurelie silently cursed Catherine for not seeing to the matter, but the woman had gone off shopping earlier, and the children's nanny was still recovering from her illness.

"Will you tell us the rest of the story now?" Michaela asked after a time, daintily wiping the last remnants of chocolate from her fingers.

"Yes, I will," Aurelie agreed, "as soon as Phoebe and Freddy tidy themselves up."

Both seemed to be wearing as much food as they had consumed, and in the end it was Aurelie who did most of the tidying. Freddy tolerated being wiped down with good grace, but Phoebe squirmed throughout.

"Now, where did we stop?"

"Emer was taking her knife to kill Fand," Phoebe said immediately.

"Knife," Freddy repeated, and scrambled off to locate a wooden saber that he had found in a chest.

"Ah, yes, at the yew tree at Baile's Strand . . ."

So, leaving behind her a trail of tears, Emer made her way to where her husband would be meeting the faery queen. Cuchulainn was there in the shade of the tree, with Fand sitting upon his lap. Around them were a bevy of Fand's servants, fey creatures playing sweet music on flutes and pipes.

The faery queen saw Emer approaching and stood up. The two women faced each other. Fand's glorious beauty made Emer blink as if she were looking into the sun. She knew in that moment she could never destroy one so perfect, nor could she hope to compete.

"This faery is without equal, Cuchulainn," she said sadly to her faithless husband. "Yet you never expressed dissatisfaction with who I am. What was it that made you think less of me?"

Now Cuchulainn did not, in truth, think less of his wife. He still thought her fair, and he loved her as much as his heart allowed him to love. He certainly did not love the other woman any more than Emer, but he was entranced by Fand's ethereal beauty and grace. She was a faery, magical and mystical, while his wife was flesh and blood—a mortal woman. Emer was, however, good and pure, and he remembered the sunshine her love had once been. Torn by his feelings, he searched his beleaguered mind for an answer to her query.

Emer bent to unstrap the dagger from her leg and dropped it on the ground at Fand's feet. "I came to destroy you and reclaim my husband," she said, looking like a proud, heartbroken queen herself, "but I cannot harm you." To Cuchulainn she said, "I will not deny you this woman, with her incomparable beauty and noble blood. Though I know she is no better that I, you have chosen her. What is new and different seems better than what we know and makes us spurn what good we have. I wish you happiness."

With that, she turned to go. Fand, seeing how much this mortal woman loved her husband, threw out a golden net, fine as a spider's web, stopping Emer where she was.

"You are a noble woman, Emer of Carraig na Siúire, and your devotion is more than a man deserves. I see you truly love Cuchulainn, so let me be the one to leave."

Emer shook her head. "I have made the choice for both my husband and myself. I will go, for it is the saddest of fates to have love unrequited. It is better for me to release him than to not have my devotion returned."

The two women stood there, each insisting the other be the one to have Cuchulainn. For, despite the fact that they both wanted him, neither could feel jealousy or hatred.

Cuchulainn sat for a long time like a stone statue, watching the two in their debate. At last, he rose to his feet and stepped between them, taking Emer's hand in one of his, and Fand's in the other.

"Why did you stop? You must tell us the end of the story, Miss Carollan."

"Why don't you tell me how you think the story ends, Michaela," Aurelie replied with a smile.

"Emer leaves Cuchulainn and finds a new, better husband," Phoebe announced decisively, and Aurelie suppressed a laugh. The child had an intelligence and self-esteem that were priceless.

"No, that is not what happened. But perhaps it should have. What do you say, Michaela?"

The girl looked pensive for a moment before answering, "I believe Cuchulainn realized what a terrible mistake he had made, choosing the faery Fand over his wife. I think he begged Emer's forgiveness, and she gave it. Then they returned to their home and lived in love ever after."

"Ah, a happy ending. Did you find a moral to this story?"

"Don't get married," was Phoebe's prompt response.

"Phoebe, that's silly," her sister scolded. "We must all be married at some point, Mama says, or we will be unhappy old maids."

Aurelie winced, then hurried to force a smile back to her lips. Michaela had not intended to say anything hurtful. The children, after all, expected her to marry their uncle soon. Still, she could not completely mask the tremor in her voice as she asked, "And your moral?"

"See the beauty and value in what you have," Michaela replied thoughtfully. "What is novel is not necessarily better and the best of treasures can often be found at home." When Aurelie merely nodded, she queried, "Was I right? Does the story end happily?"

"Of course it does. Cuchulainn returns home with his wife and they live in love ever after. There is more, too. Fand's husband, Manannen, hearing how his desertion hurt her, returns to her side. They are reconciled and find as much happiness as Emer and Cuchulainn."

Michaela smiled contentedly. "That is a wonderful story, Miss Carollan. Will you tell it to us again sometime?"

"Oh, I don't know. There are so many stories to tell. Perhaps you can tell this one to your friends, and later to your children."

And perhaps you will never know that the ending I gave you was not the complete truth. For Cuchulainn returns to Emer only after Fand's Sea-god husband gives them a drink of the Water of Oblivion, making Cuchulainn forget his infatuation with the faery queen and erasing the anger and humiliation from Emer's heart. A happy ending due to magic alone.

There was little magic to be found in Britain now that the faeries were gone from the land.

* * *

"It would take magic, my lord, of which I possess none."

Jason scowled at his valet. "It is merely a bit of raspberry tart, Girvin, not blood."

"That may well be, my lord, but it is several days old. I should have noticed it sooner, but you hung the coat up yourself."

The man's expression clearly told Jason of his opinion on the master doing such a lowly task. Not that Girvin would have been any less affronted at the prospect of removing the purple handprint from the russet superfine at an earlier date. Nor had Jason hidden it from him on purpose. He had not noticed the stain until that very morning and did not remember getting it in the first place. It must have been when he lifted Freddy from Aurelie's lap after Vauxhall.

"Well, it looks as though I will not be wearing the coat today." He handed it to the valet, accepting a pale gray one instead.

"Or ever, most likely," Girvin muttered under his breath, followed by a low curse that seemed to end with *"Children!"*

Jason did not bother to rebuke him. The man's patience had been tried sorely since the children had arrived at Havensgate. From scuffed boots to smudged cravats, Girvin's hands had been full.

It was a shame, really, that the russet was unwearable. The gray reminded him too much of Aurelie's eyes, and he did not want to be distracted from the onset. Things would be tense enough once he had to face those orbs.

He was not looking forward to their interview at all. In fact, he would rather be on his way to Almack's.

Stop in the library on the way out, he told himself. *There should be at least one shot left in the brandy decanter.*

It was three shots, actually, and he was feeling reasonably relaxed by the time he reached his parents' house. It occurred to him that he had taken to drinking at appallingly early hours since he had met Aurelie. All hours, to tell the truth. Well, if all went as planned, that would cease soon enough.

His family was apparently occupied with callers when he arrived, but the butler informed him that Miss Carollan was in the morning room. He found her curled up on one of his mother's impossibly uncomfortable settees, head buried in a book.

"Good morning."

The book hit the floor with a resounding thump. "You just took ten years off my life," she gasped, hand over her heart.

Jason chuckled. "Sorry. Next time I will be certain to make a louder entrance." He bent over to retrieve her book. "*The Aeneid*. I should have expected as much. Do you ever read novels, Aurelie?"

She deftly removed the book from his hands. "Of course. Though I must admit Mrs. Radcliffe is a bit wearing on one's intelligence." She hoped he could not see that her hands were shaking. "And even Miss Austen cannot come up with phrases like 'through the friendly silence of the quiet moon.'"

"Or *sic itur ad astra*."

"'Thus shall you go to the stars.' You know Virgil."

Jason lowered himself onto one of the delicate chairs. "Have we not had this discussion before? I thought we had reached a plateau of mutual literary admiration."

"So we had." Aurelie would have liked very much to banter in Latin for an hour or so—anything to stave off what was coming. But she'd had enough of her own cowardice for a while. "I apologize for last night. I know you wished to speak with me."

He stretched out his legs, nearly touching hers. "You seem quite recovered. Who was he?"

"Who was . . . ?"

"Come now, Aurelie, you can do better than that."

Coward! "I am afraid I really do not know what you mean."

Jason never appreciated being told a lie. He especially did not appreciate it from Aurelie. For such a convincing fiancée, she was an appalling prevaricator.

182

"The man who sent you fleeing for cover last night. The one in the awful coat." He had waited quite a long time for the man to reappear, with no luck. "Did you work for him? Did he hurt you, or try to . . . force himself on you?"

"Fenwick? Good Lord, what a thought!" Her eyes widened as she realized what she had said. Then she gave a resigned sigh. "I do not suppose you would let the matter drop if I were to ask."

"I might, eventually. Fenwick, hmm. Last name?" She merely stared at him. "Not willing to answer that one? All right. Why does he frighten you?"

Aurelie searched for any explanation that was neither the truth nor an outright lie. "He is someone from . . . home. And he does not frighten me. Not really. It is very complicated, and very simple, and all I will say is that he is not a good person."

"You expect me to let it go at that?"

"Have we not had this discussion before? I'm sorry, Jason—that was impertinent. But we agreed there would be questions I would choose not to answer. Why I dislike Fenwick is one of them. Can you accept that?"

His eyes had darkened dangerously and Aurelie was reminded of how very much he liked to be in control of matters. For a second, she debated telling him the whole, miserable tale and asking for his aid. But the deception had gone on too long for her to be truthful now, so she sat quietly and waited for his response.

"I am not certain what I can accept, Aurelie. You are, after all, my fiancée . . ."

"No, Jason, I am not. I am pretending to be betrothed to you. Nothing more."

"Fair enough." *Was it?* At the moment, he did not really think so. "In fact, it is our engagement that I wished to discuss. Though," he added grimly, "if I see this Fenwick again, I might have to hit him." From Aurelie's expression, he surmised it was an appealing concept. "What I wished to say is that I feel . . . that I . . . Oh, hell. The arrangement

183

is no longer working to my satisfaction and I believe we need to end the deception."

"End it?"

"Don't look so crestfallen. I have an idea that will work for both of us."

He was startled when she shot to her feet, even more so when she threw the book down on the settee and rounded on him. "I don't want any more of your money, Jason! I would like a week, though, to make plans before I leave."

"What are you talking about? You do not need a week. We can settle the matter here and now."

Her eyes widened perceptibly in her pale face and she made a single small, choked sound. Jason, having no idea what was going through her mind, decided conversation could wait. She looked as if she needed a drink. He crossed the room and was reaching for the bellpull when the door flew open.

"Early, come quick! Freddy's stuck!"

Now Jason would have sat Phoebe down and got the whole story out of her. Aurelie, on the other hand, was out of the room in a flash. Having little choice but to follow, he did.

Aurelie was forced to run to keep up with Phoebe. Her own distress had been forgotten at the sight of the little girl's face. Whatever fix Freddy was in had to be a bad one to terrify his sister so. When they reached the ballroom, Phoebe skidded to a halt and pointed toward the row of French doors.

"He's there."

All Aurelie could see was a line of chairs and a few potted trees left over from the ball. "Where, sweetheart? I cannot see him."

"Up there."

And up there was exactly where Freddy was. A good fifteen feet above the floor, the little boy was clinging to the valance rod, whimpering softly. Michaela was standing below him, wringing her hands in helpless anguish. Aurelie's breath caught in her throat as she noted the distance between the boy and the hard parquet floor.

"Phoebe," she whispered, "go find a footman and tell him to bring a ladder."

The child nodded and turned to go.

"Oh, I do not think that will be necessary." Aurelie watched as Jason calmly strode across the floor. "Pardon me," he said to Michaela as he took her place directly below the boy. "Tell me, young man, how did you manage to get all the way up there?"

"He was climbing the draperies again," Michaela explained. "I have told him not to, but he slipped out of the nursery."

Her voice shook with suppressed sobs, and Jason patted her cheek. "It is not your fault, sprite." Then he turned his attention back to Freddy. "Climbing the curtains, again, hmm? You must be quite an expert by now. Sorry to end your fun, my man, but it is time to come down."

"Can't," was the faint response.

Aurelie was beginning to think Jason was either a little daft or totally unfeeling, expecting the little boy to climb down. Her opinion was instantly changed when he reached his arms up as far as he could. Freddy's dangling feet were still several feet higher, but his intention was clear.

"You can do it. All you have to do is let go."

"Can't. Too far."

"Freddy, I was a soldier, was I not?"

" 'Gainst Napoleen," Phoebe chirped, her confidence in her uncle obviously far greater than her brother's. She was, however, the one standing on the floor. "With Wellington."

"Quite right. And who won the war, Freddy? Napoleon or Wellington?"

"Wellington, of course," Phoebe answered. Freddy was not saying much of anything.

"Of course. Now, Freddy, since Wellington beat Napoleon and I helped Wellington, I must be a trustworthy fellow, mustn't I?" Freddy might have nodded, but it was hard to tell. "Very wise of you to see that. Now you will let go and I will catch you. Agreed?"

Aurelie stepped forward to touch his shoulder. "He is petrified, Jason. I doubt he could let go if he wanted to. Let me find a ladder."

He merely gave her a fleeting smile. "You might want to stand back, my dear. Thank you. Now Freddy"—his voice deepened audibly—*"let go!"*

To Aurelie's astonishment, Freddy did. There was a jumble of flailing limbs, an ominous tearing noise, then the sound of the boy's sobs as his uncle cradled him in his arms.

"Good man," he said softly. "Wellington would be proud."

He glanced around to see that Michaela was crying silently, her lower lip caught tight between her teeth. Aurelie was decidedly pale, her skin exactly mirroring the white of her sprigged muslin morning gown. Phoebe, on the other hand, was grinning from ear to ear, clapping her hands in delight at the show.

Freddy's face was buried in his cravat, ruining Girvin's impressive starched arrangement with his tears. "All right, troops," Jason announced with forced cheerfulness, now feeling the thundering of his own pulse in his ears. "I think it is high time for some refreshment. I believe we can persuade Cook to provide lemonade. And something to eat as well"—he glanced over his shoulder—"before Michaela consumes her own lip."

This earned him a few watery giggles. Even Aurelie cracked a smile. As they filed out of the room, Jason felt a draft. Looking down, he found the sleeve of his coat was separated from the shoulder, displaying a rather large amount of his white linen shirt.

Not that it mattered in the least. He felt marvelous. Girvin, on the other hand, was going to have a stroke.

They were just crossing the hall when the parlor door crashed open. A screaming banshee who could have been his youngest sibling flew out, trailed closely by his parents.

186

"Not if hell freezes over and pigs fly!" Grace shrieked, coming to an undignified halt as she avoided crashing into him. "I will crawl naked over broken glass first!"

Freddy promptly stopped his snuffling and peered around the severed sleeve. Jason frowned as he surveyed his sister's flushed cheeks and snapping eyes. "I sincerely hope that will not be necessary. Care to tell me what the devil is going on?"

"Perfect choice of words!" Grace raged. "They"—she threw out her arm to point at her mother and father—"intend to see me married to the Devil himself!"

16

"I WAS NOT aware he was in Town for the Season," Jason muttered under his breath, and Aurelie poked him in the ribs.

"Hush!"

"Grace," Lady Heathfield said sternly, "such hysterics are completely uncalled-for. Your behavior is beyond unacceptable."

"Lord Fremont," her daughter retorted, "is beyond unacceptable. I will not have him!"

"You will, girl, and that is the end of it!"

"He is a fatuous popinjay!"

"He is a high-ranking peer of the realm, whose wealth and property quite exceed your own value!"

There was a moment of ominous silence where the only audible sound was the ticking of the hall clock.

Then, *"Fremont?"* Jason's bellow all but rattled the walls. He rounded on his father. "Fremont made an offer for Grace—and you *accepted* it?"

"Quite right, I did. Old money, older family—father likes fishing." The earl's bushy brows drew together as he studied his son's face. "Well, dash it all, boy—what is the matter? You said you liked the man. . . ."

"I said I *knew* the man. I never said I liked him. In fact, I believe I expressed the opinion that he was not at all suitable for Grace."

"That is hardly a specific enough reason for me to refuse his suit."

"Perhaps not," Jason snapped, "but his habit of hiring

prostitutes for the express purpose of beating them certainly should be!"

"Jason!" Lady Heathfield's gasp was nearly drowned out by Grace's shriek.

"What's a positoot?" Phoebe asked, and Aurelie recovered sufficiently from her own shock to shake her head warningly.

"Now, Father," Jason growled, "I suggest you contact Fremont and inform him that, after careful consideration, you have decided his offer is not acceptable. If you do not, I will very likely be forced to call him out . . ."

"Now see here, young man . . ."

". . . and while I am an accomplished marksman, I have never fought a duel. Fremont has, and word is he cheats. Lucky, I suppose, that you produced an heir and a spare, because Rickey might inherit the title after all."

Lord Heathfield continued to bluster, and for once his mutterings did not include *"Irish."* The conclusion of whatever he was saying was drowned out by the resounding clang of the doorbell. The butler scurried nervously into the hall and cast a beseeching look at his employers.

"Perhaps we should adjourn to the drawing room," the countess said stiffly and the group filed after her, Grace still sputtering and Lord Heathfield mumbling vague invectives.

Aurelie followed them into the room, then removed Freddy from Jason's arms and signaled for the girls to come with her. Both were wide-eyed in awe, and neither seemed inclined to depart such a fascinating exhibition. A fierce glare from their grandmother, however, set them in motion.

Their exit was blocked by the sudden appearance of the butler. "I beg your pardon, but there is a young gentleman here to see Miss Carollan."

Now eight pairs of eyes fastened themselves on Aurelie. "Who is it, Diggs?" she asked nervously, heart pounding.

"I believe he said his name was Oglesby, miss. Fenwick Oglesby."

Now her heart gave a mighty lurch and landed in the pit

189

of her stomach. So he had found her after all. "Please inform Mr. Oglesby," she murmured through stiff lips, calling on the only escape that came to mind, "that I am not here."

Diggs bowed and hurried off. Trying to fortify herself with a deep breath, she turned to face the room. She noted, with faint and hysteria-edged amusement, that the matter of the depraved Lord Fremont had been superseded by that of her mysterious visitor.

"A r-rather unpleasant acquaintance . . . from the country," she stammered. "One whom I would rather not receive." At Lady Heathfield's icily disapproving stare, she turned beseeching eyes to Jason. "Lord Tarrant knows of him."

"And agrees wholeheartedly with your assessment of his character." He had spoken almost without thinking, reacting instinctively to her distress. "In fact, perhaps I ought to inform him myself that his presence is not welcome."

"Oh, no—that is not necessary. . . ." Aurelie cried, but he was already on his way out.

He was all the way through the front door when he decided running after the man might not be the best course of action. Instead, he summoned a footman and, pointing to the receding salmon coat and turquoise breeches, instructed the man to follow and report back only when he had ascertained where Oglesby was lodging. The footman, delighted with such an unusual order, set off with alacrity.

Jason was back in the library within five minutes, planning to send the children off to the kitchens and remove Aurelie to the parlor to finish their talk. He arrived only to find she had gone upstairs with Grace, who had informed her parents in no uncertain terms that she would not come down until Fremont had been summoned and summarily dispatched.

Dinner was looking to be a dismal affair, so Jason decided to seek the relative peace of his club. He instructed Diggs to have the sleuth-cum-footman report to him there and, avoiding his parents, took his leave.

* * *

"I would call it a victory," Aurelie said to Grace, trying desperately for a modicum of cheeriness.

"You are an unmitigated optimist," was the tart reply. "If anything, it was the first of many such battles and I was saved only by the intervention of the Toast of His Majesty's army. Jason is hardly likely to step in the next time."

"And why is that?"

"Well, it is hardly his style, for one thing. And"—a flash of familiar spirit appeared in Grace's eyes—"who knows how many of my parents' choices will play fair on the dueling field. Jason only has to lose once. . . ."

"Grace!"

"Ah, now you sound like a Granville. Only members of the family can say my name with such panache. Though to truly fit into the family, you must do so with stunning regularity."

"Grace—"

"See, you're getting it already."

"Grace, really," Aurelie scolded and, hearing herself, laughed.

She sobered quickly, though, at the invasive realization that she would not, in fact, ever be a Granville. Fen had found her out and, if he came up with some clever plan, she might find herself back in Somerset, married to her own family's version of Lord Fremont.

In fact, Lord Fremont would be in very familiar company indeed should he ever meet Edwina's stooges.

Grace was pacing tracks into the carpet and Aurelie wished she would stop. It was more than a bit trying on the nerves. She wished, too—far more charitably—that she could find something truly reassuring to say to the younger girl. At the moment, she was herself finding precious little solace in either fate or Jason's protection. For a time, she had believed him to be her salvation. Now it was quite evident that she was going to have to be her own.

"Things will only improve for you, Grace. At the very least, I think you can be fairly certain your parents will be far more discerning in their choices from now on. And you have definitely proven your strength of will."

"Hah! My will has tried my parents' nerves for years. They are quite immune by now."

Aurelie rose to her feet and grabbed the girl's hands, stilling her pacing. "Your family loves you. You must believe that. They would never intentionally hurt you."

"Intentionally, no." Grace smiled sadly. "But it is a careless sort of affection that we Granvilles breed. What I mean to my family pales in comparison to what they mean to Society."

"Oh, don't say that."

Grace shrugged. "It is much the same for everyone I know. But then, they don't have sisters-in-law like you. I know you are the one who made Jason take an interest in my future. Thank you." She gave Aurelie a brief hug. "I feel better knowing you will be with us."

Sorrow, fierce and guilt-laden, welled in Aurelie's heart and she wanted nothing more at that minute than to confess all. But she could not. Instead, she squeezed the other girl's hand and murmured, "I'm glad I have been able to do something. I will remember how much it meant to you."

"Now you sound sad. It's not like either of us is doomed—yet." Grace stepped back suddenly and studied her closely. "You're not having second thoughts about marrying my brother, are you?"

Aurelie shook her head and gave a twisted smile. "I shall never change my mind about Jason."

"Right—I should hope not. I am counting on having you as an ally for a good many years to come. Now, shall we ring to have supper sent up here? I'm hungry, and I am not leaving this room till I am certain the devil has been dispatched back to the netherworld."

"Now tell me one more time, Mr. Oglesby. What business do you have with Miss Carollan?"

Jason's grip on Fenwick's cravat made it difficult for the man to speak at all, but he managed to croak, "I've told you, my lord. Aurelie is my cousin. I only discovered by chance that she was in Town and thought I would stop by to pay my respects . . ." He broke off with a gasp as Jason tightened his fist and shook him.

"In the middle of the evening? I know it is a foolish concept to make morning visits in the afternoon, but it is bloody rude to make them at seven o'clock."

"But I only learned of her direction this evening . . ."

"You were there last night."

"I was several places last night . . ." Fenwick reached up to disengage Jason's hold but a blast from molten eyes stilled his hand. "Yes, my lord, I was."

"Uninvited."

"I came with . . . friends. I do it all the time—well, sometimes. Very rarely, actually."

"But on this very rare occasion, you just happened to invite yourself to an affair at the house where your cousin was staying. You expect me to believe that? Come now, Oglesby, do I look like a stupid man?"

This had been going on for far too long, and Jason's annoyance quite matched his disgust. Fenwick's face was now the same bright hue as his coat. "Yes, my lord . . . I mean no, my lord. You do not look stupid. But yes, er . . . no—I did not know Aurelie was there. I didn't know until today when I joined a group in the park discussing your sister's fete. The fact that you were to marry a Miss Carollan entered the conversation. You must believe me—I had heard nothing of the matter before."

Jason could not resist shaking the man once again, but his heart was not in the act. The damnable thing was that most of the worm's story rang true. He knew of Somerset and Aurelie's grandmother, more perfectly reasonable details about the Carollan family, in fact, than Jason himself knew. Beyond that, Oglesby clearly knew a great many things he was not telling.

He would. Lying effectively was obviously not one of his strengths, if indeed he had any. Nor could he hide the fact that the end of this interview could not come soon enough.

Jason, on the other hand, prided himself on both coolness and patience. With that thought, he graciously released Fenwick's cravat and watched impassively as much of the pent-up color receded from the naturally florid face.

The man sat down heavily in the nearest chair, sending up a faint cloud of dust. The footman had provided Oglesby's direction, which proved to be a marginally disreputable inn near Covent Garden. Glancing around the dingy room, Jason was reasonably certain of the knave's purpose in seeking out his cousin.

"Did you think to take advantage of my pockets, Oglesby?"

"What?" The word was croaked rather than spoken, and Jason figured the man would have a mildly sore throat for a day or so. The concept did not bother him in the least.

"I sincerely doubt Miss Carollan would have considered giving you money, let alone asked me for it. She does not think too highly of you, I am afraid to say." Oglesby looked genuinely surprised. "Have I shocked you? What a shame. How disconcerting it must be to discover one's cousin would prefer to consort with poisonous reptiles."

"No doubt of that. We can't stand each other. It was the bit about the money that got me."

Pleased to have at last provoked a genuine response, Jason prodded, "How so?"

"Why, Aurelie has no need of your money, my lord. Though I expect she will make use of it. Even an heiress will marry a fortune, given the chance."

"An heiress, did you say?"

Fenwick blinked, then gave an unpleasant chuckle. "Who'd have thought it? My ugly, sharp-tongued cousin catching herself a husband without having to use her inheritance as a lure. Mother will be livid, after all that clever conniving. . . ."

He gasped as Jason captured his neck again. "And what is that supposed to mean?"

"About her scant attractions? No offense, but my cousin is hardly much to look at."

"Oglesby, you are an ass. Tell me what you meant by your mother's conniving."

It took a good five minutes of alternately squeezing and shaking for Jason to get any response at all. Finally Oglesby sputtered, "Mother picked suitors for the girl. They would have paid her had a marriage occurred. Only fair, you know, as they would be coming into a good deal more money after."

This time, Jason did not shake him. Instead, he gave a sharp push, sending man and chair tumbling backward with a resounding crash. Fenwick's howl turned into a suspicious snuffling. The urge to plant his boot in the blackguard's stomach was fierce, but he controlled it.

"I amend my earlier statement, Oglesby," he spat. "You are not an ass; you are a pestilence on the ass of an ass." He bent over then, getting as close to the man as he could tolerate. "Hear me well. Not only will you stay away from my parents' house and Aurelie, but if I ever so much as catch a glimpse of you in London again, I will personally deliver you, chained and beaten, to one of the navy's indenture ships. Is that clear?"

Oglesby groaned something that sounded acceptably affirmative.

"Good. I am so glad we understand each other. Now, you will settle your bill with the landlord and take yourself back to Somerset tonight with this message for your parents: Aurelie is under my protection. Should your father try to assert his rights as guardian, he will soon find himself up against my considerable money and influence, not to mention my rather formidable wrath. You might not believe this, Oglesby, but I am not ordinarily a violent man. I am, however, the worst enemy you could ever imagine. Tell your parents that as well."

He left Fenwick blubbering on the floor and headed out, not bothering to close the door behind him. As he was descending the stairs, a portly man came huffing up. "I run a respectable establishment, I do. Won't have no brawling. If there's anything damaged, I'll be expecting res'tution. . . ."

He was not wearing a neckcloth, but Jason made do with his shirtfront. "Take the matter up with Mr. Oglesby. And if I ever hear of you giving him lodging again, I shall see your respectable establishment reduced to rubble. Understood?"

"O'course, m'lord. At yer service, m'lord."

Jason snarled and pushed him away. The man lost no time in scuttling back the way he had come. A clock chimed in the distance and Jason cursed as he sprinted for his carriage. He was expected to escort the ladies to some dismal affair at eleven. It was a nauseating concept in light of the evening's events, but there was no way around it.

A glance down reminded him that he was still wearing his ruined coat and there was a Freddy-sized footprint in the middle of his chest. No wonder he had gotten more than one odd look from his White's clubmates. Fenwick, too, had been slack-jawed at his appearance, and that even before the inquisition began.

He would have to stop at his own house for a change of clothes. Girvin would have a fit at the state of his apparel. If the man knew what was good for him, he would keep his mouth shut and do his job quickly. Even then, Jason would be late and he was hardly in the mood for one of his mother's icy glares. He was feeling less than kindly disposed toward his parents at the moment, and did not expect that to change in a hurry.

He was frankly appalled that his parents would have even allowed a rotter like Fremont in the front door, let alone considered him an acceptable match for his sister. Grace deserved far better than the dissipated earl. So much better, in fact, that Jason was hard put to think of a single man who was good enough.

He had always known his parents were a cold, self-centered pair. Hell, he had learned the finer points of aristocratic reserve from them. But to treat their own daughter with such callous disregard was inexcusable. Once he and Aurelie were married, he would demand that his sister spend much of her time at Havensgate. . . .

Once he and Aurelie were married.

It sounded so simple. They were already betrothed, damn it. But they were not. It was not that he had not intended to have dealt with that minor inconvenience by now. In fact, he had been trying to propose to her for a full day already. He had made a royal hash of it, to be sure, but he had not counted on steady interference from all directions.

And now he had Fenwick's words with which to contend. So Aurelie was not an impoverished governess after all. No, it appeared she was the daughter of landed and wealthy Somerset gentry. An heiress. His anger at her deception lasted only until he had settled himself in the carriage.

He wondered just how much money she actually had—or would have once her birthday was past, and found himself hoping it was a piddling amount. Otherwise, he thought with no small amount of concern, she might not feel the need to marry at all. And especially not him.

What could he possibly offer to an independent woman? A title, yes, but he did not think Aurelie cared much about that. A family? Yes, but one comprised of wild children and ever squabbling adults. It was true she seemed to like Grace, Rickey, and the children, but she had never really been facing the prospect of continued contact with any of them. The Granvilles were enough to try a saint's patience.

There was, of course, himself. *Ah, the ultimate selling point.* An unsociable, rigid viscount with more ice in his veins than blood. All things considered, he was quite probably everything Aurelie did not want, and nothing she needed. He found laughter difficult, knew nothing of Celtic mythology, and never, ever stopped to look at ants.

By the time he arrived home, his spirits were about as high as the Oglesbys' morals. He snarled at Kenyon when he opened the door and all but pushed him out of the way. He should have known better. The butler, quite Strawbridge's equal when it came to getting his job done, followed him up the stairs.

"Begging you pardon, my lord, but there is a message from your mother." By this time, Jason had stalked past a gaping Girvin and was rifling through the armoire. He viciously pulled out a fresh shirt and shucked his ruined coat to the floor. "I believe you will want to hear it before . . . er, changing your clothes."

"Well, damn it, man, what is the message already?" Girvin rushed forward to assist him with the shirt, only to jump back as Jason's elbow narrowly missed his nose.

"There has been a change of plans, my lord. Your family will not be going out this evening. The countess sends her regrets and hopes you will not be terribly inconvenienced."

There was no question of his mother having said the last bit. Kenyon, however, was a firm believer in politeness. "Like hell she did," Jason muttered, letting the now-wrinkled shirt drop into his valet's hands. Then, ignoring the startled expressions on the faces of his retainers, he stalked out the door, bare chested, and headed downstairs to the brandy.

He had been given a reprieve of sorts. There would be plenty of time to talk to Aurelie on the morrow. Which meant he had approximately twelve hours to think of what he could possibly say to a woman, who had nearly been sold into marriage by her own family and battered by his own, that would make her want to stay with him, as his wife.

It was only eight hours later that he found himself standing in his parents' foyer with his hat in his hand and his heart somewhere in the vicinity of his feet.

"What in the hell do you mean—*she is not here*?"

Diggs cowered before him, wringing his hands in distress. "She is not in her chamber, my lord, and her maid says the bed has not been slept in. She also says one of Miss Carollan's valises is gone, and some of her possessions. No one saw her leave, but there is no one about during the wee hours."

Grace appeared at the top of the stairs then, still in her

wrapper and rubbing her eyes. "What on earth is going on, Jason? Your bellowing was enough to wake the dead."

As if on cue, his parents appeared behind her.

Jason looked at them bleakly. Any hope that they might know what had happened was effectively doused. "Aurelie has left," he said dully.

She had said she would. It had been part of their deal, after all. Only she had done it in the middle of the night, several hours before he had come to change that deal.

And she had done it nearly two months too early.

17

THERE SEEMED TO be no escaping the noxious smell of the mineral waters, even at the relatively dry Pump Room counter. Aurelie, sipping at tea rather than the dubiously curative water, tried to smile pleasantly at her companions while edging away from the glasses they held.

"Bothering you, is it, my dear?" Lady Fielding chuckled. "I assure you, 'tis every bit as wretched tasting as it smells, but marvelous for the heart."

Aurelie rather doubted anything could cure what ailed her heart and had been able to avoid partaking of the marvelous stuff thus far. She had also been able to avoid bathing in it. It was bad enough to be near a glassful, but to actually submerge one's body in the steaming, foul-smelling pools seemed an act of unnecessary torture.

Mrs. DeLancey swore by the baths and had recently joined them fresh—if that word could be used—from her second dip of the day. She looked quite invigorated, if a bit more wrinkled than usual, and was smiling contentedly. "Splendid temperature this morning, not too warm. Yesterday was a bit on the toasty side. I very nearly fell asleep."

"Wouldn't recommend that," her sister said dryly. "Burroughs might take it upon himself to rescue you."

The elderly Mr. Burroughs had come to Bath to take the waters for his gout and had been hovering around Mrs. DeLancey for some days now. It had become a joke among the three women, though the sweet-tempered Felicity was loathe to be rude to the persistent widower.

"Yes, he insisted on watching me throughout my bath

earlier, waving whenever I mistakenly caught his eye." She sighed. "For all the advantages of widowhood, there is the unfortunate drawback of appearing to be fair game for lonely widowers. I am rather afraid I shall have to change my custom and use the Queen's Bath in the future. Men are not allowed there."

Now that, Aurelie thought wistfully, was an interesting concept—a place where men were not permitted. Perhaps she ought to join Mrs. DeLancey at the Queen's Bath and take up residence there. Maybe then, surrounded by pampered, whining women, she would not find herself thinking of Jason every moment.

Not that there was much chance of that. He had haunted her thoughts from the time she had crept out of his parents' house at dawn and, in that shadowy form, had followed her to Bath. She had spent the first few days terrified that someone would recognize her and send word of her presence back to London, but Lady Fielding had informed her she was quite safe.

The ton apparently used Bath as a training ground for future debutantes, and as a sort of purgatory for widows and for girls who had managed to do something scandalous. The city was respectable enough to be frequented by Polite Society, yet tame enough to serve as a temporary repository for those not currently welcome in or ready for Town.

After nearly a month, Aurelie felt reasonably secure and moderately comfortable. She missed the Granvilles terribly, even Lord and Lady Heathfield, and woke up on too many mornings with damp cheeks and a heavy heart. Jason not only invaded most of her waking thoughts, but her dreams as well.

For their part, the sisters delighted in her presence and were charming hostesses. They questioned her little and she was tremendously grateful for their forbearance. As long as they thought her hiding from an unwanted marriage, she would not have to speak of the matter. Lately, however, she was beginning to suspect that the sharp ladies were not so convinced of her resolve. Perhaps it had to do with the countless unfinished letters—consisting of nothing more, really, than salutations to Jason or Grace at the top of the page, which she threw away.

It was not that she wanted to be in contact with the people she had left behind. Well, that was not precisely true, but after what she had done, she could hardly go back. What could she possibly say? *I am terribly sorry that I lied, and crept away like a thief in the night. But Jason is, after all, going to marry someone else, and my utterly charming relatives could have descended upon us at any moment. All in all, it might have been a bit awkward all around if I had stayed—don't you think?*

Beyond all that, her guilt at her furtive flight was eating at her and she felt compelled to explain somehow, to someone. But the letters were never written, and she had very nearly resigned herself to living with the misery and self-censure.

In another four weeks she would be able to go home to Granny Carollan and their simple life. Odd, to think her own home was only a county away. Perhaps she would bring Granny to Bath later in the summer if Lady Fielding and Mrs. DeLancey were still in residence. She rather thought the three older ladies would get along smashingly. Her grandmother was not nearly so refined as the sisters, but possessed every bit of their wit and spirit. She would undoubtedly feel out of place, however, amid Bath's rather pretentious society.

"*Ní dheanfach an saol capall rás d'asal.*"

"I beg your pardon, my dear?" Mrs. DeLancey said curiously.

"Goodness, girl, what a sound. Are you unwell?" was her sister's addition.

Aurelie smiled. "It is an old Gaelic saying of my grandmother's. Something about not making a fine race horse out of an ordinary donkey."

"How interesting," Mrs. DeLancey commented.

"Hmmph," her sister sniffed.

Later, with Mrs. DeLancey having decided another bath

202

would make her look decidedly prunish, the trio strolled down Milsom Street, peering into the shops as they went. Aurelie declined what would be the fourth trip within a week to the milliner's—Lady Fielding being extremely fond of elaborate hats—choosing instead to visit one of the city's several libraries.

There were numerous books to be found, even some of her favorite classics, but she bypassed them in favor of the London papers. This had become something of a daily ritual, and she rationalized it as being merely an intellectual interest in the news of the day. The truth was that she skipped everything except those pages which contained the latest *on dits* of Society.

Each time, she searched for word that Lord Tarrant had announced his betrothal to Lady Eleanor DeVane. Each time she did not find it she assumed it was because the papers arrived in Bath a day late and the announcement had been made that very day. It was a macabre activity, but she could not seem to give it up no matter how she scolded herself.

She had just managed to ascertain that Jason had not been mentioned in the previous day's *Times* when her companions joined her. Lady Fielding shot a shrewd glance at the hastily discarded newspaper, but held her tongue.

"A new acquisition?" Aurelie asked lightly, pointing to the hatbox in the woman's hand.

"Gray silk Kutuzov with a blue ostrich plume. Very military." No one could say the stylish widow did not keep up with current fashion. "I am always on the lookout for the newest ... er, object of interest."

Her sister was no less astute. "And you, Aurelie? Did you find anything of interest?"

Feeling decidedly like a child whose mischief has been discovered yet who insists on continuing the chicanery, Aurelie rose to her feet. "There is always something intriguing to be found here. I do not feel like choosing today, though, so if you would care to leave, I am ready."

As it turned out, she heard something of great interest

later on, and the *Times* had nothing to do with it. She was watching the nightly ritual of posing and posturing from her vantage point near the windows in the New Assembly Rooms, wondering as always why the people did not expire from the sheer tedium of Bath's evenings. The sisters were sitting several feet away, regarding the scene with similar disinterest.

Nothing out of the ordinary had occurred in the past hour, unless one could count a rather remarkable chain of snapping corset ties as unusual. Considering the rotundity of many of Bath's denizens, Aurelie had long since decided such an event was thoroughly typical.

Then, like the sudden rising of a faint breeze, something began to circulate through the room. Ladies fluttered their fans and whispered amongst themselves in small groups before one would break away and pass on the tidbit to the next cluster. Another girl arriving in the wake of a scandal, Aurelie thought, and watched the delighted buzzing with wry amusement.

"Aurelie," Mrs. DeLancey called out some minutes later, "Lady Willoughby is telling the most entertaining story. Would you not care to hear it?"

In fact, the matron who seemed to have started the breeze was sitting to the lady's right, near to bursting with ill-suppressed excitement. As Aurelie approached, she noted that neither sister looked particularly entertained. In fact, they wore identically tense expressions and she quickly understood her presence was required—not requested.

"As I was saying," Lady Willoughby explained for Aurelie's benefit, "my niece has only just arrived from Town this evening. Her grandmother's ninetieth birthday party, of course." To be distinguished, of course, from a young miss arriving in Bath for less respectable reasons. "And she brought the most delicious rumor. It involves one of the jewels of Society. Can you guess?"

"No," Aurelie replied dutifully, "I confess I cannot."

"Lady Eleanor DeVane. Apparently she has got herself betrothed, though no one will confirm to whom. Tarrant, most likely, though I heard he was attached to someone else for a bit. The Town is all abuzz about the wedding of the Season. It is all so very mysterious and romantic, is it not? Makes one want to rush out and buy Mr. Lane's latest."

It made one young woman want to rush out and scream.

Using every bit of willpower she possessed, Aurelie remained where she was.

"Most certainly," she managed through stiff lips.

Apparently satisfied that she had done her job there, Lady Willoughby got up and trundled off to spread the delicious, mysterious, romantic news elsewhere. Aurelie promptly sank into the vacated chair.

"Not exactly a weight off your mind, is it, girl?" Lady Fielding asked gruffly.

Aurelie could not find the words to express how she felt, nor would she have used them if she could. "It is just so . . . sudden."

"You have been gone a month. The ton works with speed and repents at leisure."

"Really, Constance." Mrs. DeLancey leaned over to pat Aurelie's hand. "Men's hearts are not affected like ours, dear. Besides, there is nothing to suggest it is truly Lord Tarrant."

Aurelie gazed sightlessly out over the merry crowd. "No, but neither is there anything to suggest it is not."

Jason signed the last of the papers and set them aside for his solicitor. As far as he could tell, everything was settled and he could leave for Havensgate without worrying about loose ends.

The door opened as he was cleaning his pen. "Ah, Phillips, good. These can be delivered to Quigley this afternoon."

"I am afraid visiting your solicitor is not among my list of errands today."

Jason looked up in surprise. "Rafe. Isn't it rather early for you to be up and about Town? I thought we were to meet at Tattersall's this afternoon."

"So did I, Tare. So did I. But apparently you are going to be well on your way to Newhaven by this afternoon." At Jason's muttered oath, Rafe commented, "Good of you not to insult me by denying it."

"How did you find out?"

"Ran into Rickey last night. He assumed I already knew."

Cursing his brother for his loose tongue, Jason rested his elbows on the desk. "I'm sorry. I should have told you I was leaving. It is just that I expected you would try to talk me out of it."

"Now why would I do that? Your actions these past weeks have been so very rational, after all."

"That's just it, damn it. It is my life to live and I am bloody well sick and tired of you and my family interfering."

Rafe leaned back and surveyed his glossy boots. "Has it occurred to you that all the interference comes from the fact that we care about you? That we don't want to see you doing anything stupid? You've been an odd creature lately. I mean, look at yourself, Tare. Your cravat is crooked. And you said it yourself: neatness of dress implies neatness of mind."

"There is nothing wrong with my mind."

"If you say so."

Jason knew he ought to be annoyed, angry even, at his friend's meddling insolence. But he was not able to summon up much annoyance. In fact, he was feeling blessedly emotionless these days, and it suited him just fine. "Just what is it you wish to say to me, Rafael? I am in rather a hurry to be on the road. Wiggins sent word that the river is rising again and I want to have a look before dark."

Now the bounder was surveying his shirt cuffs, tugging at one to bring it to its proper place. When he looked up, it was to fix Jason with the sort of smile one employed with a recalcitrant child. "We are still friends, Tare. In fact, I suspect we shall always be friends. In many ways you are the brother I never had."

He paused, and Jason cut in dryly, "You are warming my heart. And wasting my time."

"There, you see. That is the way one speaks to a brother, is it not? Not having one of my own, I have only your behavior on which to base the assumption. Yes? Well, anyway, we have always been loose in our banter and I trust you will not be any more offended than usual when I tell you that you have turned into a prime candidate for Bedlam."

"Now you are becoming redundant. Get to the point."

Rafe leaned forward. "I don't know why she left. No one knows. But I do know it tore you apart. I also know you have dealt with the pain in the worst ways imaginable. Instead of going after her, or even trying to find out where she is, you have . . ."

Jason's fist hit the desktop, rattling the inkwell. "Enough, Rafe. I get the point. In fact, I have gotten it loud and clear for weeks. Silly of me to insist that you elaborate." He rose to his feet. "Yes, we are friends. Yes, you are like a brother to me. And, as with Rickey, I will be as open and reasonable as possible. I will not, however, be made to feel guilty because my actions do not coincide with what you expect of me. If you will excuse me, I need to prepare for my journey."

Rafe, too, got up from his seat. "All order and reason. It has always been order and reason for you. God knows it's one of the things that has made our friendship—you choosing to live with so much rigid control and me choosing to live with so little. But you have got to leave some room for genuine affection, Tare. Both for yourself and from yourself. It is crucial, you know, for the family and friends you have and those you will have in the future."

"Do you know what Grace calls it, the caring in our family? Careless affection. She managed to get that in in the midst of blistering my ears for letting Aurelie leave."

"Astute of her, I would say."

"Perhaps. But she sees it as a problem; I do not. Duty, responsibility, respect—those should not be careless, for they endure and are rewarded. Love, my friend, is a waste of energy, a fallacy created by merchants to increase sales."

Rafe actually had the gall to laugh. "Clever words, those, but you don't believe them."

No, I do not, but they work for me now. "What's the difference?" He shrugged. "Duty calls—in the form of a rising river. I shall see you when I return."

He was back in the library two hours later, trying to make some sense of the information Phillips had given him. The secretary, to his credit, had not written the reports, but his transcription left a good deal to be desired. Jason ground his teeth and resigned himself to another hour of lost time. He had dispatched Phillips on several errands, including the visit to Quigley, Bates, and Fergusson, Esquires. Now he heartily wished he had waited.

When Kenyon entered some time later, he was ready to tear his hair out. "Well, man, what is it?"

"Begging your pardon, my lord, but there is a message from Lady DeVane."

Jason took the note and scanned its contents. "Hell and damnation."

"Yes, my lord."

Jason did not even bother to scowl at him. He was far too busy scowling at the elegant lines of Eleanor's summons. She was being polite, deferential even, undoubtedly knowing all the while that he could not possibly refuse the request for his presence.

"Have my horse saddled," he ordered wearily.

He arrived at the Ramsden house in a decidedly black mood. At this rate, the river would have flooded all of East Sussex by the time he got there. The duke's dour butler met him at the door.

"Good day, my lord. Her ladyship is in the parlor."

Eleanor was there all right, a golden vision in blue silk. Seated next to a golden vision in blue muslin.

"Hullo, Jason."

"For God's sake, Grace, what are you doing here?"

His sister tilted her heart-shaped face and gazed at him

208

angelically. "What an odd question. Eleanor and I are, after all, well known to each other. We were merely discussing the merits of long sleeves versus short."

And Sally Jersey has a conscience. "I hope you came to a satisfactory conclusion." He dropped a kiss onto the top of her head and bent over Eleanor's hand. "I came as soon as I received your message."

"Thank you, Jason. I know you are busy."

"Never too busy for you, of course."

An amused glimmer appeared in her aquamarine eyes. "Of course. Though I appreciate your presence nonetheless."

Jason turned to his sister. "I do not suppose you would wander off for a few minutes."

"No," Grace replied cheerfully.

"Grace—"

"There is no reason for Grace to leave," Eleanor announced. "In fact, it was as a result of our earlier conversation that I contacted you."

"Ah, you want my opinion on sleeve length." No annoyance, just tiredness.

"Don't be impertinent, Jason," his sister scolded. "We are fully aware that you are off to Havensgate today. This should not take up too much of your precious time."

"Indeed?" He raised his eyebrows at Eleanor.

"Indeed," she replied with a smile. "Though I do not want to be rushed. It is very important, you see, that I get it right."

"Now you are making me nervous."

"Now *you* are teasing." Eleanor turned to Grace and asked her to ring for the butler. "I think perhaps tea might be in order." Then, to Jason, "I meant to pass this on some weeks ago, but everything became so hectic after the announcement. I do hope you'll forgive me."

"I expect I will." Jason darted a glance at the mantel clock. "Once I hear whatever it is you meant to pass on."

"Now don't look at the clock again. You will be out of here soon enough." The butler appeared in the doorway.

"Oh, good. Tea, please, Cameron, and perhaps some pastries. Are you hungry, Jason?"

"Eleanor," he growled.

"Quite right. Shortbread, I think, Cameron, rather than pastries."

"Very good, my lady." The butler backed out of the room.

Eleanor smiled at Grace, then turned back to Jason, who was trying very hard not to reduce his molars to dust. "Now, I have a story to tell you, and I trust you will listen closely and not interrupt till I have finished. I heard it nearly two months ago and was quite moved by it. It is called 'Emer's Choice.' "

18

Clonakilty Cottage, Somerset

"B OTTOMS UP!"

"Happy Birthday, Aurelie!"

"Good to have you back, girl."

Aurelie raised her own glass of cider and saluted the room. Her birthday was nearly two weeks past, but Granny had organized a party nonetheless. The faces gathered around the table were familiar and beloved. Looking at the people who had been her friends all her life, London and Havensgate seemed very far away indeed.

"Sláinte chuig na fir, agus go mairfidh na mná go deo," was her grandmother's toast.

"What in the devil does that mean?" Sir Percival Reade, the village's resident curmudgeon, asked sharply. "Can't stand it when you spout that Irish rot, Kate!"

"It is just my grandmother's favorite toast," Aurelie said affably. *"Go raibh maith agat,* Gran. Thank you." It was her favorite as well: "Health to the men, and let the women live forever."

"Tell us again about the fireworks at Vauxhall," Meggy, their neighbor, prompted.

"No, no. Tell us about the fine cattle and phaetons," her young husband demanded.

Aurelie had done her best to describe her "travels," choosing those things most guaranteed to amuse her friends, some of whom had never been to London. In this way, it had been easy to avoid speaking of the Granvilles.

The weeks since she had returned had gone quickly, filled with familiar and peaceful activity. Now, surrounded by warmth and security, and with the memories of her time away still fresh in her mind, she managed to ignore the fact that the future stretched out long and quiet before her.

"I say we have another drink," Mr. Bigley, the vicar, suggested jovially, and Granny refilled his glass.

Her grandmother certainly had not changed in three months. She had greeted Aurelie at the door with a fierce hug and lively tale of how she had run the Oglesbys off with a pistol when they had come looking for the girl.

The house, too, looked the same. Granny, all those years ago, had flatly refused to move into her son's grand home. When he and his wife had died, it had seemed the most natural thing in the world for Aurelie to move right in with her. Her bedroom, with its narrow bed and sloping ceiling, seemed smaller somehow, but it was home.

"Will you be going back to London soon to visit your friends?" Meg asked after a time. "How dull this all must be after experiencing the Season in Town."

"No," Aurelie said quietly. "It is almost heaven." *Almost.*

Later, as she walked the elderly and slightly drunk Mr. Bigley back to the vicarage, she tried to convince herself that happiness could be found as easily as it was lost. She had attended two assembly balls in the village, lively affairs that gave her the opportunity to reacquaint herself with the other young people of the area and to wear pretty clothes.

The lovely rose ball gown had been left in London along with most of her new wardrobe, but she had taken a full valise. For the first time in her country life, she found herself quite the toast of the local crowd. It was not the same, to be sure, as being an Original in London, but it was gratifying nonetheless.

The men were suitably attentive, too. Many were young, some were handsome, and a few were utterly charming. She liked them all equally and none especially. Perhaps, she had thought at the first assembly ball, one would someday strike her fancy and she would consider marrying. The thought had lasted only until the end of the first set. Her husband was in London, marrying the wrong woman.

She left the jolly vicar singing at his door and, as she headed home, his slightly slurred baritone followed her. "O I once knew a lass name of Jean, whose vision was none too keen. So I put in her hand an object so grand, and told her 'twas stone from the stream . . ."

Not a hymn, by any stretch of the imagination, but Aurelie was hardly in the mood for musical homilies. She hummed a lilting ballad of her grandmother's as she walked, thinking no place in England had moonlight so beautiful as Somerset. Pausing beside a gnarled oak, she gazed up into the sky. As always, Orion was the easiest constellation to find.

And despite the fact that she was more than a hundred miles from London, he blazed with the same fierce elegance as he had that night at Vauxhall.

"Tell us again about the fireworks at Vauxhall."

Well, they came just as he was going to kiss me, when his face was so close that I could see the scar above his lip, even in the soft night. His hand caught my gown and I was held fast, between him and the wonderful, rough bark of the tree.

She took a few steps, closed her eyes, and leaned back against the oak's sturdy trunk.

He was foxed, and teasing, and so impossibly beautiful. And had he given me just one small sign, anything to tell me that the moment mattered, I would probably not be here now.

A cow bellowed in a far field, and Aurelie reluctantly opened her eyes. No lanterns, no rowdy dandies cavorting on the lawns. Just Somerset, with its moonlight and earthy smells. She pulled her shawl closer around her shoulders with a sigh and resumed her trek home.

Granny had undoubtedly gone to bed, but she had left the lamps burning for her. Aurelie reached the front door and turned back for a last glimpse of Orion, unwilling to let go of the reverie just yet.

Granny's laugh drifted from inside. It appeared not all of the guests had taken their leave. Well, there was nothing to be done for it but go in and pretend to celebrate a bit more.

She entered the parlor to find her grandmother chatting animatedly with someone whose identity was hidden by the high back of her grandfather's old wing chair. One glass of sherry rested on the table. The other was waving through the air as the older woman made a point. Granny looked up as Aurelie approached, her eyes bright in her fine, Irish face. No, she had not changed—not much, in fact, as far back as Aurelie could remember. Her thick hair was snow white now, and there were lines around her eyes, but anyone looking deep into their vivid, silvery depths would have no trouble imagining the fiery red that her hair had once been.

"Still celebrating, Gran?" Aurelie asked cheerfully, draping her shawl over a side table.

"I might be that. Depends a good deal on you."

"Oh, and why is that?"

Her grandmother gestured toward the other chair. "Our guest brings interesting news. 'Tis betrothed to him he says you are, *caílin*. Is that true?"

Aurelie's heart missed a beat as Jason's head and shoulders appeared over the top of the chair. Yes, it was Jason, though his hair was ruffled, his cravat was crooked, and there was a dramatic smudge on the lapel of his coat.

"Hello, Aurelie," he said gruffly, coming to stand in front of her.

The urge to reach up and smooth back the dark hair from his forehead was almost overwhelming, but she kept her hands at her sides. "My lord."

"Well?"

"Well what, my lord?"

"Is it true?" Jason was having a damnably hard time keeping his hands to himself. So many times he had imagined her with him and here she was, that infernally sharp gaze fastened on his face and her hair glowing with fire in the light from the hearth. "Are you not betrothed to me? I

214

admit the disappearance of a fiancée could be regarded as a sign that the betrothal was off, but I have always been one to settle matters with words."

He could read nothing in her eyes as she replied, "That is precisely why I left." When he merely looked at her blankly, she continued, "You were going to send me away with your words, Jason. I made it easy on you."

Neither heard her grandmother quietly leave the room.

"Send you away? What could possibly have given you such a crackbrained idea?"

Something very much like hope fluttered in Aurelie's chest. "They were your own words: settle matters. I thought you wanted to end the arrangement earlier than we had originally agreed."

"Well, yes, I did . . ."

"So I went—leaving you free to marry . . ."

". . . because I was going to ask you to marry me."

"I did not want to be dismissed flat out and . . . *What did you say?*"

He ran both hands through his hair, sending it into greater disarray. "I was going to put an end to the farce by making the betrothal real. Not that I was convinced you would have me, but I knew I had to try. Then, when you left, I went half-mad, knowing you couldn't have felt anything for me after all . . ."

He broke off with a grunt as she hurtled herself into his arms. He stood motionless for a moment. Then, with a groan, he hugged her to him with fierce tenderness, vowing as he did never to let go. "Can I take this to mean you might have accepted my proposal?"

Her voice was muffled slightly by his waistcoat. "Without a second's hesitation. Oh, Jason!" She started shaking then, and it took him a minute to realize she was crying.

"Good Lord, Aurelie, what's this?"

"Why couldn't you have come after me sooner?" she gasped. "Before it was too late."

His hands tightened on her upper arms and he pushed her

roughly away from him. "Are you telling me you have attached yourself to another man?"

"Of course not! How could I? But what of your betrothal to Lady Eleanor?"

His brows drew together in a frown. "Eleanor?"

"I heard about the announcement when I was in Bath. Lady Eleanor was to be married in the wedding of the Season. I assumed . . ."

"Eleanor," he interrupted roughly, "is to be married next month to Alexander Symington."

She was having a very hard time processing this information. "Who is Alexander Symington?"

"He is the second son of the Earl of Wentford. Apparently he and Eleanor have been in love since they met several years ago but, as he was a younger son with limited prospects, they knew Ramsden would not consider the match."

A glorious warmth was creeping upward from Aurelie's feet. "What happened to change things?"

Jason grinned. "Eleanor decided several months ago that she did not give a damn what her parents thought. She threatened to run off to Gretna Green with the man. It worked. Ramsden gave his blessing, albeit grudgingly, and announced the betrothal. His future son-in-law will not have the title, but he has money in his own right and a very distinguished military record behind him."

"So it was this Symington all the time."

"All the time." Jason promptly captured her hand and dropped to one knee before her. "As you have been for me. Will you do me the honor of becoming my wife, Miss Carollan?"

Aurelie's eyes glowed as she looked down at him. "Does this mean that you do care for me a little bit?"

"A little bit? Good God, woman, I have been head over heels in love with you for months. Probably from the moment you made me look at ants."

She was crying again, but smiling at the same time. "And I think I have loved you from the moment you

216

looked." She bit her lip then. "But I lied to you, Jason. About who I was."

"I knew who you were," he said softly, rising to his feet and again taking her into his arms. "You were the woman with the golden heart and pure soul. So pure that you made a choice for both of us. One you did not need to make."

"I allowed you to go on thinking I was a governess."

"It was my stupidity that allowed me to go on believing that. I should have connected you right off with Sir Warren Carollan. I knew of his rise to the top of the king's diplomatic corps and how he was instrumental in keeping peace with the dissident Irish factions. Your mother was Lord Aldrich's daughter, was she not?"

Aurelie nodded. "They died in a carriage accident while acting as the king's emissaries."

"I know, and I'm sorry. I am fully aware that my parents are poor replacements, but they are fond of you."

"No, they are not. They wanted you to marry Lady Eleanor."

"At first. But they have both been like bears with sore heads since you left. Grace has stopped speaking to me, and the children are inconsolable. Even Rafe has taken to treating me like a pariah."

It occurred to Aurelie that she ought to tell him about Rafe, but he beat her to it. "I know he proposed to you. And when I tried to flatten his face for it, he said some very nasty things about me that I understand now were his way of explaining why."

She buried her face in his waistcoat, savoring the wonderful smell of him. "You really do want me to marry you, don't you?"

"More than I have every wanted anything in my life."

She sighed happily and murmured, "What took you so long?"

"You can be a very hard woman to find when you want to be lost. I imagine the Oglesbys would agree wholeheartedly."

"You know about that, too?"

"I do indeed. And I did hit Fenwick. You don't mind, do you?"

"Not in the least. I wish I had been there."

Jason chuckled. "I think I could arrange a repeat performance if it means so much to you."

Aurelie's response was to shake her head and hug him tightly. She looked up after a time and raised her fingers to his lips, gently tracing the upper slope. "I have been meaning to ask you something for the longest time."

"Let me guess—you wished to ask me to kiss you senseless."

"No. I mean, yes, but ..." She laughed, the glorious sound he remembered. "I wanted to ask how you got the scar."

He reached up to feel the mark himself. "Funny, I had forgotten it was there."

"Was it during the war?"

"Lord, no. It was more than ten years ago."

"A fight?"

He gave a wry chuckle. "Not precisely. It was Grace."

"Grace?"

"Apparently that was her day to play David. Unfortunately, I was the most convenient Goliath. I have always been rather grateful her aim was so poor."

"How poor could it have been? She hit you in the face."

"So she did. But it was a very large rock and she was aiming for my forehead."

This time, Aurelie kissed her fingers and raised them to the faint scar. "I am awfully glad her aim was off. I love you, Jason Granville."

"And I adore you, Aurelie Carollan. Will you ask me now?"

"Hmm?"

"No, perhaps I ought to do the asking. I believe Catullus said it best: *Da mi basia mille, deinde centum, dein mille altera.*"

So she gave him a thousand kisses, then a hundred, then a thousand more.

Cuchulainn surveyed the two women whose hands he held, Fand to the left and Emer to the right. The faery queen illuminated the Strand with her glorious beauty, her hair shining bright as the gold of Lugh's shield. Emer's visage, he saw, illuminated nothing but him. She was very lovely, but her glow came not from the exterior. It was her heart that was gold, strong and warm, and his for the asking.

In that moment, he saw with complete clarity what a fool he was to have been so dazzled by something no more true or lasting than a magic mirror. In his wife he had all of what any man could possibly wish for in a lifetime. Or—he had once had it.

Cuchulainn did not realize he had released Fand's hand until he stood facing Emer with both of her hands in his. Desperate and humbled, he sank to his knees and bowed his head. "If you will but give me one kind word, one small sign that you could someday love me again as you once did, I will swear by my father's light to cherish you till the stars fall from the skies and my heart stops beating in my chest."

Emer stood still as stone for a moment, her own heart beating like the wings of a rising bird. Then she bent low and gently coaxed her husband's face up to hers. The love she saw shining in his eyes was enough to keep her warm for the rest of her days.

"We were meant to be, my Cuchulainn. And you have proven yourself full worthy of the love I cannot help but give you, that is as much a part of my life as breathing. Rise, my heart, and let us go home. There is a lifetime for us to cherish each other and I want to waste not a minute of it."

Cuchulainn stood and, taking his wife into his arms, kissed her with all the passion and promise in his heart—long and deep and unending.

Meanwhile, Fand's husband, Manannen, had arrived

219

to reclaim his place at her side. She, too, forgave him and went willingly into his arms. As Cuchulainn and Emer turned to go, Manannen offered them a drink from the magical flask he carried. In it was the Water of Oblivion, and he thought to ease the pain they had suffered with its soothing power.

First Cuchulainn and then his wife declined the flask. For Emer had made her choice, and nothing could ever seal them together more completely than the simple power there.